D S Johnson - Mills

Choosing Love

Woodbridge Publishers
1200 Century Way, Thorpe Park,
Leeds, LS158ZA

Copyright © 2024 D S Johnson - Mills
All rights reserved

First Edition

ISBN (Paperback): 978-1-916849-94-5

ISBN (Hardback): 978-1-916849-95-2

This novel is entirely a work of fiction. The names, characters and incidents portrayed in it are the work of the author's own imagination. Any resemblance to actual persons, living or dead, locations or events is purely coincidental. No part of this publication may be reproduced, stored in retrieval system, copied in any form or by any means, electronic, mechanical, photocopying, recording or otherwise transmitted without written permission from the publisher. You must not circulate this book in any format.

If applicable
Cover Design by Woodbridge Publishers.

WOODBRIDGE
PUBLISHERS

For my Grams, Jane.

Table of Contents

Prologue 1

Starting over 10

The middle ground 29

The first chapter 54

Kizzy and me 83

Scotland 113

Heroics 141

Changing seasons 152

Repercussions 180

Going home 195

Healing 244

New sensations 267

Yellow Diamond 298

Changes 311

Traction 338

Mirror 370

Eirith manor 388
Kizzy's choice 416
Leap of faith 471

Choosing Love

The shift

It feels like waking from a deep sleep; your eyes open,
and everyone you love is there.
Time stands still in that moment; the circle of love
surrounds you to banish fear.

And in his arms, I would find peace.

Prologue

Boston, June 1998

The smell of death is everywhere. It touches the walls, the wooden pew, the pulpit, the flowers, encases in my hair, in my skin. With every breath I take, I suck it into my lungs, and it chokes the very life out of me, tightening my throat, squeezing until there is nothing left.

There is nothing but the glossy exterior of the white lead-lined coffin, barely visible beneath the spectacle, and the rainbow colours of all the flowers she loved. All except one.

Choosing Love

"Kizzy, they forgot the white hydrangeas," I turn to my sister sitting next to me.

"Grams specifically asked for those not to be in the church," she replies, her usually cheerful voice now colourless.

"They were her favourite," I say.

"And yours, Dilly. She didn't want them on her coffin. I think it is so that they will continue to be your favourite. You can't associate them with her death, only her life."

My sisters' words portray the essence of our grandmother. It would be just like her to ensure that she is looking out for us, even after she has gone beyond. I reach for her hand, and she squeezes gently.

This is the best of my sister. She has taken care of it all. The funeral arrangements, answering letters of condolences, the caterers, the flowers, all done by her. Daddy and I walk around in a vapour; a cloud of mist that renders us both incapable.

We've both been looking to Kizzy. She'd picked

out our outfits, brushed my hair, comes to my bed, and holds me when I cry. I don't know how she does it. Grams used to say Kizzy thrives best during times of stress.

"It's time," she whispers.

Kizzy and I stand together. I smooth the folds of my billowing dress, and she adjusts my pill box hat, pulling the veil over my eyes. I didn't want to dress up today. I didn't want to leave the house. But Kizzy reminded me that we are her granddaughters, and she would never shy away from anything she had to do.

After the service, daddy stands at the door; Kizzy and I walk down the aisle to join him. We go through the motions, greeting the friends who have come to say goodbye. Grams had just turned eighty-three, and she was an only child.

Our great aunt Francine, her sister-in-law, is the only remaining relative attending. I hug her close as she is all we have left. And then I correct myself and think of Lily, our mother and Gram's only child. She

Choosing Love

should be here today. But this is the sum of it. What is left of the Johnson clan: Four women. No cousins or long-lost uncles.

Aunt Francine's only child was still born, and her husband Frank died a long time ago. It is only her, and she lives as a recluse in a remote part of Vermont.

"I had to come for Rosie. I don't know how much time I have left myself," she says.

"Grams would have loved that you came," I say, holding on tight.

It is at that precise moment that I notice a woman sitting alone in a pew at the back of the church. I am distracted with the well-wishers, paying their respects, but I keep my eye on her. She wears a broad-brimmed hat that completely obscures her face. But when her delicate fingers flutter to touch the pearls at her neck, I know it's her.

"Lily," I whisper, no longer able to hold in my glee.

I go to her. My heels slapping against the bare

stone floor of the nearly empty church. The pall bearers will be here to pick up the coffin in an hour to give her family private time to say goodbye. The rest of the guests will make their way to the reception venue for refreshments before moving on to the cemetery. Lily looks up at me and smiles, and my heart becomes full.

"Mom. I'm so glad you're here," I cry, falling into her arms, into a sea of warmth and comfort.

"My darling. I'm so sorry for your loss," she says.

But this makes me cry more. My sobs are loud, echoing up to the high rafters. It's her loss, too. She has lost her mother. She has lost so much. Papa Kit died five years ago, so my mother is an orphan.

"What is she doing here?" I hear Kizzy hiss.

"Kizzy. Lily is here to say goodbye to her mother," daddy says.

I pull out of Lily's arms and hold her hand, determined that I will fight for this today.

"She already said goodbye to Grams. The night

she left her baby in a hospital. Leaving her to pick up the pieces of the life she abandoned," Kizzy retorts.

Her voice is soft, but the vitriol is no less potent.

"Kizzy, don't start. She has every right to be here, just as much as you and me," I say.

"Kizzy," daddy puts his arm around her shoulder, but she shrugs it off, and I brace myself for the wave that's about to hit.

This is my sister at her worst.

"No, daddy, she does not belong here. I want her to leave."

"I want her to *stay*," I reply, pleading with daddy.

I already know he will not take my side. He never does. Not because he does not love me. I know he does. My father can never see past the tiny, helpless baby, *his* baby, who was left without a first suckle at her mother's teat. He was not there when it happened and has been forever trying to make up for this. And so, he always puts Kizzy first.

I love him for it, even when it's not fair to me.

But today, I stand my ground. Since that awful day three weeks ago, when my sister called to tell me our grandmother had died after a routine surgery, I have been inside a black hole. Everywhere I turn, it is dark and cold, with no possible way of escaping because I didn't have the chance to say goodbye...

Grams did not reveal she was going to have surgery the last time we spoke. I was at my London university preparing for finals, and she was here, three thousand miles away. Our last conversation was a happy one, and there were no signs, nothing to indicate that the woman who is my guide, my saviour, would be cruelly snatched away.

Today, in my mothers' arms, I find the strength to crawl out of the never-ending despair and embrace the first flicker of hope. Daddy looks like a wounded bird living in a cage, never to take flight; his clipped wings keeping him a prisoner. He has both arms around us. One for my sister, the other for me, but he stares at our mother; the woman he was not brave enough to fight for.

"Please, daddy," I say, daring to think that for

once he would fight for his other daughter.

After all, I was left too. Though, no one seems to remember that detail.

"No, daddy. The prodigal daughter does not get to show up now," Kizzy says.

"Grams would want her to be here, Kizzy. This is not your call. I want my mother here."

"Your mother is dead," she says.

A scream starts in my lower back but does not escape.

"Girls. Please don't argue. Not over me. Not today. Mama wouldn't want this. Kizzy, I'll go. I'm sorry to upset you."

No, Mom, I want you to stay for me. I want you. I forgive you. I love you. The words attach to the scream, forever lodged inside me, with all the other unspoken words I will never say out loud. I hold them in and cry instead. Once again, I am beaten, defeated in my quest to have the one thing I have craved all my life.

"I'm sorry, my darling Dilly," Lily says, and I turn, walking swiftly back towards where Grams lies forever silent.

I am consumed by such rage, such hate for them, it leaves me breathless. The surface of the coffin is cool. I rest my head against the hard marble, and the heat inside me evaporates, replaced by a peace that is silent. The hurt, the angry words, all dissipate and break into tiny fragments, escaping with my tears.

Am I destined to lose everyone I love?

Starting over

The heavy rain beating against my window is loud, and I wake with a start, my heart racing before I realise where I am. Sleeping in my old bed in my tiny apartment. I had only been to the sprawling Penthouse for a week, but already, I was used to its silence. At his place, the walls are soundproof.

I sit up, reaching under my pillow for his note. Smelling it and reading it again. The words are beautiful, and they help to dull the ache in my heart, but for the ache in my bones, I have no remedy.

Slipping on my robe, I head to the kitchen to make a hot beverage. My appetite has disappeared, so I've been sipping warm water with lemon, ginger, and a touch of maple syrup.

When I step out into the hallway, I notice the door to my spare room is pulled to, and a sliver of light shines under the doorway. I walk to the room and stare at the frame of the tall man sleeping peacefully. My best friend, Toby. I don't remember that he stayed over. But if I am honest, yesterday was a write-off. I was in a bit of a state.

He twitches when I switch off the light. He is not wearing a shirt, and I briefly wonder if he is naked under the covers. His incredibly long lashes flutter against the top of his high cheek bones. I reach my hand to brush across one perfectly shaped thick eyebrow. I sigh. Toby is considered an exceptionally beautiful man, but now, watching his face as he sleeps takes my breath away.

It reminds me of another face. The face of the man I love. It's not the same. Toby's looks always attract attention. Markus is handsome in an understated way, but I have seen the beauty hidden beneath the façade he shows the world.

'After I'd made love to you. I sometimes lie awake and watch you sleep for hours.'

Markus' sweet words echo in my head. He was expressing one of the things he loves about me.

Hot tears spill over, and I leave the room quickly, not wanting to disturb Toby. He spent the best part of yesterday comforting me. Today, I want to repay him for his kindness. Food is the way to his heart, so I will make him a hearty breakfast. He was kind enough to replenish my groceries when I could not face it.

The rain is relentless. I open the tiny window in my kitchen and listen to it. The sound is oddly comforting. The warm tea soothes my parched throat. Just seven short days ago, I was worried about starting a relationship with a man I barely knew. I needn't have bothered. It was over before it even began. Not for the first time, I feel robbed, bereft of something beautiful.

I start making pancakes for breakfast, and the warm smell of cinnamon fills the small space of my kitchen.

"Good morning, beautiful girl."

Toby makes an appearance. Bending his six-foot frame to kiss my forehead.

"Hey. Thanks for staying over, but you didn't have to."

He reaches out and pulls me into his arms, and I breathe in his clean scent.

"I wanted to make sure you were okay," he whispers, kissing my hair.

"I'm a big girl, Toby."

"Why don't you take a few days off work?"

I pull out of his embrace and turn down the fire.

"No way. I'm fine. Yesterday was tough, but work will help. It will distract me from feeling sorry for myself."

He stares as if he wants to say something but then changes his mind.

Choosing Love

"What is it?"

"When you left my place on Friday, I was sure you two would work things out."

I move around him to set the table. The pancakes are ready.

"How can we? It involves more than just us," I say, not looking at him.

He walks over and takes my hand, forcing me to look up. He arches one eyebrow.

"A relationship is between two people."

"Precisely. I'm the third wheel," I shrug my shoulders.

Toby sits across the table, so his eyes are level with mine.

"*You* are the woman he loves."

"She is having his child."

"She betrayed Markus. And in the worst way. I don't think he'll be reuniting with her anytime soon."

He speaks with conviction, and I wonder briefly

if they have discussed it in finer detail. Toby's position in this situation is rather unique. He is my bestie, but he is also Markus' friend. They went to school together.

"He loves her, and irrespective of the circumstances, she is pregnant with his child. It is not over between them. The baby makes them connected. They're a family whether he chooses it or not."

"Okay," he says, holding up his hands, "What if it's not his?"

I sit, suddenly breathless.

"Then, we can be together. If he still wants to."

"Markus will always want you. He gave you his heart."

Tears spring to my eyes, but I don't allow them to fall.

"And he has mine."

Toby reaches across the table, catching a determined tear.

Choosing Love

"And if the baby is his? What then? Is it the end for you two?"

I shrug my shoulders. Looking away from his piercing brown eyes. The rain cascades down my window. This is the worst situation for me. My own mother left when I was barely two. My sister was hours old. She broke my father's heart, and I spent my life pining for her to the point where it consumed me. The idea of putting another human being through that kind of pain does not bode well with me.

"I don't know."

* * *

A multicoloured three-dimensional kite floats precariously in the sky. It reminds me of happier days, playing on the beach outside our childhood home with my sister and grandfather. Papa Kit loved to fly kites. He had a collection, but after he died, Grams could not bear to have them in the house.

The wind has picked up, and my hair whips around my face, so I secure it at the nape of my neck in a loose ponytail. It's my lunch hour, and I am sitting in the little park across from work. I come here every day now. Markus and I used to have lunch right in this very spot when we first started seeing each other. It was not clear to me back then, but now I know for sure. It was where I fell in love with him.

When the sun touches the kite, the colours are vivid. The emerald hues are the same shade as his eyes. I see them everywhere. Hear his voice. Feel his touch. Every second, I miss him more, but it's only been five days.

Five days in which my phone has remained silent. It was my choice to leave, but I thought I could handle the pain. This is so much worse than I imagined.

When Grams died two years ago, I thought my world was over, but I was saved. Toby came into my life like a wonderful force of nature. But now, this is a different kind of pain, and not even he can dull the ache in my heart.

"Markus," I whisper.

Letting it out into the atmosphere. I do it often

Choosing Love

when I am alone; just say his name. I wonder if he's with her. When she showed up at his sister's house in the pouring rain on his birthday to reveal she was pregnant; it was the moment of truth. An ugly kind. She also revealed, no doubt for my benefit, that she still loves him.

They had been together twelve years, and she admitted to deliberately entrapping him by coming off the pill without his knowledge. I know it is not his fault. I know that he loves me. I love him, too, but for me, this is a deal breaker.

I'm a product of a broken home, so although I love him with everything I am, I cannot go on. It was difficult to remove myself from the situation, but she is having his baby. Nothing is more important than family.

My phone rings, and my heart almost stops. I rifle in my bag with hurried fingers to retrieve it. The ringer is turned up to maximum volume, as I did not want to miss hearing it. I stare at the caller ID, my fingers trembling and disappointment like bile is bitter in my throat.

"Hey Kizzy," I answer, tears spring to my eyes.

"Dilly!" she shouts excitedly, "The great lady finally came calling!"

"What?"

"Harvard. Dilly, I got in."

"Congratulations. I am so proud of you."

The tears start falling for real. This is a big moment for my sister.

"Daddy won't thank me. The fees are double."

"Kizzy. I will help. I got a promotion at work just last week."

"Did you? Wow. Congratulations," she shouts in her Kizzy way, "I really appreciate your help, Dilly, but I plan to work the summer months. I've applied for an RN position at Mass General for the fall in the maternity unit, so if I get that poor daddy won't have to work all the time."

I sigh. It means she will not come to London as planned. I swallow my disappointment. My sister is on a mission. She completed her undergraduate degree in three years instead of four, and she is currently on a partial scholarship at Dartmouth for her first year of medical school.

Harvard was her first choice, but her application was deferred, and now she is in. This is the brilliance of my sister.

"Whatever it takes to achieve the end goal, right? Daddy and I are with you Kiz, every step of the way."

"Hey, Dilly. Are you alright? You sound a little off."

"I didn't sleep very well, Kizzy, that's all."

"Who needs sleep? I haven't slept in four years. It's Friday. Aren't you going out dancing with your friend Toby tonight?"

"Not tonight. But we're going to an open-air theatre production tomorrow."

A clock chimes on the other end of the phone, indicating the hour. I need to be back at my desk.

"I've got to go now, Kizzy. Grams would be so proud of you. I love you."

"Thanks, Dilly. I love you."

I end the call, packing up my blanket and rushing out the gate. I glance up at the sky and notice the kite is no longer there.

* * *

The chilly spring breeze coming off the River Thames is unseasonably cold for late May. His car is not in its usual spot, but I pretend not to notice. I am here to collect my belongings. It is no longer my business where he is. The security guard watches me from head to toe as I walk inside the building. The glass walls offer instant relief from the cold. I smile politely, and he nods. I walk to the lift. My heels clapping against the tiles.

A sinking feeling grows in the pit of my stomach. It's like coming back to the scene of a crime. My hand trembles as I open the door with the key card. I step inside, and the familiar smell assaults my senses.

It smells like home.

The view of the river greets me outside the glass

walls, but I try not to look. A vase of freshly cut yellow daffodils sits proudly on the sideboard. His domestic helper Sarah has been here cleaning.

The first time he brought me to his place, I wanted to leave immediately. The sensation of stepping into the clouds was too much to take.

I didn't want to fall in love with the high ceilings, the glass walls, the spacious kitchen filled with every appliance, his king-size bed, and the rooftop garden, and I certainly did not want to fall in love with him.

It was a moment when I should have listened to my head telling me to run away from the beauty of all this.

An impossible type of dream.

Instead, I listened to my heart, giving in to the pull of him and the life that he laid out before me. I was foolish, and now I pay the price.

I don't know how long I have been standing at the door to the balcony, mesmerized by the activities on the water. But the door to the apartment opens, and I gasp in surprise when Markus comes through the door. He is dressed casually in a windbreaker-style outdoor jacket and cargo trousers.

I stare. My memory did not serve me well.

He is utterly gorgeous.

His skin flushed with a healthy glow. His hair is cropped short in his preferred style. He notices me, and his face splits into the most heavenly smile.

"Dylan."

He drops his bag to the floor in a most un-Markus-like move, and taking long strides, he whips me into an embrace, and my heart is full.

* * *

He orders Food from Nates, telling me I look far too thin. His hug distracted me. His warmth obliterated the coldness from my bones. I forgot why I came. We sit at the kitchen Island on the stools facing each other; his eyes roam over my face. My fingers entwined with his. I want to tell him the reason I am here, but his touch is everything. I glance over towards his discarded bag. His eyes follow my gaze.

"I was in Scotland. I needed some time to think. I came to your place to tell you, but your neighbour said you were out."

"You didn't go to your birthday party?"

His parents were planning a celebration for Markus and his twin sister, Savannah, at their house last Sunday.

"No. I couldn't face it. But they are having it this Sunday. I'd love for you to accompany me."

He smiles happily and kisses my hand.

"Markus..." I start to say, but the buzzer rings.

He rushes off to answer it.

"The food is here. I'll go down," he says, coming over to kiss me quickly on the lips before pulling on his trainers and heading out the door.

As soon as he disappears, I exhale my held breath.

Scotland.

Relief floods through me.

I thought he was with her.

I take his bag to the laundry room, where Sarah will find it when she comes to clean again on Monday. I then go next door to the bathroom to wash up and check my face in the mirror.

My café au lait complexion is a little pale, but my eyes are shining. I brush my hair, as it is a little windswept from earlier, and pull it back into a loose ponytail. The pulse in my neck is racing, so I undo the first two buttons on my blouse but then notice that it exposes my cleavage, so I redo it. I've already given him the wrong impression, so I don't want to add fuel to the fire.

I can hear he has returned, so I go back out to join him. My mouth waters from the smell of the food. Vegan korma with naan bread. He sets two places on the marble top of the kitchen Island and dishes up. It was where we ate the first night I stayed here with him. I notice his phone on the coffee table. He must have had it replaced. I smashed the last one

Choosing Love

a week ago. I want to address the invitation to his parents' house, but my tummy rumbles painfully, so I dig in.

He talks about his trip, and I listen. His face lights up. When we first met, his face was always passive, and I could never tell what he was thinking. I still can't, but I try to read his eyes and his body language. He has removed his Jacket, and underneath, he is wearing a beige t-shirt that shows off his lean muscles. He opens a bottle of merlot, pouring himself a glass and then topping up my lemon water.

"I can't wait for my family to meet the woman I love."

I stop eating and place my utensils to the side.

"Markus?"

He gazes over at me with such trust in his eyes; I almost change my mind.

"I had only come to pack my things."

Watching his eyes shift from happiness to realisation is hard. I immediately want to put the smile back on his face. He seems a little stunned.

"Well. Your note seemed so final, and I hadn't heard from you all week, so I thought things had been decided."

My voice sounds heavy in my ears.

He exhales sharply, his eyes boring into mine for what seems like ages. He holds my gaze, and I am powerless to break it. His eyes are always my undoing; the emerald irises flashing with understanding.

"I've decided that If I let you slip away, I'd be the biggest fool."

"Markus..."

"I'm so sorry about all of this."

"It's not your fault. I know that."

"Is there nothing I can say? Am I supposed to just watch the woman I love walk out of my life?"

"I don't know what else I can do."

He nods sharply, excusing himself and standing quickly. He walks over to the balcony door. It is dark

Choosing Love

outside, so I can see his reflection in the glass. When the first tear slides down his face, I am up in a flash. I touch his arm, the muscle flexing under my hand. He does not look at me, but his fingers grip mine. The warmth spreads through my limbs, and slowly, I thaw, wrapping my arms around him. He does not hesitate; he wraps me in, burying his face in my hair, breathing my scent.

"I missed you," I whisper.

"Then stay."

His hand moves to caress my hair, and I am melting from the gentle strokes. My body tingles from head to toe. I want to ask him about her and the baby, but I leave it for another day.

When his lips press against mine with the lightest touch, I am lost.

D S Johnson - Mills

The middle ground

The room is completely dark when I wake up alone in his bed. I did not make a conscious decision to stay, but there was no way I could leave him again when he was so unhappy. To cheer him up, I lit the candles on his week-old birthday cake, and he made a wish and then ate almost half of it. I smile to myself, now remembering. It is so easy to be with him, and If I am honest, it felt good to fall asleep without the sense of despair.

I hurry to shower and dress in dark red jeans and a blush pink halter-neck top. When I go downstairs, he has left me a note to say he's gone to his club. It is almost eleven a.m. My favourite green smoothie is in the refrigerator. I drink it down, swallowing my disappointment that he's not here.

I wonder if he will go to see her.

I sigh.

"You have to trust him, Dylan," I say out loud to myself.

I have a few hours to kill before I meet Toby, so I go up to the sky garden. The day is bright and sunny, and I sit on the bench. There's a lovely breeze, and the water feature adds to the soothing atmosphere. The heat of the midmorning sun is very welcome against my skin. Its rays touch my exposed shoulders. I unhook the straps of my top so I can tan evenly. I close my eyes, put my head back, and sigh.

"Dylan?"

I open my eyes, and he is standing in the doorway, focused on me. I sit up and refasten my top as he approaches. He sits next to me on the bench, and his eyes take in my outfit.

"Are you going out?"

"Yes."

The sun shines on his heartbreakingly beautiful face. His green eyes are illuminated.

"Are you seeing Toby?"

I nod my head.

"You look pretty."

"Thanks," I say softly.

I reach for his hand, and he comes closer and puts his arm around me. I lean my head on his shoulder. It feels as if he's wrapping me in a warm coat on a cold winter's day. He has made no attempts to ask for more. He did hold me in his arms last night. I could sense he did not want to assume. But falling asleep in his arms only rekindles the fire. In my head, I list all the reasons why I love this man.

His warmth, the way he holds me as if he's afraid I'll disappear. He makes me feel safe and loved. Above everything else, this is what I crave the most.

I invite him to come with us, but he's reluctant to

Choosing Love

intrude.

"Toby won't mind. Come on, you deserve it. You've had a stressful birthday."

I take my pink corduroy jacket, just in case the weather changes. I wear comfortable wedged heel sandals, as I plan to do lots of walking.

"We can take the car," he says.

"How about we wing it?"

Toby is waiting for me at the Embankment Pier. His face splits into a huge smile when he sees Markus and me approaching while holding hands.

He hugs us both simultaneously.

"I'm going home to feed the cat," he says.

"You don't have a cat," I reply.

"I don't, but my neighbour does, and it's about time I did a good deed."

I roll my eyes. We hold on to him, Markus and I, and drag him along with us.

I sit sandwiched between my two guys.

We barely watch the show as the crowd is rowdy. They clap, stomp and whistle in appreciation of the actors on stage.

Toby joins in, and Markus laughs at his antics. London works its magic and pulls us back together. No one stays sad in Toby's company for long. I watch the two men goofing around.

We buy street food and eat out in the sunshine, and then we walk along the embankment eating ice cream. We each like different flavours —chocolate, strawberry, and non-dairy vanilla for Markus. Toby and I try some but find it's far too sweet. I grudgingly eat my strawberry and tell them about my favourite ice cream.

"It has rum, but you don't drink," says Toby.

"I know it's weird, but rum and raisin taste the best," I say.

We walk leisurely along the canal, and I hold hands with Toby. Markus slowly walks behind. We have not touched much today, but I sense his presence, our connection.

Choosing Love

As if Toby can read my mind, he turns and pulls us both together. When his arms enfold me, I hang on, closing my eyes. The warmth radiates through my entire body, and I never want to let go.

"This is my stop," says Toby.

Markus and I break apart as we're outside the train station.

"Let's take a river taxi back," I suggest, but Toby protests, so I look to Markus.

He convinces Toby to come with us, and we make our way home via the river. We hop on at the Embankment Pier, sailing to Greenwich Pier. I stand at the front of the boat, leaning onto the railings and looking out at the water. Toby and Markus sit nearby, talking.

We sail past Tower Bridge and the Tower of London. I think back to the night not long ago when the three of us went to the boat party on the river.

I become nostalgic for Boston when we sail past the Marina filled with moored yachts.

Toby laughs loudly and breaks me out of my reverie. His laughter is infectious. I turn to face them both. I wonder what Markus could be saying to him which is so funny that he has tears in his eyes. I smile and shake my head. Toby does have a flair for the dramatic.

We disembark at Greenwich Pier, and Markus hails a black cab. We drop Toby home first. On our way back to Canary Place, we don't speak, and we don't touch, but the tension between us is electric.

The past few months finally make sense. I quiet the noise, ignoring the shouting in my head that cautions me from taking this bold new step.

I am more afraid than ever before. When he reaches for my hand to help me out of the cab, my movement is symbolic.

I leave all my fear and doubts behind and take a step towards my here and now; to live in the moment. I imagine this is what Grams would say if I could pick up the phone and call her. Markus appears to have exorcised his demons, and now he is free. I see this

Choosing Love

in the way he gazes at me.

He is mine, and I am his.

Much later, when we fall into bed, exhausted from our day, I make my intentions clear. Reaching for his hand, I guide it lower, and his eyes never leave mine. When we finally kiss. I savour the sensation of his mouth on mine. He opens for me, and I taste the warm sweetness as I drink him in. I hear his soft moan, and I wrap my arms around him and pull him closer still. The warmth radiating from our closeness is exquisite.

With every touch, his words come back to me; all the reasons why he loves me, and I want to demonstrate a few reasons of my own. I don't speak the words; I want to show him, and I know he hears me. I bare my soul, giving all that I am, until he breaks apart, sobbing in my arms.

* * *

The next day, he takes me to meet his parents. Surprisingly, my nerves have not made an appearance. I dress in white jeans and a dark blue cold-shoulder top.

In the car, Markus glances at intervals toward me. He's wearing black jeans with a black and grey polo shirt. His clothes fit him so well, showing off his slim physique, and he completes the look with his Ray-Bans.

He turns the radio on to my favourite station, and I laugh. I'm self-conscious, so I don't sing along to the songs as usual. He starts singing, and it's very funny. He knows the songs very well and is pitch-perfect.

He pulls into a wide, leafy street and drives until he comes to wrought iron gates at the end of a cul-de-sac. He makes a call, and the gates open. Tall conifers line the path up to the house, which is nestled at the end of the drive. Tinted bay windows add character to this cottage-style house. He parks the car next to what must be Savannah's green Jaguar.

"This is quintessentially English."

It's a beautiful house, right out of a period romance novel. He holds my hand and rings the doorbell. A young boy, maybe fifteen, opens the door. His mouth falls open when he sees me.

"Josh?"

Markus introduces me, and I say hello. His face goes bright red, and Markus and I laugh as he's lost for words. Markus takes my hand, and we push past him.

"Markus!"

A young girl, I'm guessing seventeen, screams his name and comes over to hug him.

She has a chin-length wavy bob. She's very pretty, with dimples in her cheeks.

"Hello, Holly."

She gives me a hug when Markus introduces me.

Holly leads the way to the back of the house.

The interior is exquisite, and it looks much larger on the inside. The rooms are spacious and wide with high ceilings. I hear Savannah's voice.

I do notice some nerves now, as when we walk out in the garden, I am floored by how vast the grounds are. The front of the house is deceptive. This is not the small, quaint English home I first thought about.

This is the type of house that would feature in magazines as a show home.

I meet Matthew and Connie, his dad and aunt. They're both tall and fair with striking green eyes. Savannah comes over, and I'm happy to see one face I recognise. They all greet us with hugs and kisses. Connie's husband, Robert, is tall and of a stocky build. He has a jolly laugh.

Meeting Markus' mom is eerie, but I'm surprisingly calm as she comes over to meet me. If I were not wearing heels, we would be the same height, but everyone else towers over us. She looks so delicate, but her body is lithe and supple.

She wears a floaty white dress with long sleeves, which falls to her ankles. I notice her dainty ballerina flats. Her eyes are chocolate brown, her face is pear-shaped, and she has full lips like Markus. Her dark hair is very short and styled in a boy cut. She is pretty in an ethereal sort of way, and I like her immediately. She greets me before she greets Markus.

"Hello, Dylan, you're so lovely. I'm Helen."

"Hello, Helen, thank you."

She holds my hand and reaches for Markus. He bends and kisses her.

"Hello, Mama."

Savannah puts her arms around Helen and kisses her hair.

"Markus, take Dylan to meet Becca," she calls out as she leads her mother away.

Markus takes me back into the house and to the kitchen.

"Becca is our fairy godmother."

"Markus, my boy, good to see you," says a voice with a strong Caribbean accent.

She is of medium height and slim, with short jet-black hair styled fashionably. Her features are strong but quite attractive. She is perfectly coiffed from head to toe and looks out of place in the kitchen.

Markus greets her with hugs and kisses. Becca looks at me with huge eyes. She must be in her early forties, but it's hard to guess. Her eyes are like pools of wisdom.

"Who is this beautiful lady?" she says, taking my hand.

"Becca, meet my Dylan," he replies, and I smile warmly.

"Nice to meet you, Becca."

"You're American?"

"I'm from Boston. You're from Grenada, right?"

"That's right, honey. Have you been to my Island?"

"Yes, a few times. My dad has a band. He travels and plays the carnival seasons."

"Which band?"

"Two Great Bobs."

"Are you serious? Spice Mass '92 I was home and went to hear your dad play, and right up on the stage, there were two young girls —one fair-skinned, and

Choosing Love

another a little brown-skinned, pretty little things. Was that you?"

"Yes, that was me and my sister."

I'm astounded, and so caught up that I forget Markus is standing there. He stares at me.

"Small world," I say, shrugging.

"Indeed," Becca says, shaking her head.

"Well, darling, I'm just finishing up. You go and enjoy the sunshine."

I offer her some help, but she declines by telling me that I am an honoured guest, so she won't hear of it. I laugh and follow Markus to join the others.

"How weird is that?" I ask.

"If only Becca had brought you back home to me, you would've been mine much sooner."

"Er, I was fifteen; Underage," I remind him, and he laughs.

"Besides, I found you all on my own. It was written in the stars."

"I believe that one," he whispers, taking my hand.

I enjoy the day with Markus' family. His cousin Joshua recovers enough to talk to me and explains that he thought I was a famous singer.

"I get that a lot," I say.

Becca joins the family party. She tells everyone that she saw me when I was a young teenager, and they make a fuss about it. I gaze at Markus; he's sitting next to me with his arm across the back of my chair.

"Come with me?" he whispers in my ear.

He takes my hand as I stand, "Mama, can you excuse us?"

Helen waves us off.

He leads me along the path towards a gazebo at the end of the walkway. There is a large pond at the back. We sit, and I take in the beauty all around me. I like seeing his family home.

"Thank you," he whispers.

"For what?"

Choosing Love

"For coming here with me today. It means a lot."

"I like your family. They seem to adore you."

"It's probably because they hardly see me. Absence makes the heart grow fonder."

I stand and move towards the bannister, looking out towards the water. A gentle breeze blows and moves my hair. I sigh, loving the silky warmness against my skin. I turn to face him. He sits with his legs extended, gazing at me intensely, then he stands and walks slowly towards me. He pulls me closer until our bodies touch, and my pulse races.

"Have you kissed many girls right here in your gazebo?"

His lips touch mine gently.

"Only one," he whispers.

"Do you expect me to believe I'm the first girl you've kissed at your childhood home?"

"You asked about the gazebo."

Music floats over to us, and he groans.

"What?"

"Mama likes to dance."

We head back over to the rest of the family.

His mom is already dancing on the makeshift dance floor in the middle of the lawn. Markus goes over and dances with her. The moment is incredibly sweet.

His dad, Matthew, comes over to me and takes me onto the dance floor. It's such good fun. I even dance with Joshua, who is astonishingly shy. It's too funny.

A little later, Becca lights a huge cake, and we sing Happy Birthday to Markus and Savannah.

Becca asks me how I cope with cooking for Markus, and I tell her I don't mind. I like the challenge.

It takes a lot of planning, but I plan for fun. Markus tells them I plan what I'm wearing a week in advance and that I even plan to have a plan. They crack up.

We head home soon after, but I'm sad to leave

as I've had such a good time. We say goodbye and promise to visit again soon. Becca hugs me and turns to Markus.

"No pressure, but I like her. Make it happen."

* * *

My gynaecologist's office is on a quiet street close to London Bridge. As I walk over the bridge, I don't notice the scenery as I usually do because Stacey and the baby invade my thoughts.

Markus and I have taken no precautions during sex since we became a couple. My mind is troubled that he would have been just as careless with her.

I don't have the facts, but I wonder how far along she is and when he was with her last. There was no mention of the sordid affair at his parents' house.

She must have been on the pill, as I recall her words to him.

Why did she not tell him when he saw her in Paris? Why reveal her actions in such a public way?

Now that I have been with Markus, it's not hard

to guess her motives for taking such measures.

As I wait at the reception, I notice the posters about pregnancy. Shiny, happy women with glossy smiles advertising the joys of motherhood. There are no equally thrilled males in any of the pictures.

For me, it represents the reality that I could be facing in a few months' time. Averting my eyes, I think of my own sister, abandoned merely hours after her birth, and I shudder to find myself in such a situation.

"Dylan Weekes?"

"Hello, Dylan. I am Dr Amy Forester. Please call me Amy. What brings you here today?"

I tell her.

"The pains you are experiencing during sex, you say this only happens with certain positions?"

I nod.

"Can you describe the pain? Is it during penetration or after?"

"Umm, after he is inside, it feels like he is hitting

against an obstruction."

"Sometimes pain can be caused due to the size of the penis."

"I don't have pains if I am on my back or on top if I position myself just right."

"And you take no oral contraceptives?"

"No. Well, this is my first sexual partner, so I'm not on anything."

"How often would you say you have unprotected sex?"

"Almost every day, sometimes twice a day."

"For how long?"

"Since Easter, so five weeks."

"When did you last menstruate?"

"Two weeks ago, on the twenty- second of May."

"I would like to do a pregnancy test first."

"What?" my voice comes out loud.

"It's normal procedure, Dylan."

The check-up lasts longer than I expect.

The nurse prods, pokes, and looks around inside me, and I hate it.

Finally, I sit in Dr Amy's office and wait for the diagnosis.

"The pregnancy test is negative."

A fleeting pang of disappointment rises into my chest, taking me by surprise, but I don't have time to process this unexpected feeling.

"But Dylan, there is a problem."

She tells me I have submucosal fibroids, which, if not removed, could affect my ability to conceive. She also says they're causing me to have pains during sex.

I'm not sure what to do with this information. My mind is a mixture of emotions as I try to process the news in the taxi on my way home. The irony is not lost on me. My boyfriend's ex-lover shows up pregnant with his child, and now I find out that I potentially cannot conceive.

Choosing Love

I tell Markus the news that night. He's cleaning up the kitchen after dinner, and I'm sitting at the breakfast bar.

"I went to see the gynaecologist today."

He stops his movement, staring at me blankly.

"Sorry. I forgot about that," he says, "Is everything okay?"

"It depends on how you look at it."

I exhale. Now is not the time to be funny, I guess, but there is no stopping me.

"The good news is that we don't have to worry about me becoming pregnant. We could just go crazy and do it every day like rabbits."

I laugh, but he is not amused.

"Do rabbits do it every day?"

I don't know the answer. I decide to be serious and tell him.

"Like a tumour inside of you?"

When he puts it like that, it does sound scary.

"Yes, but they're benign and quite common."

"What's the prognosis?"

"I can have them removed. She suggests I do, as they'll become larger in time."

I speak quietly, as for me, this is the scary part. I don't want to have surgery.

We stare at each other. He comes around the island and touches my face, then pulls me into his arms.

We go to bed soon after.

I've already showered, so I brush my teeth and dress in my new shorts and camisole silk pyjamas. I crawl into bed and wait for him to come to me. The anticipation is always so sweet that I'm already aroused. This is the effect he has on me. He comes out of the bathroom, naked.

He pulls his bottoms on. I leave them for him at the foot of the bed as I love watching him dress. He comes to my side and removes my shorts. I don't know why I bother to get dressed for bed.

He pushes my camisole up and examines my tummy. My heart rate spikes and my breathing is harsher.

"How many?"

"Seven."

He palms my tummy. I'm no longer self-conscious as I know why it pokes out. I say this to him, and he shakes his head. He leans down to kiss me there.

"I didn't notice that your tummy pokes out."

"It's not flat like yours, but it used to be. The changes started a few years ago."

"I love your body, Dylan. Every inch of you."

His kisses move lower. My breathing is louder as I know where he will end up. Markus does not disappoint me. I do a special job down there, taking extra care in my twice-a-day cleaning, just for this occasion.

It's not so much the act that feels exquisite, but the way he seems to enjoy feasting on me. He eats slowly tonight, but I have learned that patience is a virtue. When the release finally comes, I feel it in every inch of me.

The first chapter

Summer arrives with a heat wave, and I find creative ways to stay cool. The days are hot, but my nights are even hotter. I break out my summer clothes to deal with the daytime heat, but I have no solution for the nights.

All day, I think about the moment when I can come to bed and make love with him.

His touch is like fire, leaving me in a heap of smoking embers night after night.

I can't complain. I love him more with every touch, every glance, every kiss, and every moment we are together. If we were to part, I would be broken.

It's the most frightening feeling to put so much trust in another human being and give him everything I am. Yet, I'm willing to risk it for one moment in his arms.

Today is the longest day of the year, and even though it's midweek, we invite his sister over. We order food and sit in the garden. Another water feature was added a few days ago, and it helps to keep us cool. Markus opens the parasol, and it blocks the sun. London is burning, and my skin is already a few shades darker, but Savannah is sitting in the sunshine, soaking up the rays.

"Savannah, who looks after Bruno when you're out?"

"I have a sitter. She stays with him until I'm home, or if I'm away, he stays at her house."

I laugh, "Are you serious? I've never heard of such a thing."

"That dog is spoilt," says Markus.

Choosing Love

"Everyone has a dog sitter, don't they? I mean, how would one be able to have a life? You can't take them everywhere."

"I prefer cats. They take care of themselves," I reply.

"Would you like me to get you a pussy?" Markus asks, and I almost choke on my water. Savannah cracks up.

I tell her that her barbecue chicken is from Nate's restaurant.

"This is so tasty," she replies, licking her fingers.

I've not had chicken for a while. I only tend to cook what Markus can eat.

"Vana, that is absolutely disgusting!"

"I do apologise. What do they put in that sauce? Markus, it's such a shame you'll never taste anything this good ever again. I mean, grass just doesn't cut it."

"I beg to differ, Vana. I tasted something sweet for breakfast," he winks at me when he says this.

"Bloody hell, would you two like me to give you a moment?" Savannah says.

She tops up her Sauvignon Blanc. It's her third glass, so one of us will have to drive her home. I take all the empty plates and run down to put them in the dishwasher. When I return, Savannah comes and sits across from me under the shade.

"Where are you going on holiday this year, Dylan?"

"I usually just go home to see my family."

"I've never been to America. Maybe you can take me with you one day. I brought you some brochures from the holiday I just booked."

The glossy writing in bold reads "Europe's hidden gems".

"I've never been anywhere else in Europe apart from London and Munich."

"Trust me. You should take charge of booking the holiday. You leave it up to Markus, and you'll be camping in the great outdoors with giant mosquitos devouring your lovely skin."

"Do you go home for Christmas as well?" she asks, pouring more wine into her glass.

"I go home for Thanksgiving weekend and Christmas every year."

"Oh, that's a shame. I thought you could come skiing with us."

She touches my hand, and I glance at Markus. He is playing with my hair, deep in thought.

"Let me come back to you on that," I say.

Markus and I have not made any plans, but I'm hoping to be wherever he is.

"Where are you planning to go?" I ask.

"Davos, Switzerland," she whispers and giggles.

I think she might be a little tipsy.

Markus soon leaves us and takes the bottle of wine with him. Savannah grins sheepishly and asks for some tea.

"I think I've had too much of your white," she

says.

I make a whole pot, and Markus takes it up to the garden for me. I thank him, and he goes back inside. I'm enjoying his sister's visit. It makes me realise I don't have enough women in my life. A little voice in the back of my head cautions me from surrounding myself with only people from Markus's life.

"Mama loves you, Dylan. She and Daddy think you're perfect for Markus."

"Do they know about Stacey and the baby?" I ask without thinking.

She sighs, "Yes. Markus told them a few weeks ago."

I feel bad for prying behind his back, but we don't talk about it anymore, and I don't dare to ask him.

"Do you know what's happening?"

She looks towards the door, probably checking the coast is clear.

"Markus is rather shell-shocked, as we all are. Mama and daddy are quite upset about it."

Choosing Love

I didn't consider how they would feel, but I know Markus is sad. I sometimes wake up in the middle of the night, and he is not in bed. I glance down at the brochures on the table.

Perhaps a change of scenery is just what he needs, what we both need.

I change the subject, not wanting to ruin the relaxing evening with any more talk of babies.

"Are you taking anyone on holiday with you?" I ask, and she grins, nodding.

"Nothing serious, of course, but beggars can't be choosers. I work very hard, so I think it's only fair someone should work me even harder."

I laugh out loud. I never imagined she would speak in this way. The change of topic was a good call. We chat and laugh until the sun goes down and the evening becomes cooler.

She does not appear to be affected much by the alcohol after four glasses, but Markus drives her home in her car, and I follow in his.

She hugs me outside her door.

"Good night, Dylan. Let's have lunch next week."

She holds onto her brother, and he takes her up the stairs. I think back to the last time we were here when Stacey showed up.

"Did you have a nice evening?"

Markus pulls into the parking spot back at his apartment.

"I did. She's good fun. It's so nice to have a girlie chat."

I miss my sister.

He puts his arm over my shoulder, and we go upstairs.

* * *

I sit on the Chaise Longue with his laptop on my knee, trying to book a holiday from the brochures his sister gave me. When I mentioned the idea to him, he seemed excited.

"Our first holiday as a couple," he said, and I smiled.

Choosing Love

"Have you been wild camping before?" he then added, and my smile disappeared.

We made a compromise. He agreed we would go away to some exotic location of my choice, and I've promised to try wild camping in Scotland.

I know I'm doing this very last minute, but I blanche. I slam the lid and put the laptop on the floor.

"What's wrong?" Markus asks.

"I can't find anything suitable. Let's just go camping; I don't mind."

He picks up the laptop and opens it up, sitting next to me.

"How about this one? I like Budapest," he scrolls through the options.

"Yes, but the price is ridiculous, Markus. That's my entire year's wage, and I haven't even booked the flights or bought my bikini."

"Which bikini will you be buying?" his eyes fall on my breasts.

"None after I pay for *this* holiday. I'll have to go naked."

"In that case, I better make sure we have the beach all to ourselves," he reaches over to kiss me.

"Dylan, I'll pay."

He goes to fetch his wallet, pulls out a black MasterCard and passes it to me.

"Pick a holiday you like," he says, and then he whispers in my ear, "I'm thinking red for the bikini, but I know you'll surprise me."

His words travel straight to my core. He walks away to finish dressing while I book the holiday; four days on a luxury yacht in Croatia, three nights in Budapest and five nights in Rhodes, Greece. I search for the flights, and I check if he is happy with the times.

"Why is it such a long wait?"

"It's what's available."

He comes over and looks at the screen, and then he looks at me.

Choosing Love

"I've never travelled economy before," he says.

"Am I sleeping with the Prince of Wales?"

I just spent thirty thousand pounds on a holiday. Surely, the card is maxed out.

"I'm not being a snob, Dylan. I can't do the waiting. The summer Olympics are on; it will be chaos."

Nausea chokes my response. I've only ever spent this much money to buy my apartment.

An asset that I would own for life, not on a holiday that would be over in a few days. I purchase the tickets: six flights in total, as there is one interchange, for two adults, first class, and another twenty thousand pounds.

* * *

"Are you okay, D?"

Toby and I are at Mare Street Market. I chose this one today for a much-needed dose of reality, as yesterday was spent in a bit of a daze.

"Not really," I say, and he takes my hand.

"What's wrong?"

His face is serious.

"Markus and I are going away on a holiday."

Toby cracks up. He sounds so happy that it makes me smile. I tell him about the cost of the holiday. We sit on a bench, and he watches me, seemingly slightly bewildered, shaking his head.

"He lives in an exclusive penthouse, and he drives a luxury car. What did you think, D? He's rich!"

"I know, Toby. Spending the money brought it home to me."

I start biting my thumbnail, but he pushes my hand away.

"It seems so wasteful, just for the two of us."

He puts his arm around me.

"I know you think I'm foolish, but I just like being with him. I don't need all the extras."

He kisses my cheek.

Choosing Love

"You're a diamond in the rough, D. I don't think you're foolish. Where are you going?"

I tell him about the holiday and the little magical black card.

"You'll have everything catered to you and quality time together."

"Have you sorted out your wardrobe yet?"

I shake my head to indicate no.

"What?" Toby exclaims, and I giggle.

"Up you get, no more food shopping. There is no way I'm letting you head off on holiday, not looking your best. You still got the magic card? Let's go."

* * *

As my holiday approaches, work is busier than ever. June is my year-end, so I spend the first two weeks in July going into the office at the crack of dawn and sometimes leaving at eleven p.m. Markus is shocked and tells me I'm crazy to work like this.

"Markus, this is the nature of my job. I love it."

He's been taking cabs to and from work as he's let me take the car, spending obscene cash so I can park in the city, but I appreciate being able to arrive home in record time.

Today is the last day of the madness. My team and I go out for lunch with the auditors, then they sign off the accounts, and I'm free. I can go off on my holiday to recharge my batteries.

My head hits the pillow at two a.m., but I am so wired that I can't sleep. We haven't had sex this week, and my body is missing him. I'm not sure if it's the heat. This environmentally friendly penthouse has one flaw. There is no air conditioning.

I could go up to the garden, but it's late, so I start to touch myself. My nipples are tight, and they hurt. Markus opens his eyes and looks over at me. The next second, he is inside of me, with his mouth on my body and his hands touching me everywhere. My moans are loud in the stillness of the morning. He doesn't make a sound, but from the intense look in his eyes, I know all too well; he's doing this for me.

Choosing Love

I wrap my legs around him, and his warm hands grip my tender flesh. The stress of the past two weeks melts away as my man caters to my needs. I'm hungry, and it's feeding time.

His lips find mine, so he kisses me deeply and moves back to my throbbing nipples. I explode loudly and shamelessly; he comes soon after.

It's several minutes before my heart and breathing regulate. He pulls out of my body, wraps me in his arms, and I drift off.

* * *

I lose all sense of time somewhere between Budapest and Rhodes. I've always wanted to travel the world. I find something that I love in every city I visit. This moment in my life is pure bliss, and I'm past caring whether the balance is out of sync. Maybe this is how it's supposed to be. We're all allotted a certain amount of happiness, and this is mine. It would be foolish not to own it, so I do.

I've been on the journey of discovery for the past few months with Markus as my guide. I let him lead me now; he can take me anywhere he likes, and I will go. All my senses are engaged at present. The food, the people, and the history are all blended to create the perfect getaway. I make one new discovery. I say new, but it should have been obvious all along.

Markus is extremely kind. He shows respect to everyone he meets, even if they're pushy or rude. He is always polite; it must be the British in him. I don't make a fuss or let him know that I've noticed, but I think to myself, *if a man is kind and says you are the woman of his dreams, does that mean he will love you forever?*

The days are not long enough to see everything, and Markus says we can come back another time. I love the way he speaks as if it's a done deal. He hires a moped, and we roll around the city with my arms around him; this is my favourite part —holding on for dear life as we zoom past the scenery.

He's nervous because I couldn't fit the helmet on my head, as I'd had faux locks done for this trip. They are long and thick and very blond. When I came home from the salon with my new look, his face was priceless.

He tells me my dreads are sexy.

"Hold on tight. Don't let go!"

"Don't worry. If I fall, the hair will protect my head!"

He laughs out loud at that one, and I see yet another side to him. He seems so young and carefree. Our first four days are spent on a luxury yacht off the coast of Hvar.

Apart from the crew and catering staff, we have the entire boat to ourselves. It's brand new and on its maiden voyage. We swim, explore the nearby island, make love in the Adriatic Sea, and watch the sunrise and the sunset.

We don't talk much. I opt instead to spend long moments absorbing the world around me, and he does the same, so we are quiet mostly, but always touching and always close. I start a journal on our first night in Budapest. Sleep eludes me, so I write down everything I'm feeling. Whatever happens in the future, I want to remember this time, so I take pictures every day.

The women are some of the most beautiful I have seen. I say this to Markus, but he disagrees. He tells me the most beautiful woman he has ever seen is me. I suppose it helps that at the time I'm wearing a strapless red dress. It's sunset, and we stand on the balcony just before dinner, taking it all in.

We gaze into each other's eyes, and the world around us disappears. It's just us two.

I kiss him softly and wipe my lipstick off his lips. Toby had given me strict orders. He picked out this dress and told me that it cannot be worn without a matching lip colour. I repeat this to Markus, and he smiles. There is a live band playing, and after dinner, Markus and I dance into the early hours of the morning.

* * *

I lie in bed wide awake for hours. It's our last night in Budapest, and I decide to write in my journal. We're catching a late afternoon flight to Rhodes tomorrow. Opening the sliding doors and

Choosing Love

stepping out on the balcony, I listen to the sounds of the city below.

The room is hot, but I keep it this way as my hair dries easily.

"Are you okay?"

I turn, and he is standing naked in the doorway.

"I can't sleep."

He moves closer and wraps me in his arms; his arousal pressing into my flesh.

"I can see your body through your nightgown."

"It's much cooler outside."

He lifts my gown over my head and puts it on the balcony wall. The cool breeze caresses my overheated skin. His hands are vice-like on my hips, and my legs fold around him; then he slides me down onto his erection slowly, and I grab the wall for support.

"I've got you," he whispers, and I let go.

He moves us over to a chair in the corner. My legs are on either side of him as I move my hips in a circular motion. With his hands on my thighs, he nibbles gently on my ripened nipples. I gasp as the erotic sensations travel through my body.

My core muscles spasm and tighten around his throbbing shaft, and he moans loudly. I do it again, and he swears. I sit up straight until my legs touch the floor. Sharp pain like hot heat sizzles across my back, and so I ease back a bit, clenching tighter around him again, and he ejaculates deep inside of me, swearing as he loses control. I smile and kiss his lips.

He stands and cradles me in his arms. I reach out to grab my nightgown, but it falls off and flies into the wind. We laugh, and he takes me to bed. He falls asleep almost immediately. I drift off much later.

In the morning, before breakfast, he wakes me to make love.

"I want to make up for last night."

"There's no need, Markus," I say, but he trails kisses down the back of my body, his fingers sliding inside of me, and I can't speak for several minutes.

We catch our flight for the last part of our

holiday. We're dressed identically in white tops and blue jeans with matching Ray-Bans, my faux locs wrapped in a white scarf.

We hold hands as we board the plane, and all throughout the flight, we smile at each other, and he kisses my hand. We're the only ones in this section of the aeroplane. The flight attendant brings us magazines with pictures of expensive jewellery and perfumes.

I skim through the pages, and my eyes linger on a stunning solitaire diamond ring. It looks very similar to the one Sam gave me when he proposed.

"Do you wear jewellery, Dylan?"

"Not really."

Grams left her small jewellery collection to our mother. I did inherit a stunning emerald broach from Aunt Francine, but I never wore it, so I gave it to Kizzy.

"Is that by choice?"

"I can't afford jewellery, Markus."

"So, it's not because you are opposed to diamonds?"

My throat is suddenly tight, and no sounds emerge. I'm wondering what kind of *diamonds* he is referring to. My eyes drift back to the page of the glossy magazine, showcasing the engagement ring, and my heart rate accelerates.

"Are you alright?"

I drink from my glass of water.

"I'm good."

I cough in an un-ladylike manner.

He taps me on my back, looking concerned. I exaggerate the coughing a bit to make sure he does not talk about diamonds anymore. Politely, I close the magazine and place it on the chair in front of me.

We touch down in Athens, and Olympic fanfare is at a fever pitch. The flags of the participating countries are on display all over the airport as we make our way to the connecting flight from Athens to Rhodes.

Choosing Love

Our villa is on the beach. Only the sound of the waves can be heard for miles. I step outside onto the pristine sandy beach. A white hammock sways gently in the breeze, and the ocean is the colour of his eyes. Markus hugs me from behind.

"Do you like it?"

"Yes, very much."

"Let's go for a swim," he whispers in my ear.

* * *

The shower is hot and soothes my aching body, and I liberally apply the moisturiser all over.

He watches my every move, but I don't look at him. It's day four, and I'm beyond sore. Pulling on a long nightgown, I crawl under the crisp, fresh sheets.

"You are so beautiful."

He kisses my shoulder.

He cannot be serious.

"I'm sore."

"Are you?"

He reaches under the sheets and caresses between my thighs, and I roll away from him onto my side.

"Yes. It tends to happen if you are having sex multiple times a day!"

"I'm sorry, Dylan. Why didn't you say I was hurting you?"

His lips are close to my ear. His hand caresses the gentle slope of my hips, and my body responds. Wet heat pools along my thighs. I sigh...

"I enjoy when it is happening, but after, I feel the effects. Especially today."

We've had sex four times already.

"I apologise, Dylan. I see you in your bikini, and I can't seem to resist. That yellow one with the strings was particularly brutal. It barely covered you."

"It also doesn't help that when I do this," he runs his fingers lightly down my arm, and my nipples tighten and poke out, "that happens."

He bends and takes one into his mouth, and my

breathing changes.

"You're always so ready for me."

His kisses trail down my body. He disappears under the sheet, positioning between my thighs. *He is being so gentle...*

I moan with utter delight when his tongue touches the fleshiest part of me.

"Mmm...You taste like nectar."

He reaches up to fondle my breasts, his fingers stained with the juices of my love. Our moans are carried on the evening air.

I run my fingers through his hair, and he grabs my hand and interlocks his fingers with mine. I can't see him, so it makes our lovemaking more salacious.

I should complain more often.

My intimate muscles spasm and contract before releasing me, and I float along to the sounds of the gentle waves lapping on the edges of the soft sand. He reappears and lies next to me, pulling me close.

"You're so good at that," I say, still catching my

breath.

"You smell heavenly."

"You like it?"

"Yes, very much."

During my afternoon massage, my masseur had organic sweet almond oil, which I'd applied to my skin tonight. He supplied me with enough to last a few months. Sated, I purr as my eyelids droop.

"Sleep, my gorgeous girl," he whispers, and I drift.

When I wake the next day, it is past one in the afternoon. Markus' side of the bed is empty.

My body hums deliciously from the long sleep. My skin is glowing, and my face looks fresh. I shower and choose a floaty white midi dress that caresses my skin. Wrapping my hair up in a red scarf, I step outside. Markus is lying on the hammock. He gazes at me as I approach, reaching out to lift me into the space next to him.

We rock slowly as the gentle sea breeze drifts

over to us.

"Hello."

"I missed breakfast and lunch."

"Hungry?"

"Famished."

He moves away to order my food. He wears all-white shorts, a t-shirt and handmade jewellery on his wrist that he bought from a stall in Budapest. His skin is golden brown.

He walks back over to me.

I'm a lucky girl.

"You're gorgeous," I say.

"Ah, Dylan."

"What?"

"I've ordered your breakfast so now you reward me with compliments."

I stare at him. His green eyes sparkle in the sunlight. He climbs back onto the hammock and pulls me into his arms.

"What are you saying?"

"Food and sex. Those are your vices. In that order."

"I'm seriously outraged."

"No complaints from me. It's an easy life when I know how to keep my woman happy."

I turn, and he adjusts so we can lie facing each other. The hammock sways gently.

"Is that how you think of me, as your woman?"

"Yes," he whispers, "There'll never be anyone else for me, Dylan."

The little voice inside my head wants to remind him that very soon, it may not just be us two. There's another life that is eminent. Soon, he will become a father, and responsible for another human being. He'll be forever connected to a woman he tries to forget. A woman who is not me.

But I don't utter those words. Lying here with him at this very moment, I can believe another way is possible, and if not, then perhaps this is how it should be. Two months ago, I was ready to walk away, but now he has made it impossible. To leave this man is to lose myself.

I hear the sincerity in his voice, and I'm moved beyond belief.

This, too, feels like more than love.

I stare into his eyes, mine suddenly moist from the emotions playing havoc with my pulse.

He must see my fear showing on my face, so he changes the topic.

"Do you want to do any sightseeing today?"

"Can we visit the old town?"

There is a gentle knock on the door.

"Sure," he kisses me lightly on the lips and goes to answer the door.

Kizzy and me

Toby and I are sitting at a small café at the edge of Portobello Road. He's just returned from visiting his mother in Jamaica.

"How was Gina?"

I regret asking immediately. He sighs.

"It was the first time in my life she looked disappointed in me."

Tears form in his eyes, and his voice breaks.

"Gina thought you and I would be together."

"Did you tell her that I did try?" I say to cheer

Choosing Love

him up, but he barely smiles.

"Give her time. She loves you. You're her only child, and you two have a close bond. She'll come round."

"I just hope I haven't disappointed her for nothing. This relationship with Nicolos, it's the scariest thing I've ever done."

"Scarier than the first time you shaved your head?"

"I wish that I could tell you it will all be easy. If it's what you want, you'll have to put in the effort," I say.

"I'm not sure what to say at work," he says.

"Why don't you ask Markus for advice? I know it's not his field, but perhaps he could ask someone at his firm. Surely, there must be other professional people who are gay."

"That's a good idea. I will."

He opens his box of Godiva's and takes one. He offers me the box, but I decline.

"How does Nicolos make you feel?"

He finally cracks a smile.

"When you start feeling stressed, try to focus on this. That's what I do."

He nods, and we finish our coffee. The market is about to close, so we head to the tube station waiting to catch the next train.

"Is Markus okay about you going to your place when your sister visits?"

"No. He doesn't understand why, so I gave up that idea. My sister will stay with us at his place. I don't mind; he has more room; this is how he always puts it."

"I think he's afraid if you left, you might not go back."

Toby hits the nail on the head.

"He goes away on business, and I don't give him grief, even though I miss him."

The train pulls in, and we step on.

"It's a nice problem to have," Toby says, smiling.

Choosing Love

* * *

I am practically bouncing in my seat.

"Dylan, you're like a kid going to the candy store."

We're on the way to the airport to pick up my sister. She will be with us over the bank holiday weekend. Her semester at Harvard will be starting in a few days.

Even though I'm excited, I'm nervous for when Markus will see her. He makes such a fuss about my looks, but honestly, he is in for a surprise. The most annoying thing is that my sister not only looks good, but she also knows it.

As we approach the arrivals area, I whisper to Markus.

"Do me a favour; don't sleep with my sister."

"Dylan, why would I sleep with your sister?"

He tries to meet my gaze, but I keep my eye on the gate, checking the flight details. He sighs and takes my hand instead.

When Kizzy appears, I groan. She's wearing a trouser suit that fits her to perfection. Her hair is cut in a short bob with bronze highlights. She is simply breathtaking despite the long flight.

Markus laughs and covers his face with his hands. Kizzy sees me and squeals, and I run into her arms.

"Dilly!"

"Kizzy, I like your hair. When did you cut it?"

She looks so beautiful it is a crime.

I pull her out of the way of the crowd and take her over to meet Markus. He can't take that smile off his face. Her eyes go wide.

"Dilly, you have a boyfriend?"

"Louder, Kizzy, because no one can actually hear you."

"It's good to meet you, Kizzy. Yes, I'm Dylan's boyfriend. Although, it seems she forgot to mention me."

She stares at him with her mouth open.

"Wow, say that again. I love your accent."

Choosing Love

She pulls him in for another hug, and it goes on for longer than I'm okay with, but this is Kizzy. What's mine is usually hers.

We help with her bags and suitcases, and Markus gives me an amused look.

"Yes, she's only here for four days. Kizzy never travels light," I say.

Kizzy and I sit in the back, so we can have a proper catch-up. She's super excited, and I'm soon caught up in the magic that is my little sister.

I have a full itinerary for her visit. I'm taking her shopping to all the major stores in central London. It's carnival weekend. We're going to a Soca rave tonight. Then, onto Borough Market tomorrow. I'm also planning on throwing her a party to celebrate her amazing achievement.

We reserve Sunday and Monday for the carnival, and she leaves on Tuesday. That's the plan. I'm hoping we will achieve it.

When Kizzy and I are together, the inevitable ugliness always rears its head. My resentment towards my little sister comes to the surface.

I know it's not fair to either Kizzy or myself; what happened to us as children. We had no say in the matter. Our mother left us with a broken father. Our grandparents tried hard to make it up to us, but they, too, had lost a daughter, their only child. It was as if when our mother left, she took all the happiness with her.

Our father and grandfather spoilt my sister. It was their way to compensate for the way she was left. Even I would indulge her every whim. Only Grams insisted that Kizzy and I be treated equally. She wanted us to support each other.

Whenever we fought, she was never interested in who started the fight. She would punish us both. Her message was clear: you're sisters. I try to remember that now. I want this to be a drama-free visit.

We dress for our night in the town. Kizzy helps me pick my outfit, styling my hair, and applying my makeup. My red strapless dress shows off my full figure. Markus is practically drooling when he sees

Choosing Love

me, but when Kizzy walks into the room, I feel like I disappear.

She is wearing a white dress and has a red rose in her hair. She is simply classy and breath-taking.

She steals the show every time.

Even Toby, who meets us at the dance hall, cannot take his eyes off my sister.

We have a blast, all four of us. Kizzy and I love dancing, and Soca music takes us back to fun days on the road with our dad. The night ends for me on an extra high as Markus, who is besotted, has eyes only for me. We don't make it to bed until three a.m., but it's another forty minutes before I can finally sleep.

"I heard you and Markus early this morning, Dilly."

Kizzy and I are at Borough Market, sitting in a café. We're both drinking lemon water.

"Markus assures me the walls are soundproof."

"Not if the door is open."

"I guess not."

"Did he take your virginity?"

I look around the café to see if there is anyone listening.

"Yes."

"When? I can't believe you didn't tell me?"

She shakes her head, and her wooden earrings jangle.

"Five months ago."

"It all happened so fast. I'm still trying to process what I'm feeling, you know."

"Well, he's lucky to have you. Make sure he never forgets."

"What about you? Left any broken hearts at Dartmouth?"

"I've no time, Dilly. I've not had sex in ages. This drought is giving me dry skin, and here you are in London with all these gorgeous men."

We hail a taxi back to Canary Place and start cooking for the barbeque party tonight.

Choosing Love

We've invited Toby and Nicolos, and Markus has invited Ryan, a young man from work.

He has just moved here from Spain and doesn't know many people, so Markus thought he could hang with Kizzy.

I tell Kizzy about Markus' diet, and she shares some ideas with me about what I can cook for him.

"Lots of people at college are going vegan, so it's not a new concept."

Kizzy is a great cook and not afraid to experiment. She prepares vegetable skewers for the barbeque and makes a special sauce and a garden salad. She works so hard that I tell her she can go and relax. She skips off to the sky garden to stock up on her vitamin D.

Markus comes through the door with our guests in tow.

I greet Nicolos warmly. Since he and Toby have officially become a couple, I want to encourage their relationship. At work, I hear the whispers behind Toby's back.

Markus' advice was for Toby to be upfront and honest as he has the top job, so he made an announcement to the entire staff. I thought my friend was brave.

This is where my mind is as I wrap my arms around Nicolos and lead our guests up to the roof.

Markus' role is to fire up the grill. When we arrive in the garden, Kizzy is lying on a sun lounger, sunbathing topless. Her eyes are closed, and she sings along to the music coming from the speakers.

"Kizzy!"

She looks up and smiles apologetically, pulling her dress over her head. Despite my annoyance, we have a lovely evening. I catch up with Nicolos and leave Kizzy to chat with Ryan. By the time everyone has left, I'm still fuming.

I excuse myself and go down to bed, leaving Kizzy and Markus chatting on the roof. I'm tired after the late night yesterday.

In the morning, I decide to go for a run. Markus is asleep next to me. I run along the canal. The early morning rays glisten on the water, a beautiful sight. I end up being out for a couple of hours. The morning air is cool. I arrive back home with a clear head and run up the stairs of the building. It's just after ten, so I expect Markus to be up.

I run up the stairs to ask him what he wants for breakfast. As I approach the ensuite, I can hear Kizzy's voice. My blood runs cold as I walk towards the open door.

Markus is naked in the shower, while Kizzy leans against the marble top across from him, and they are both laughing. I go nuts.

"Markus?"

He looks over at me. Ever calm.

"Dylan, Kizzy is just leaving."

"Why are you in here?"

"I'm sorry, I was just messing around."

Markus comes out of the bathroom with his towel wrapped around his waist.

"What's the point of covering up now?"

I storm out of the bedroom, slamming the door. Kizzy comes down the stairs.

"Sorry, Dilly."

I don't want to see her face.

"You couldn't wait to ruin this for me!"

"No, that's not true."

"This is typical of you."

I know this is a low blow, but I don't stop.

"Dilly, don't be so dramatic. Nothing happened, he loves you."

She sounds upset. I know my words hurt her.

"Yes, he loves me and that kills you."

I'm shouting now, and tears of fury cascade down my face.

"You think it kills me that he loves you? Everybody loves you. I said I'm sorry!"

"You see, that's the problem with you, Kizzy, you're always sorry. How about for once trying not to do anything to be sorry about?"

Choosing Love

I wipe my tears, but they keep flowing.

"I don't have to listen to this. Nothing happened with your precious boyfriend!"

She turns to go as Markus comes down the stairs, now fully dressed. He walks over and tries to hug me.

"Don't touch me!"

"Dylan, stop this. Nothing happened."

He tries again, but I push him away.

"You think nothing happened, but I know differently. This is what she wanted, to humiliate me."

I am past caring what either of them think.

"Are you so insecure that as soon as anyone gets close to your man, you think the worst? You've lost your edge, Dylan. You came to London and got fat. Guess you're no longer the beauty queen."

She storms out of the room. Markus is looking at me, and I can't read his face. Kizzy comes back and then leaves through the front door. Markus goes after her, and I go upstairs to shower.

We were going to watch the children's carnival parade today. I dress in an outfit that Kizzy had picked out for me yesterday. I sit at my dressing table, brushing my hair. Markus comes into the room. Our eyes meet in the mirror.

"What just happened?"

"Why don't you tell me? I found you naked in the shower while my sister was there watching you."

"Dylan, I told you. Nothing happened."

"That's not what it looked like to me!"

"Are you saying you don't believe me? Do you think I would lie to you?"

I don't respond.

"Kizzy came into the shower room, and I asked her to leave. I could tell she was only messing around. I think, at first, she thought it was you in the shower, but then she saw me, and I guess she had the idea to try it on."

I glare at him.

"Try what exactly?"

Choosing Love

"Try to see if I was true to you," he shrugs, "she needn't have bothered."

My resolve breaks, and I start to cry. He pulls me into his arms.

"Dylan...don't cry. You must know I love only you."

"And Kizzy loves you too. Last night, after you went to bed. She talked about you and how amazing you are. We agree on that."

"Did she tell you where she is going?"

"She was already in the lift, so I have no idea."

I move away from him and try her cell. It does ring but goes to voice mail. She's not going to answer my calls right now anyway; I'll have to give her time to calm down. Her stubborn streak is legendary. Kizzy can hold a grudge for a lifetime. I know this. I lose my cool quickly, but I'm also quick to forgive.

"Why did you think I would sleep with Kizzy? Has that happened before?"

I shake my head no.

"Then why did you say that?"

He appears puzzled. I'm not sure why, though. He has been with me long enough now to know I'm nuts. I shrug my shoulders, feeling silly.

"I thought you'd find her attractive, and I knew she would flirt with you."

"I like Kizzy. She's intelligent, and yes, she certainly is attractive, but she's not *you*. If I didn't already know you, and I walked into a room and you were both there, I would still pick you."

I move into his arms, resting my head on his shoulder. I don't expect him to understand, but I try to explain.

"Daddy and I, we always make concessions for Kizzy. Whatever she wanted, she got. It's always been that way because we both wanted to make up for what Mom did to her."

I wipe my tears away in frustration.

"My life here in the UK with Toby, with you, it's off limits to her. I'm ashamed to say I moved halfway around the world to escape my sister."

"Have you spoken to Kizzy about how you feel?"

I pull out of his embrace and shake my head.

"No. I don't talk about how I feel to Kizzy. We argue, we make up. The vicious cycle wore me out."

"So, this is why you left?"

"London gave me my freedom."

"I hate to break it to you, but Kizzy mentioned moving to London after she graduates."

"Better start planning my move to the land down under."

"As long as you take me with you."

* * *

Whenever Markus and I have a heart-to-heart, I feel like a huge weight is lifted off my shoulders. I say this to him.

"I'm here for you, Dylan, always."

We spend the day close to home. Eating out at a new Japanese restaurant on our street. I try to relax and enjoy the meal; the ambience is very laid-back, but my tummy is tied up in knots.

I'm constantly checking my phone and glancing out the window, hoping to see Kizzy. Markus knows I'm distracted, but he doesn't try to force me to snap out of it. He's also on the lookout for my sister, and I love him more in this moment than any other time since we got together.

He squeezes my hand as we go up in the lift, heading back home. It's eight p.m., and the light will soon disappear. I try Kizzy's phone again, but it goes straight to voice mail.

Dejected, I sit on the couch and turn on the flat-screen TV, keeping the sound off. Markus comes and sits next to me, reaching for my hand. I cuddle up to him. Around ten thirty, he suggests we go to bed.

While he showers, I call daddy. He answers on the second ring.

"Dilly, how are you?"

"I'm fine, daddy. Did Kizzy call you?"

Choosing Love

He sighs.

"What happened?"

I'm disappointed when daddy already expects that Kizzy and I would have a fallout.

When will my sister and I be able to just be sisters without the drama?

"We had an argument and she left."

"Dilly, go to sleep and don't worry about your sister. Kizzy can take care of herself."

"Dad, if you hear from her, just tell her I'm sorry and to call me, please."

My voice comes out in a croak. I'm tearing up again.

"Okay, Dilly. I will. You try to rest. I love you."

"I love you too, daddy."

Markus is sitting on the bed when I turn around. I go straight to the shower and cry my eyes out. By the time I come out, I'm mad.

"She could at least call to let me know she's okay.

She's so selfish!"

I'm worried sick, and my imagination is running wild. Markus comes and helps me to bed. He wants to cuddle, but I push him away. I can't be touched when I'm a bag of nerves like this. He drifts off after a while, and I stare out the window.

I must have dozed off as a piercing sound wakes me up.

It's my phone. I don't recognise the number. Panic-stricken, I answer.

"Kizzy?"

"Dilly!"

I start to cry.

"Kizzy, where are you?"

"I'm not sure. Can you come for me?"

Markus takes the phone, and I start to dress quickly, throwing on some jeans over my nightgown. Markus ends the call.

"She's in Shoreditch. Dylan, let's go."

Choosing Love

My man takes over. I'm a bag of mess. I run out to the corridor with no shoes and then run back inside to get shoes, but Markus comes out with my sneakers and helps me put them on. He also pulls a hoodie over my head as I didn't put on a top, just tucked my nightgown into my jeans.

We're in the car and on our way. Markus is focused on driving. He's breaking all the speed limits tonight. If we're pulled over, and he gets a ticket, I will murder my sister. It's two a.m., according to his dash. I imagine my sister alone in a dark and deserted alleyway.

Markus pulls up outside a building, and there are crowds of people spilling out onto the street. He dials the number on my phone.

"Kizzy, we're outside. Come downstairs."

I am already out of the car and waiting to cross the road. Markus swears loudly.

"Dylan!"

I don't stop. I'm on a mission to find Kizzy. He grabs my hand as I am about to enter the building.

A scantily dressed woman is standing at the door, eyeing us up. I could imagine what this must look like, so I stop. I don't want her to think Markus is attacking me.

Kizzy appears at the top of the stairs, and I scream her name. She comes running out and straight into my arms. Markus guides us back to the car, and I jump in the back with Kizzy.

"Sorry, Dylan."

"It's okay, Kizzy."

Relief washes through me, and I hug her close.

"Sorry, Markus."

"Your sister was worried about you all day."

"I lost track of time, lost my wallet and my phone at the carnival."

"How did you call us?"

"I borrowed someone's phone. I guess I could've done that earlier, but I was upset."

Her voice is quiet, and I smile. He's not a pushover like me and dad. He passes her my phone.

Choosing Love

"You should cancel your cards and let your phone provider know you lost your phone."

"Yes, I will. Thanks, Markus."

She takes the phone and is subdued for the rest of the drive home. I hug her and rub her back. Markus pulls into his parking spot.

"Are you hungry?" I ask, and she shakes her head no. I help her to her room.

She removes her clothes and goes to the shower. We have that in common. I text my dad to let him know she is home. I hug her, and she tells me she's sorry again, but I'm happy she is safe. Her head hits the pillow, and she is out. I smile and kiss her. This is typical Kizzy.

Back in my room, I undress and climb into bed. I roll over to kiss him goodnight, and he pounces on me. He takes off my nightgown and throws it on the floor. My body responds immediately. My nipples, like obedient soldiers, stand to attention.

He penetrates deep, my flesh yielding to his powerful strokes. He is breathing hard, and my moans are deep, husky. The pent-up emotions of the day ripple through my body, and I fall asleep in his arms.

I awake feeling refreshed. I dress in a burnt orange sleeveless top and dark blue shorts. I'm famished, so I head downstairs.

The smell of fresh muffins greets me as I enter the kitchen. Markus is sitting at the breakfast bar, and Kizzy is in the kitchen cooking up a storm. They are laughing and chatting easily. As I approach, she beams at me.

"Love your outfit, Dilly."

"Thanks, Kizzy."

Markus turns and looks me up and down. He gives me his signature smile, and I know he likes what he sees. I grab a muffin and start to eat.

"I've never seen you eat starchy carbohydrates."

"Kizzy made these, so I know they are low carb."

Kizzy confirms they are made with almond flour. I wink at him. She is wearing a fitted white dress, and she looks so pretty.

Markus grabs his phone, sending a text message.

"Are we going to the parade?"

"Yes. Savannah is picking us up in twenty minutes."

"I thought the roads were closed."

"Yes, most of them are closed. She'll call us when they are close by, and then we'll go up to the helipad."

I think he is joking. He's not. Savannah has arranged everything. We are flown by helicopter to another building in Notting Hill and watch the parade from the balcony.

"Sometimes it's good to know you."

He's standing behind me as we enjoy the spectacle in front of us. Kizzy snaps away with her camera and fizzes with excitement.

"Dilly, this is so amazing! Daddy won't believe this."

Savannah passes out glasses of Sauvignon Blanc

and offers one to my sister. Kizzy smiles and takes the glass. I stare at her, shocked.

"When did you start drinking, Kizzy?"

"College life does this to you," she replies.

"I'm sorry, Dylan, I didn't ask if Kizzy is old enough to drink," Savannah says.

"I'm old enough," Kizzy says.

I explain that college in the US is the same as a university.

"Kizzy is starting her second year of medical school."

"I never would have guessed, Kizzy. You look so young. What field of medicine?"

"Obstetrics. It was always the plan, right, Dilly?"

"It sure is," I reply quietly.

"Beautiful and smart women. Markus, darling, is there anything more powerful?"

She sips her wine and offers him fruit from her platter.

Choosing Love

"Nope," he replies, popping a strawberry into his mouth.

Savannah and her pilot drop us back to Canary Place soon after. We have a bird's eye view of the carnival, and the crowds form a long S shape along the streets.

The colours of the rainbow are on display, and from our vantage point in the skies, we can make out the costumes.

We are on a high after our day. We eat dinner and clean up the kitchen. Kizzy goes to pack, and Markus is on his laptop organising last-minute arrangements for our Scotland mini-break.

"Dilly, can I brush your hair?"

Kizzy appears at the top of the stairs. We go out to the balcony. The sun dips in the sky, preparing for its daily descent. I sit on a chair and close my eyes, enjoying the sensation of the brush on my scalp. Markus joins us on the balcony.

"Markus, Dilly's hair can grow all the way down to her bum. I was always jealous. When we were kids, it was so thick, Grams used to take ages doing her ponytail."

"She had arthritis and struggled to braid my hair."

"Poor Grams, but she did it every day, putting in our ribbons," Kizzy says.

"Do you remember when daddy made you cut your hair because I was upset mine was not as long?" she says.

"I was such a brat," she laughs, and I don't disagree.

"It was a nice bob haircut, but you hated yours and cut it even shorter. I was so scared dad would make me cut my hair even more," I confess.

"Well, you looked pretty with the long bob, and it didn't look good on me," she admits.

"Are you having it out like this for your Scotland trip?" she resumes brushing my hair.

"Yes. I didn't have time to do anything with it, to be honest. I'll wear hats and wrap it up."

Choosing Love

"I can do a goddess braid for you, and it will last a few days, if you want."

"I'd love that, Kizzy."

She goes inside and returns with her tools. Kizzy does an intricate hairdo with smaller braids all around my hairline, finishing with a fuller braid around the halo of my head.

Markus is intrigued. He puts on the light for the balcony as the sun has long gone down. He stands next to her, holding pins and helping Kizzy do her work.

"You look like an African princess," he says.

"Good job, Kizzy!"

She beams at him.

Scotland

We take Kizzy to the airport the next day to catch her flight. I'm sad to see her go. I hug her at the departure gate, and as usual, the tears threaten to fall. This always happens when I say goodbye to her.

"See you for Thanksgiving, Dilly. I love you!"

"Take care of yourself, Kizzy," Markus says, and he pulls her in for a hug and kisses her.

"Look after my sister."

"Always."

She heads to her gate and turns to wave. I blow

kisses to her and wrap my arms around Markus.

"Was that just a four-day visit? It felt like four months," he says, laughing.

We stop off at Blacks to stock up for our trip tomorrow. Markus is hiring a Range Rover, and we will drive to Scotland and return on Sunday. He tells me he spends a minimum of two weeks in Scotland, in the great outdoors, every year. It's a special trip for him as he can also spend time with his second family.

Back at the apartment, Markus is focused and serious. He has a large map on the table with markers outlining where we're going and telling me what to do in case of emergency.

He packs our bags with dehydrated food and water cans, flare guns, and knives. I'm overwhelmed.

"Markus, what's the point of a trip like this? No one will be having any fun!"

"Dylan, it's fun. We just need to prepare in case something goes wrong. When you fly in an airplane, don't they run through the safety procedures?"

I roll my eyes.

"No one pays attention to that!"

"Please take this seriously, Dylan. This is your first time, and I don't want you to get hurt. I know how to take care of myself, but if I'm to keep *you* safe, I need you to do everything I say."

He's not joking, so I sit and listen to him.

He makes me write all the emergency numbers inside my jacket pockets and my shoes. Demonstrates how to use the flair gun and runs through the first aid steps. There are portable batteries for our phones, compasses and all sorts of gadgets and gizmos.

When he ignores my attempts to have sex later in bed, I know he means business.

"Dylan, we're leaving at five a.m. The alarm is set for four."

"I'm not tired. I need help to sleep."

I say, moving closer.

"Goodnight, Dylan."

Choosing Love

I sigh.

His serious energy makes me nervous. Earlier today, I popped down to the spa and beauty clinic in our building. My gel nails have been done in all different colours. He cracked a smile when he saw my nails, and I told him they will help us get discovered quicker if we got lost.

Once we set off, I offer to share the driving, but he declines. Keeping him entertained soon goes out of style, and after a few hours of monotonous driving, I fall asleep.

He is still being the focused Markus, not saying much, deep in thought. The annoying thing is, I find it sexy, but after last night's rejection, which I must admit stung as I'm not used to it, I leave him alone.

When I finally awake, the clock on the dash says twelve-thirty. I've been asleep for five hours. Markus assures me we did stop a few times for him to stretch his legs.

"Did you eat?"

"I had a couple of the cereal bars Kizzy made us.

They were quite good."

The temperature has dropped. Looking out of the window, my breath stops for a moment.

"Oh wow. It's so beautiful!"

We're surrounded by tall, lush green mountains and not one building in sight. The mountain air is cool and fresh as I open my window. Markus had mentioned that the temperature can sometimes drop below freezing in the evenings, but now the weather is pleasantly mild.

"We'll be there soon."

He pulls off the main road and continues to drive for another ten minutes along a completely deserted road.

"This is Loch Lochmond," he says, indicating the Loch to our right.

It reminds me of our visits to Maine in the US. He eventually comes to a dead end and there, nestled in the woods, is the most charming log house.

A beautiful border collie runs up to greet us as

we step out of the truck.

"Hello, Skye," Markus ruffles its ears and the dog barks.

An older man approaches, smiling warmly. He has sandy blonde hair, a muscular build, and looks to be in his early fifties. His skin is tanned and leathery, as if he spends all his time outdoors.

"Cameron!" Markus calls to the older guy.

"Markus, laddie. Good to see you!"

They embrace while I stand, taking in the view. The house is set further back from the road and faces the Loch. The blue, tranquil waters sparkle in the sunlight.

Markus introduces me as *his* Dylan. I offer my hand to Cameron, and he takes it and pulls me in for a hug.

"Good to meet you, lassie!"

"How charming is this place. I imagine this is what paradise looks like," I say.

"I've lived here so long, I hardly notice

anymore," he replies, his accent heavy.

The men go straight to business, unpacking our gear.

Cameron calls out in a funny language, and a slender lady, who also looks to be in her fifties, with long red hair, comes out of the house.

"Fe!" Markus says, running over to greet her.

"Put me down, laddie!" she says, laughing as he spins her.

"You're more gorgeous every time I see you."

"You need to have your eyes checked, laddie."

"Come and meet Dylan," Markus replies, laughing boyishly.

Her blue eyes dance merrily as she invites me into her home. I feel at ease in her presence. Inside, the house is cosy and inviting. The décor is made of stone and timber. The fire pit is lit and roaring, and the smell of food cooking makes my mouth water. She takes me up the wooden staircase to our sleeping quarters and leaves me to freshen up. The room is spacious, with minimal furnishings. Lush green mountains loom in the distance.

I wash up and head back downstairs.

"Can I help you with anything?"

"Dinner is thereabouts, so I was just about to set the table."

"I can help."

"Thank you, lassie, that's very kind. There are five of us."

I am wondering who the fifth person is when he appears. His voice greets me, and I jump, startled.

"Hello."

"Hi, I'm Dylan."

His face split into a huge grin when I jumped.

"I'm Benjamin. Everyone calls me Ben."

"This is our son. Benjamin, this is Markus' young lady," Fiona says.

Ben looks no more than sixteen, tall and lanky with blond hair, like Cameron's. He helps me to set the table, and we bring the food in. Markus and Cameron appear soon after, and we all sit down to eat bean stew with rice.

After dinner, Cameron stokes the fire, adding wood.

"We are caught in the winds from the loch and the mountains, so the house is very cold at night," Fiona says.

"How long have you lived here?"

"I've been here since I married Cameron thirty years ago. He was born in this house."

"Your home is lovely. We lived in a seaside house in New England, and winters there would be brutal, but in the summer, it was always hot."

"Oh, very much like my summers growing up in Glasgow," she says, sighing softly.

"How did you two meet?"

"Pure chance."

"The best day of my life," Cameron says.

"Cameron was a young marine at the time when

he walked into my family's pub; the rest, as they say, is history."

I smile at the older couple as they reminisce on their early days.

It is clear their love for each other is still strong after all these years.

Benjamin, standing in the doorway, stares at me for a moment too long, and I am slightly unnerved by it. Not wanting to appear unfriendly, I smile at him, and he smiles back.

We have an early start, so I am the first to turn in. When Markus comes to bed later, I mention the staring, but he assures me Benjamin means no harm.

"He's seventeen, Dylan, and the way you looked sitting there in the firelight, it's only natural he'd want to stare. I've known him all his life; he won't hurt you."

Sleeping in the warm house lulls me into a false sense of security. The next day, the reality of what is in store for me is an eye-opener. We set out early on foot. Ben and Skye come with us. I try to be friendly and chat with him as I soon realise he's here to help me and keep up with my pace.

The beauty of my surroundings keeps me captivated for most of the day. We walk past green foliage and crystal-clear streams. Markus and Cameron have long disappeared, and I can no longer see them up ahead. Ben shows me where we are headed to camp tonight on the map.

The memory recall is vague, but I remember Markus pointing out the same route to me yesterday. Despite the cool temperature, I'm sweating profusely out of every orifice, and I need to use the toilet something fierce.

After a few hours, I relent and tell my guide. When I realise I must go in the bushes, I begin to fume internally at Markus.

What is the point of trekking all day when there is no place to relieve myself?

I make mental notes of all the things I'm mad at him for. Fiona had made us sandwiches, and we sit to eat them. They're delicious, and I'm jolly again once my belly is full.

The sun makes an appearance over the hills and floods the entire valley below us, and a sense of calm descends as I take in my surroundings. We walk past streams flowing downhill, and I stop to wash my hands and face.

The water is not freezing cold, as I expected. It is cool and refreshing on my sweaty skin. I mention this to Ben. He tells me that the water comes from the campsite higher up, which is heated when the sun comes out.

After eight hours of walking, my legs refuse to work. Ben comes over and tells me to lean on him, and we carry on like this at a slower pace. He starts to slip as he is bearing most of my weight. It is a struggle to adjust myself.

His dog, Skye, runs off up ahead, and a few minutes later, Markus comes running towards us. With the relief that floods through me when I see him, all my anger and frustration disappear. He removes my backpack, lifts me up and carries me in his arms back to the camp.

"Are you hurt?" he asks.

I smile and shake my head no, and he smiles and kisses me. It's the first affection I've had in days. I glance back over his shoulder to check for Ben. He is making his way up the steep incline.

Markus and Cameron were not idle. The camp is all setup, and Cameron is cooking over the fire. Markus sets me down in one of the chairs and removes my boots and socks to check my feet. They're swollen and red. Ben arrives at camp. I am relieved to see him.

"How are your feet?"

"They hurt, but the doctor is seeing to them."

Markus lifts me up and takes me through the dense woodland.

"Are you taking me off to have your way with me?"

"I'm going to try to soak them in water for now to help ease the swelling."

Choosing Love

"You don't seem to be struggling to carry me."

He walks on for another few minutes, and I can hear the water gushing before we see it. The air is warm in the sunshine, and birds are chirping.

The afternoon sunlight shines through into the crystal-clear water as we approach. As we move nearer, I'm floored by how vast the body of water is.

He deposits me on a large rock with a flat surface; removing my jacket and hanging it on a nearby branch. Underneath, I'm wearing a lightweight top with long sleeves. He is all business again, but I don't mind. I take in the wonder that is around me. I close my eyes as the sun shines down, heating my face. He rolls up my trouser legs, and I exhale as his hands touch my calves.

"Come closer and put your feet in the water."

I ease my feet over the side of the rock and submerge them in the water.

My achy feet find immediate relief, and I sigh. My tummy rumbles.

"Does Cameron need some help with the cooking?"

"No, Cameron has been cooking for me on these trails since I was nine years old. He takes care of the cooking, and I set up the camp."

"You did good today, Dylan."

"There were times I wanted to quit and go back."

"It was nerve-wracking for me to bring you here. I changed my mind so many times."

He is rubbing an odour-free ointment over my calves.

"Why?" I sigh with relief.

His hand on my skin is exquisite.

"Having you out here in the wilderness. If you went off on one of your stubborn streaks and something happened to you. I don't know what I'd do. It was Cameron's idea for Ben and Skye to accompany you. He thought I would hover too much."

He removes my jacket from the branch and puts

it over my shoulders. I snuggle into the folds.

"What time did you get here?"

"Ten. It's a short trek. I didn't want to take you too far up."

"Ten?"

I'm shocked. It's almost three p.m. I arrived an hour ago, so it took us double the time.

"We left extra early to give you more time; the light will be gone by eight-thirty. Come on, let's get you something to eat, and you can sit by the fire." He lifts me up and carries me back to camp.

* * *

The men talk in hushed tones while I sit staring into the open flames. Heat radiates as the fire cackles and spits. Ben and Skye are next to me. The temperature has dropped a few degrees, so I'm wearing a woolly hat. Markus wraps me in a thermal blanket so I'm warm enough, and my eyelids droop. Cameron made a hearty leek and potato soup, and I ate two bowls. Ben has a bag of nuts that he shares.

"I hope I didn't slow you down too much today, Ben."

"It was okay. I thought, for the most part, you had a good pace."

I think he's being modest.

"I'll be much quicker tomorrow, Ben."

My legs are elevated, and the swelling has eased a little.

"Tomorrow, we're going upstream on the kayaks," Ben says, and panic rises in my throat.

I would rather walk than go rowing in a boat.

As if he senses my distress, Markus comes over, and I make room for him.

He had gone to wash up earlier, after we ate, and is wearing clean clothes. My own experience of washing in the open air was interesting, to say the least. We have a portable solar-powered shower that is mildly tepid.

"Are we going on the water tomorrow?"

"Yes. That's the best part," he replies, "Don't

Choosing Love

worry, you'll be fine."

He adjusts my blanket and wraps his arms around me. I rest my head against his chest.

"Are you tired?"

"I'm so tired, I could fall asleep sitting here," I reply, stifling a yawn.

"Bedtime then."

He lifts me off the chair, and I wish goodnight to Ben, Cameron, and Skye. My voice is too loud in the eerie stillness. I was hoping to hold out to watch the sunset, as the men said it was a sight to behold. I say this to Markus, and he tells me we can watch it tomorrow. He takes me to our tent, and the moment my head hits the mattress, I pass out.

* * *

The next day, I wake up to the effects when my body is achy. Markus is not next to me. My head spins with a dizzy spell as I sit up, so I lay back down, counting to ten in my head.

After a moment, I try again, slowly unzipping the

tent. Cameron is walking up from the edge of the loch with a bucket of water.

"Good morning, lassie!" he calls, beaming at me.

"Good morning, Cameron!"

I smile at his friendly face. I'm still wearing the woolly hat, so I remove it. He comes over and passes me a hot cup of tea.

"Thank you," I reply, gratefully.

I place the tea on the floor and head off to wash my face. I dig in my pack for my compact mirror.

Once I feel human again, I go back to drink my tea and eat breakfast. Cameron gives me a bowl of coconut milk and mixed berries.

"Where is Markus?" I ask, just as he appears, coming out of the forest, carrying wood under his arms with Ben and Skye right behind him.

He smiles when he sees me.

"Hey, sleeping beauty."

He comes over and kisses me. I feel stubble on his face for the first time after two days of not shaving.

Choosing Love

Markus once told me he removes all the hair from his body quite often because he runs so much. He looks sexy with the facial hair.

"I like this," I say, "Can you keep it?"

"I tell you what. I'll keep it until we're back home."

"Hi Ben, hello Skye," I call out.

Skye comes over to greet me. Markus offers me a protein bar, and I ask for more tea.

"How're your legs feeling?"

"Heavy and achy."

"Today, we'll take it easy. We'll camp here again tonight and leave tomorrow."

I can't believe my ears.

"We have a couple of Kayaks, and there is somewhere I want to take you. If you feel up to it."

* * *

Markus helps me into the boat, and I sit facing him as he rows. Ben is in the other boat, but he rows in the opposite direction.

"Is he not coming with us?"

"No. I'm taking you somewhere to have my wicked way with you."

He gives me his signature smile. He's wearing a sun visor with sunglasses, and the muscles in his arms ripple as he rows. His skin is golden brown and glistening in the midday sunshine.

I remove my shirt. Underneath, I'm wearing my yellow string bikini, the one that barely covers my breasts. I apply sunblock to my skin as it's quite warm in the sunshine.

"So beautiful," I whisper.

"Look over there, Dylan," Markus says, pointing ahead.

I turn in my seat to look. We are heading towards what looks like a secluded beach.

The water is crystal-clear, and the sand is dotted with tiny pink and grey stones. I'm astounded that this little beach could be right here. Markus steers

Choosing Love

the tiny boat onto the shore.

He jumps out and pulls the boat closer to the beach, dropping an anchor to keep it steady. He lifts me out and grabs his backpack. I've already removed my shoes. We hold hands as we run up the beach, and I look back at the boat.

"Don't worry, it won't disappear."

He spreads out a blanket and I remove my tracksuit bottoms and sit, applying more sunblock.

"We only have a couple of hours before the tide changes," Markus says.

"This reminds me of Croatia," I say, laying back and stretching out my arms over my head.

He removes his visor and sunglasses, and I can see his eyes are burning.

"Dylan."

He runs his hands up and down the side of my body, and I close my eyes, enjoying the warmth of the sun and his touch heating my skin. I've no idea how secluded this beach is.

I'm about to ask him when his fingers loosen the strings on my bikini bottoms, exposing me. The sun heats my already overheated flesh. He looks like he is deciding if he should do it. It takes him only a few seconds to make up his mind. I'm already there, breathing hard.

"This is going to be quick," he says, kneeling in front of me.

He opens my legs wider and, unzipping his pants, sinks into my warmth, swearing as he slides all the way in, and I cry out.

"We could get arrested for this."

He can barely say the words. He pushes my bikini top to the side and sucks on my throbbing nipples, and I'm going wild beneath him.

Heat spreads throughout my entire body as his strokes go deeper and faster. The risk of exposure makes this hotter, and we both explode at the same time.

Afterwards, we lay panting, and it's a few minutes before either of us can speak.

Choosing Love

Markus ties my bikini bottoms and adjusts my top. His hands are trembling. He stops and sighs, running his hands through his hair, then pulls a t-shirt out of his bag.

"Cover up, Dylan. That swimming costume is just trouble."

"I'll wash up in the water," I say, smiling.

The cool water is perfect against my skin and I sink lower. As I head back to our blanket, Markus doesn't take his eyes off me. I pull his t-shirt over my head, and it reaches to the top of my thighs.

"Better?"

Standing, he walks towards me, kissing me swiftly on my lips. He strips and goes for his swim, diving into the water and staying under for so long it makes me nervous.

"We should head back," he says as he emerges.

"So soon?" I'm enjoying my time in this tranquil place, just the two of us.

"The weather is changing."

He smiles and kisses me when he says this, but I sense his urgency. I'm so in tune with him these days; I can read his body language. I dress quickly, and he pulls out a jacket from his bag, and I put it on. It's still bright and sunny, but the wind has picked up.

We make it back to camp in record time. Cameron is busy cooking. Ben rushes over to help Markus with the boat while I go to see if Cameron needs help.

Dinner is nearly ready, but I'm happy when he asks me to fetch water for boiling. I sing as I carry out my duty. The atmosphere at camp is fun.

Cameron and Markus have such a good camaraderie. Dinner tonight is roasted vegetables, and I fill up on carrots, beetroot, and sweetcorn.

They tell me stories from when Markus and his Grandpa Joe used to camp here every summer. Markus appears to keep the people he's known the longest closest to him.

Ben sits on his log, and Skye is next to my feet. I think he is now used to me, as he no longer stares.

Choosing Love

I'm drinking copious amounts of tea, so I must keep running off to the bushes, but I'm rewarded as I stay up long enough to watch the sunset. Markus pulls me onto his lap, and no one speaks as we take in nature's most spectacular display.

Much later, in the middle of the night, I wake up, as nature calls. I don't want to disturb Markus, so I rummage for the flashlight and go alone. The night is pitch black, and a light drizzle has started. I don't loiter.

I do my business and clean myself up, then I crawl back into our tent.

"You, okay?" Markus is awake, and it looks like he was about to come and find me.

"I needed the toilet," I say, zipping the tent closed.

"You went by yourself? My brave girl."

He pulls me into his arms, and we fall asleep.

By morning, the light rain has turned into a full-blown rainstorm. The wind howls as if in pain. It's warm and cosy in our tent as Markus and I huddle close together, but all too soon, he's up dressing in his waterproof jacket and pants and going out into the storm.

He says he's responsible for packing up the camp, and although I offer to help, he kisses me and tells me to stay put. I do my bit by repacking our rucksacks as neatly as I can, then packing up our bedding, and letting the air out of the mattress.

When the rain eases, I leave the tent to wash up, lugging my rucksack over my shoulder.

When I return, Markus has already packed up our tent. There's a nervous energy among the men this morning; even Skye seems restless.

I sit on Ben's log, nibbling on dried fruit.

"What's wrong?" I ask Markus as he rummages in his rucksack.

"The weather's not looking good. We should make a move."

He removes his toiletry bag and heads off; I

assume to wash up. We're packed up and ready to go a few hours later. Markus and Cameron are loaded down with most of the bags, and I start the journey back with Ben and Skye. The rain has stopped, but the trail is slippery.

Determined to keep up a good pace, I don't idle, as I did on the way up. It's easier going downhill. We're all wearing hi-vis vests over our jackets. My hair has come loose from its intricate do, so I'm wearing a cap. I try to walk carefully where the path is less saturated.

Suddenly, without warning, heavy fog descends and cuts off my visibility. It's so thick; I have the sensation that I am drowning. Every breath is like pulling water into my lungs. My heart slams in my throat, and my movements become jerky. Cold fear grips me; I scream as my legs give way, and I tumble forward.

Heroics

"Dylan!"

I hear the panic in Markus' voice as he shouts my name. Blood pounds in my ears, and my head swims.

"Markus. Stay calm!" Cameron says.

"Benjamin?" Cameron calls out.

"I'm here," Ben replies.

He sounds far away from me.

"Is Dylan with you?"

"No. She fell forward, so she must be further along

the path."

"Take Skye and find her. We are right behind you, Ben."

I try to sit up. My rucksack helped to break my fall, but my hands have been scraped and they sting. My left ankle throbs.

"Dylan?" Markus calls.

My throat is swollen with fear; no sound comes out.

Skye finds me in no time. I feel his warm body as he comes near, sniffing me. Relieved, I hug him. I hear a sharp fizz and see a faint flash of red in the sky above me. A few seconds later, Ben crouches next to me.

"Are you okay, Dylan?"

"I think so," I say, finding my voice.

"Are you alright?" I reach out to touch him. "Yes," he replies.

"Markus is coming."

"Ben?"

Markus is closer now, and a choked sob escapes.

"We're over here. Skye, can you help Markus?"

Skye's paws hit the soft Earth as he runs off.

"He's so clever," I say.

"He's a trained rescue dog," Ben replies.

"Dylan?" Markus calls softly.

"I'm here."

I reach out my hand towards the sound of his voice. He touches me, and I almost weep with relief.

"Are you hurt?" his voice shakes.

"My hands and my ankle, I think I twisted it."

He touches me everywhere, removing my backpack. He starts to work on my ankle first. I try to be brave, but whimpers escape when he tries to straighten my leg.

While he is patching me up, Cameron instructs Ben to carry Markus' bags. I feel bad for causing this fuss.

"I'm sorry, Markus. I lost my balance."

"It's alright, Dylan. Try to relax; your heart is racing."

I try to take deep breaths. I am much calmer now,

so I'm not sure why my heart is beating so fast. He cleans up my hands, and I can smell the alcohol on the wipes. He wraps bandages around them. The fog lingers, and I sweat profusely.

"Drink?"

"When will the fog clear?"

"There is no way to tell," Cameron says.

I assume we'll wait until the fog clears before continuing down the mountain, but Markus lifts me in his arms.

"We're going to carry on down the trail," he says.

"But the fog is so thick. How can you see?"

"Dylan, I know this trail so well I can find my way in the dark. We all can."

I realise then that I'm the one he's worried about.

"I can walk, Markus."

"You sprained your ankle," he replies.

"How much farther do we have to go?"

We were walking for a couple of hours before I fell,

so we must be halfway.

"It's another ten kilometres," he replies.

I do the math. He'll be carrying me all the way for two hours.

"Can you make a walking stick that I can use?"

"You hurt your palms. Dylan, just relax, please, I can carry you. It's downhill all the way, so it will be easy."

The men have worked out a system. Cameron is in the lead, telling Markus where to walk. It's slow going at first, but the fog starts to clear after about fifteen minutes. Finally, I can see his face.

Markus stops to rest a few times. I make sure he stays hydrated. My ankle throbs painfully, but I don't complain. The others have gone ahead, so it's just us. I can tell he's fatigued. I sit under a tree and look over at him. His breathing is laboured.

"I've finally worn you out," I say softly, and he smiles.

* * *

Smoke rises in the distance, and I sigh with relief.

Choosing Love

I'm desperate for Markus to be able to rest.

"We're nearly there," I encourage, and he nods.

"Thank you," I whisper fervently and kiss him on his neck.

It tastes salty, and I do it again. We look at each other, and he winks at me. My heart swells with love.

Cameron runs up the hill, relieves Markus and carries me back to the house. I look over his shoulder. Markus is on his knees, breathing hard to recover.

"Let's look at that ankle, Dylan."

He deposits me on the porch swing. He tends to my ankle; It's quite swollen. Fiona comes out with an ice pack, and I look back to check on Markus. Fiona brings him a drink, and I am grateful to her.

Once he's recovered, we clean up. My ankle is wrapped in plastic. He removes the bandages from my hands. The hot water stings, but the scrapes are not too bad. We stand in the shower together and he washes my hair. Then he helps me to dress and dries my hair until it falls in soft waves.

He runs his fingers through it and kisses my neck; I put my arms over his shoulders and kiss him back ferociously.

He fondles my breasts, trailing kisses down my neck. I forget and put pressure on my ankle, and that is what breaks up the kissing. I also want him to eat, so I tell him I'm hungry, adding "*for food"* when his eyes start to blaze.

At dinner, I apologise again for causing trouble, but Fiona assures me that she's seen worse come down that mountain. They start telling me stories: the year that Cameron broke his collar bone and had to be airlifted to the hospital, Ben, and the unfortunate stinging nettle incident. Markus is quiet, so I ask about his mishaps.

"Markus is always the hero. One year, he ran all the way down the hill carryingMaggie. She was struggling to breathe and had fainted, poor lass," Fiona says.

"Who's Maggie?" I ask.

"Our eldest, she lives in Glasgow."

She passes me a photo from the sideboard. In the photo is a lovely redhead. She's smiling at the camera.

"She's sixteen in the picture," Fiona says.

"She's pretty. She looks like you," I say.

"Markus ran all the way down the mountaincarrying her?"

Cameron recounts the story.

"Scariest day of my life. It was Maggie's first time, and we took her further up the ridge. She was thirteen, so Markus, you must have been eighteen or so."

"It was the summer of '91," Markus replies.

"We'd only just arrived when it all kicked off," Cameron says.

"Markus has been an honorary guest in this house since then," Fiona adds.

"Skye came a few years later. He comes with us all the time now," Cameron says, and I thank my lucky stars.

Skye is also my hero of the day. They all are. It was impressive the way they worked together as a team. This is the second story of heroics that I've heard where Markus is the man of the moment.

***

The heavens open once again in abundance. I lay back on the crisp, cool cotton sheets with my injured ankle propped on a pillow. The rain, as it falls on the roof, sounds like wild horses running free, their hooves falling together in perfect harmony.

Neither of us is speaking, and I watch out of the window as the trees bend and sway. Markus lays next to me, one hand behind his head. I'm wearing my white camisole and panties, and he is shirtless, wearing only his briefs. I'm looking at the rain, and he's looking at me.

"I thought I'd lost you today," he whispers.

"When you screamed, and then we heard nothing, I felt real terror. Once I knew for sure you were fine, I was so emotionally drained I struggled to carry you."

"I thought that was because I'm so heavy."

"I love you, Dylan."

"I love you, too."

"I wanted to bring you here because I thought it

would help you."

"I'm beyond help, Markus," I joke to lighten the mood; he seems rather intense.

"Dylan, sometimes you are insecure, conflicted. There's the carefree, happy you and then, the anxious you."

"Is that why you're always so calm? Because a few times a year, you come to Scotland and become one with nature?"

"Markus, I would come again."

"Not with me; my nerves can't take it."

I stare at him.

"Are you serious? I thought you especially had fun on the beach yesterday."

"If I hadn't panicked when the fog came, I wouldn't have tripped over."

"I thought you said I did good. Cameron thinks I did a good job."

He kisses my forehead.

"If I lost you, my life would be over."

His voice is full of emotion, and I don't try to make jokes now.

I realise what he's saying, and I link my fingers with his. The wind and rain cause havoc outside but inside this room with Markus, there is a perfect kind of storm brewing.

Changing seasons

Autumn rolls in, and London glows in a multitude of colours. I have the best seat in the house. I watch from the lounge as the river changes colour to reflect the trees blowing in the wind; beautiful hues of red and orange.

The foliage back home in Boston was always the most spectacular at this time of year, so to be able to see this from the apartment in the sky is special. I make warming apple cider and sip as I look out at the display, pondering on the turn of events.

Some days, I'm seized with such fear I'd lie in

bed, unable to move. There are times when it becomes so consuming I must go off and be alone. I go to my place in Essex and clean, but I'm starting to realise that I'll have to figure out what to do with my apartment.

Toby suggests I rent it out for now. The idea of someone living in my space does not appeal to me, but I must accept that things are becoming serious with Markus, and I need to make some decisions. He wants to go home with me for Thanksgiving to meet my dad.

He makes appointments for me to see his Harley Street doctor to discuss my fibroids; he wants to know what my chances are to have children.

This annoys me at first. I feel it's my choice to decide and refused to go. But much later, when I melt under his careful administrations, when he holds me close, tells me he loves me, and whispers for me to give him a girl that looks just like me, I relent.

I talk to Kizzy, and she tells me I can have noninvasive surgery as an outpatient. I like this option, so I arrange to have this done when I go home. As we make plans for our future, I start to wonder about Markus' past.

He hasn't mentioned Stacey or the baby since that night many months ago. I have no idea if he's losing sleep over the whole sordid affair. He's cool, calm, and as collected as ever. I occasionally have a burning desire to ask him, but I never feel brave enough.

I start practicing Tai Chi. There are sessions in the gym in our building, so I go twice a week. It helps to clear my mind and calm my nerves. As if he senses my preoccupation, Markus comes to bed with another level of fire. It's as if, with every kiss and every touch, he wants to reassure me.

I'm distracted, but it doesn't stop the dreams. They started a few weeks ago.

When I fall asleep at night, I can hear a baby crying. It wails loudly as if in distress. I run around trying to find it. I want to help. I walk into a room devoid of furniture, apart from a large crib in the centre of the room.

The cries are louder as I approach. I reach into the crib and then freeze as terror drains the blood from my body. There, in the crib, is the cutest little baby.

She smiles up at me, the image of my sister. I jolt out of my sleep, suffocating in a cloud of despair.

* * *

Grams used to always tell us there was a time and a season for everything. I interpreted those words to mean that all things happen in good time.

September rolls into October, and I notice my clothes are looser.

The dreams have intensified. I convince myself that the baby has probably arrived, and Markus is keeping this from me.

"You've lost weight," he says one evening.

I sit across from him, picking at my dinner.

"Have I?"

Choosing Love

"Do you feel unwell?"

"No, I feel fine," I reply and excuse myself from the table.

At times like these, I would call Toby, but he's gone to Brazil on business. I know I could still call him, but I don't. I already know what he'll say. I think of calling Savannah and asking her, but then I remember she's in South Africa.

I don't want to involve my family, so I resort to cleaning. I come home at night and clean the apartment.

"What are you doing?"

"What does it look like? I'm making the bed."

"Dylan, you don't need to do that."

"I know, but I want to."

"Sarah came today. I'm sure she would've made the beds," he says.

I turn away from him and carry on. I bend over and pull the fitted sheet over the mattress. My dress hikes up at the back.

He comes closer and runs his hands up my legs. I push him away. He sighs and leaves the room. I sit on the bed and cry.

The next day at work, a large bouquet of a dozen long-stemmed white roses arrive for me. There is a note. The ladies in my office are excited, and it does make me smile. He's waiting for me outside the building at four, just like the note said.

"Hello," he says, pulling me in for a kiss.

I go into his arms, and his warmth radiates through me.

He takes me to Nate's place and the man himself is there to greet us.

Markus is attentive and loving. I am finally convinced that there is no way he could possibly be keeping news about Stacey and the baby from me. He's just too relaxed and calm. The aroma from my meal makes my mouth water. I am famished and so I eat. When my head hits the pillow that night, I fall into a dreamless sleep.

Laying all my demons to rest, I decide to put my

trust in Markus. I believe him when he says he loves me, and so, armed with that knowledge, I move on to embrace my happiness.

I remind myself to be present in the here and now, and not worry about the things of which I have no control.

There is no doubt that when the time comes and the season changes, I will know when the sleeping monster stirs.

The phone on my desk rings. It's the office receptionist.

"Dylan, I have a Ms. St. Cloud on the line for you."

I have no idea who this is, but I accept the call, assuming it's work-related.

"Hello, this is Dylan. How can I help?"

"Hello, Dylan."

My blood runs cold. I've only heard this voice once before, but I'd never forget it. I don't say a word. I assume she is calling to share her news.

"I do apologise for calling you at your place of work."

"What do you want, Stacey?"

"I think there's something you should know."

"I'm not interested in anything you have to say."

"I'm not the villain here, Dylan. I just want an opportunity to talk. To clear up any misconceptions."

Her French lilt is very appealing, very soft and feminine.

"I suggest you keep your talking exclusively between you and Markus."

The line goes quiet for a moment, and I almost hang up.

"I'm having his baby. Surely, this involves you."

I assumed wrong. She's still pregnant. I imagine her swollen belly. My hand goes to mine, probably forever barren, never to bear fruit. I wonder if this is Markus' only chance to have a child. I make the decision. I will do this for him, not for me.

Choosing Love

"Alright."

She gives me her address in Fulham, but I don't want to go to the house they shared together.

"I have an appointment in Knightsbridge tomorrow afternoon. We could meet at the Bvlgari hotel."

This is folly, agreeing to meet her. I bring up the calendar and work out that if she is still pregnant, then he must have slept with her in March. Perhaps mere weeks before I sealed my fate with a kiss.

Back at home, Markus works on his laptop at the dining table in the evening. I tell him I'm tired and go to bed early. Inside, I'm twisted up in knots, and I don't want my face to give away my secret.

Stacey is waiting at the reception to meet me. She is more stunning than I remember.

The first and only time I saw her, she was drenched in rain, but not tonight. Her face is perfectly made up, and her long hair is glossy and shining. She wears a white dress that falls all the way down to her ankles.

She is very much pregnant. I stare at her swollen abdomen, nausea stirring in mine. I tell myself this is the reality, not the fairy tale I've been spinning for the past eight months. She smiles at me in a friendly way, her teeth perfect.

"Hello, Dylan," she greets me warmly as if we're old friends.

A short gentleman at the desk comes to take my coat. Her eyes look me up and down and I have a moments satisfaction from her appraisal. I'm wearing a fitted beige turtleneck and red leather pants. My heels make my legs appear longer.

"Hey."

I'm already regretting this. She leads us off to a small, cosy room and orders tea for two. I've already decided not to eat or drink anything, and I sit across from her on the comfortable leather chairs. This place oozes class and money.

"Thank you for coming."

She sits and cradles her bump in a tender way.

"When's the baby due?"

My voice is strong and clear. Inside, I'm in turmoil, but I don't plan to let her know.

"Early December. It's a boy."

"What is it you think I need to know?"

The tea arrives and she takes a moment to pour. She lifts her cup and takes a sip delicately before answering.

She's wearing a diamond ring shaped like an egg. I can't seem to take my eyes off it.

She notices me staring.

"It was a gift from Markus," she says in her velvety voice.

Her eyes fall to my fingers devoid of such baubles, and she smiles.

"Have some tea," she says.

"No, thank you. I don't really have a lot of time, so please tell me why I'm here."

"Alright. I suppose I was curious about you.

Markus never mentioned you. Have you known each other long?"

The question throws me, and my confusion must show on my face.

"Markus and I have a special relationship, Dylan. I'm always privy to what he is up to, who he is dating or sleeping with. You were a complete enigma. I realise now that he must be serious about you, although time will tell. It always does."

She smiles sweetly at me, but I'm still confused.

"Why would he talk to you about me?"

"It's the nature of our bond," she coos, her hand caressing her tummy.

"Were you friends or lovers?"

I don't understand.

I'm not aware that he dated any other women but her. My body shivers involuntarily as if she is pouring ice into my veins.

"We're so much more than all of that," she says, closing her eyes briefly.

Choosing Love

"You see. I understand him and his needs. Perhaps even more than he does. I knew he was troubled. He tried other avenues; other women. I want him for myself, so I allowed him to have his dalliance from time to time. In the end, he always comes back to me."

I have no words; I just stare at her.

"I've shocked you. I'm sorry. I thought you should know."

"If you're so sure he will come back to you, why the deception?"

I glare at her face, no longer wishing to hide my feelings.

She smiles.

"I can see quite clearly what he sees in you. You're by far the loveliest, and you have some fire in you. I do admit that since the baby news, he's not been very happy with me. And he has a new distraction, but we've been here before, many times. Men don't like it when we derail them. It only makes them realise they're not so much in control. He doesn't know what he wants, but for twelve long years, I've always been the constant in his life."

I stand as she says this while she remains seated and calm.

"Dylan, It is not my intention to alarm you. This is the way it is between Markus and me. He and Marta lasted almost a year, but he came back to me. He always does."

I wrap my arms around my body.

"Whose Marta?"

"They lived together at his Villa in Spain."

I've heard enough.

"Why do you want to be with a man who doesn't make you his number one? Why would you waste your time?"

I want her to know I think she is foolish.

"He is all I've ever wanted," she whispers.

I turn to go.

"Dylan..."

Choosing Love

I continue to walk away from her. I ask for my coat, and while I wait, she tries to give me a large brown envelope.

"I don't want that!"

She has no shame.

She offers to call me a cab, but I decline. She insists I take the envelope, and, like a fool, I do. I storm out into the cold November evening, wrapping my coat closer around me. I put the envelope in my bag and walk to the furthest station.

It's three miles, and it takes over an hour. The tube is heaving with Friday night revellers. I can't stand the noise of the crowds, so I come off at the next station and hail a black cab.

In the taxi, I open the envelope. I'm not sure why, as I knew it would be nothing good.

There are pictures of the two of them together. The look I love is in his eyes.

I thought that look was exclusively for me.

In another picture, he's with a different woman.

Her skin is a deep shade of mocha, and she is wearing a red backless dress, her back to the camera, her face in profile.

Her body is remarkable. Markus is facing the camera, but he's smiling at her, his hand resting on the small of her back.

I can't imagine why Stacey would have such a photo.

I stuff the pictures back into the envelope and put them in my bag.

I guess she came bearing proof in case I had any doubts. It's obvious she wants me out of the way.

I don't remember paying the cab fare or taking the journey up in the lift. I open the door, and Markus is standing on the other side.

"Dylan, where have you been?"

He reaches out to touch me and stops. I can only imagine what he sees on my face.

I'm past caring at this point. His eyes are burning. I move past him to hang my coat in the cloakroom.

"I called you a few times. I was worried."

I take my phone out of my bag and see the missed calls from him.

"Sorry," I manage.

"Are you hungry?" he asks in his warm, caring voice.

I glare at him accusingly, and I'm confused when he doesn't respond, but then I remember he's not in my head. He doesn't know I've been informed that all this is a lie. How utterly foolish I've been to think my perfect man would come along so easily, baggage-free.

"No. I'm tired. I'm going to bed."

I stand in the hot shower for ages, but the cold still lingers in my bones. Eventually, I give up. Sleep doesn't comfort me tonight. The images play havoc with my already disturbed mind. My imagination runs wild. I see him with her.

He looks happy and wild. I watch as he enters her and moves like a man possessed. His body is beautiful as always, and when it's over, she screams his name.

The screams echo through my body, around the room, and I cover my ears and crouch over, as I no longer wish to see this. I want to erase it from my mind. I sob uncontrollably.

"Dylan. Wake up!"

I come to. Markus has turned on the bedside lamp. His face is white with fear. He holds me as I cry.

"Dylan, tell me what's wrong!" his voice shakes.

I wipe my tears.

"It's nothing," I croak.

"When I couldn't reach you, I knew there was something wrong."

My tears start to flow again, and he wipes them away. His fingers tremble.

"Did something happen?" he whispers, "Did someone hurt you? Please just tell me."

I move away and walk to the bathroom. My nose

is starting to run. I clean up and wash my hands, taking longer than needed.

I don't want to face it.

He comes to the door and looks at me. I move into the bedroom, and he reaches for me. My head barely skims his shoulder when I am barefoot, and he bends to kiss me.

His lips touch mine, and I forget everything. The image of her swollen with his child, the pictures of them both looking happy and in love. Even the photo of him with the beautiful woman in red cannot touch me now as I lose myself in his kiss.

I come to my senses too late. Markus only kisses me to disarm me. I think he knows this is my Achilles heel. One kiss, and I will spill all my secrets. He lifts me, I wrap my legs around him and he takes me back to bed. He sits with his back pressed against the headboard.

I sit on his lap, and he trails kisses over my face, settling on my lips, and I open willingly. His hands caress my lower back, which is more soothing than erotic. He breaks the kiss, and when I lean in for more, he obliges.

"Dylan, tell me."

"I'm sorry that I worried you. I'm not hurt."

Not physically anyway.

My fingers trail along his collarbone and dip into the hollow beneath his Adam's apple.

"What did you dream about?"

He grabs my fingers as they move against his chest.

"What do you mean?"

I'm not sure how he knew I was dreaming.

"You were screaming earlier when I woke you."

"It's nothing. Just a silly nightmare."

"You were screaming my name. What was I doing to you?"

"Wouldn't be the first time, and you know what you do when I scream your name."

He lifts my chin, his eyes searching mine.

Choosing Love

"I love you. You can tell me anything, no matter how trivial. I'm here for you, always."

This is what breaks me. It's as if he can see into my very soul.

"I saw Stacey."

I don't look at him when I speak.

"She called me at work and asked me to see her. She is quite far along in her pregnancy. She, uh, wanted me to know about your special relationship and that you always go back to her. The baby is due soon."

He doesn't speak, and I carry on.

"She said that you've had other women; a lover, that you lived with in Spain," my voice trails off.

It's awkward saying these words while I'm sitting on his lap. I'm wondering if he is upset with me, but then he pulls me close and hugs me.

"I'm sorry," he whispers.

My hair has come loose from my silk scarf, and I remove it. He runs his hands down my tresses.

"Is it true?" I ask so softly I barely hear myself.

"Yes," he whispers, and it's as if time stops.

I move off his lap and sit on the bed. I brace myself to hear this.

"Why didn't you tell me?" I whisper as fresh tears fall, "You could've spared me the humiliation of hearing it from her."

I wipe my tears in frustration.

"I had to sit there and look at her pregnant with your child and listen to her filth," my voice goes up a notch.

"Dylan, all of that is in my past. Before I met you, I was trying to end my relationship with Stacey. We were no longer living together. She moved to Paris, and I moved here. I admit it was difficult. I have known her and trusted her for such a long time."

He stops talking and takes my hand.

"I wasn't prepared for you. You steamrolled into my life, and I'm not that weak and pathetic man anymore. You made me realise that if I am brave enough to go after what I want, I can have it. I can have you."

His voice is soft as he speaks. I leave the bed and rummage in my bag for the envelope.

"Is this your Spanish lover?"

He glances at the photo and then puts it back in the envelope. He goes to the dresser and places the envelope there.

"Dylan, none of this is important. What I have with you is so much more. No other woman has the same effect on me that you do. I was waiting for you."

He sits facing me on the bed.

"I love *only you*," he repeats with conviction.

I remind him in case he forgot, "You love Stacey."

"Not anymore," he whispers.

"What about your baby?"

"He's not my baby."

"What?"

"I don't know for sure, but the dates don't correlate. My consultant reckons from the last time we were together, she should be further along."

"Why didn't you tell me?" I shout at him, "This is the problem with you, Markus; you never talk to me about any of this. If I had known that, I would not have gone to see her."

"I never expected you to go see her. She's obviously still determined in her plans. She can't get to me, so she goes to you."

"She's convinced that you're going back to her," I whisper.

"No. Not after her betrayal."

"And never after you," he adds softly.

"Dylan, why is it so easy for you to focus on the negative?"

He lifts my chin, so I look into his eyes.

"You *know* I love you. You *know* what we have together."

"What's this relationship you had with her,

Markus?"

He's right; I focus on the negative, but this is messing with my positive. Until I understand it, I can't forget it. I must process the information, so I need all the facts. He stares at me for a while and says nothing. I huff and lay back on the bed, pulling the duvet over me.

"We started off quite young. At first, it was fun; I was having sex regularly, and that was the excitement. When I started Uni, I was attracted to other girls, so I broke things off with Stacey. But she was upset. She said she loved me. We managed to make it work. I did date other women, but she was always there for me."

"We eventually lived together for three years, and for a time, I was happy, but when she asked me to marry her, I knew I didn't want to. We agreed to take a break. I moved to Spain. I met Marta. Yes, that's her in the photo."

He seems reluctant to go on.

"Why would Stacey have a picture of her?"

"We were together, the three of us."

"What?"

His voice is soft. At this point, I'm sitting up in bed, my eyes trained on his face.

"Stacey took that picture?"

I can imagine what is registered on my face, but I don't try to adjust it. He nods.

"Yes. We were on holiday in Bordeaux. It only happened a few times, but after that, the relationship with Marta was over."

"Is this who you are, Markus?"

"No, Dylan. I'll be the first to admit things with Stacey went further than I had intended. I wasn't proud of myself, but she's right. I always did go back to her, until she was caught up in every move I made. I felt powerless, and I wanted a way out. I finally told her last Christmas, but on occasion, I would go to see her."

He doesn't have to continue. He went back to her, and now he suffers the consequences.

Choosing Love

"Markus, you knew she loved you. That was very selfish."

"I compensated in other ways, and she seemed happy," he adds, and I just stare at him.

"How do you compensate someone while you break their heart?" I speak slowly.

"I funded her lifestyle."

I'm off the bed and staring at him with my mouth open.

"Are you kidding me? Tell me you're making this shit up!"

He doesn't look at me, so I think he's maybe a little remorseful.

"Do you think if you broke my heart, you could give me money, and I would be happy?" my voice comes out shrill.

"You were going to leave her after all that as well, so no wonder she resorted to such measures, to keep her cash flowing in. You know Markus, you dug this hole for yourself. When you mess with someone's emotions, you play with fire."

I don't want to sound like I'm his mother, but seriously, this is so wrong on all levels.

"I've heard enough. I don't want to hear any more of this madness."

I walk out of the bedroom and go to the spare room to sleep. It's three-fifty a.m. and I don't even struggle to fall asleep. I'm resolved. The information has been processed, and he can sort out his own mess.

Repercussions

I wake at ten a.m. the next day and head to work out in the indoor gym. The exercise sessions are part of my daily routine, and I feel great. After my weight training, I head back up, not bothering with the lift, climbing the stairs instead.

Markus is not at home, but there's a message from him on my phone. He has gone to take care of some business and will see me later for lunch. We are off to Boston soon, so I have some last-minute shopping to finish.

The doorbell rings, and I run to answer it. It must

be someone we know, as the security team would have otherwise buzzed me on the intercom first. I think it might be Savannah, but to my delight, it's Toby.

I scream and jump into his arms.

"Toby!" I kiss him, "Stop going away and leaving me."

"Hey, D," his face lights up.

"I know. It's constant. I miss you when I go."

I take his coat and check out his outfit. He's wearing a white turtleneck and black jeans. He looks very good.

"You look gorgeous, as usual," I say.

"So do you."

He checks me out, and I beam. He offers me a small package.

"This is for you," he says, and I open it and gasp.

"Farinha. You remembered!"

I give him a hug. Its flour made from a root

vegetable. I make him a coffee while he looks at the view.

"Is Markus at home?"

I roll my eyes.

"Uh oh. Trouble in paradise? I'm sure he'll forgive you."

"Why do you think it's me?"

He holds his hands up.

"I don't get involved in domestic affairs. Especially when they're between my two most cherished friends."

We both chuckle.

"How's Nicolos?"

"Yeah, he's good. He came to Brazil, and we spent a week there together. You're so right about that place; it really is magical."

"I'd love to take Markus."

"Markus said he's already been. He mentioned it to me when I spoke to him last night."

"You spoke to Markus last night?"

"Yes, I'd just arrived home, and he rang looking for you."

Toby and I are sitting on the couch on opposite ends, facing each other. I tell him everything.

"Dylan, don't go off meeting people like that."

"It was in a safe place."

"Still, you should've told Markus where you were going. He was quite worried. He thought you'd come to see me as I was due back last night. It was almost ten o'clock when he rang."

"Did you call me?"

"No, we spoke briefly before he asked if I'd seen you, then he heard you at the door."

"He loves you," Toby says, and I huff.

"I know that, but it doesn't let him off the hook for his past misdemeanours!"

"I'm surprised. You judge him so harshly."

"Surely, you can't think all this is, okay?"

"No, I agree with you. It's certainly messy. You're always so understanding with me. When I told you I was gay, I thought you'd run a mile. You accepted me and treated me with nothing but love. It's just the way I see you."

"It's different with you."

"I can tell you anything, and you wouldn't hold it against me. Why does Markus not get to have the same from you?"

"When I came out at work, you were my biggest champion. When I came out to Gina, you were supportive. You do all that for me. You love Markus, so why don't you do the same for him?"

"Toby, you shouldn't be ashamed of being gay. It's who you are. Markus chose to carry on his sordid lifestyle, and he kept it from me."

"She was wrong to talk to you."

"Did you know her?"

"Not very well. I'd see her in the early days but not so much later. Markus and I didn't go to each other's houses."

"Typical."

"Dylan, I was on the swim team with twenty other boys, and he was the only one who didn't bully me. He was the swimming champion when I arrived, and then he was always second to me. He had every reason to hate me."

"How did you two become friends?"

"After the incident with Simon, I would go to watch him race. He trained off school grounds, and I would go down to the track and hang out with him and the guys."

"They weren't like him. I mean, he was obviously from an affluent family and all that, but he would just hang out and be normal. That's when I knew he was cool. He had a driver, and he would pick us up and drop us back to school."

I smile, imagining the two of them as young boys. I like hearing this.

"What would you talk about?"

"Sports. Our favourite athletes at the time. The friendship was not easy for me at first."

"Why?"

"Because he knew about me, and I was ashamed. I didn't want to be his friend, but once I got to know him, it was alright."

I move over on the couch and sit quite close to him.

"Did you hang out after you left high school?"

"We did all through college. After graduation, we said we would, but I went to Loughborough, and he went to Cambridge. We met up for drinks a few times over the years, but we were both busy, I guess."

"How did you start up again?"

"When he moved here, I bumped into him at the gym. I saw him in the swimming pool."

"Did you know about his extracurricular activities?"

"We don't talk about that stuff, D. I could tell he was attracted to you that first night, and he asked about you."

"He did?"

"To be honest, I told him you wouldn't be interested. I mean, you never liked any of the guys that hit on you. I didn't think he had a chance."

"I would've never encouraged you to go out with him if I didn't know he is genuine."

I sigh deeply.

"All this talk is making me hungry. I didn't have supper last night."

"What do you fancy?"

"I don't fancy cooking today."

"You're spoilt for choice with eateries right on your doorstep. Let's go out."

"Sure. I'll text Markus so he knows I'm out."

Toby lifts one eyebrow and smirks at me. I know he's thinking that I should have done this last night.

"What would I have said? Off to meet your pregnant ex?"

Choosing Love

* * *

I'm sitting next to Toby, and he's showing me pictures on his digital camera of his trip with Nicolos, when we notice Markus standing and looking at us. Toby is up in a flash to greet him with a hug, but I don't move.

"Hey, Markus."

"Good to see you, Toby."

He greets me with a kiss on my cheek, then takes the seat across from us.

"You sit here, Markus. I'll move."

"Toby. Stay put. Stop fussing. There are four chairs at the table."

"Thank you, Toby, it's alright."

I can feel his eyes on me as I cuddle up next to Toby, who suddenly jumps up to find Markus a menu.

"You look lovely," Markus says.

I'm wearing a mustard-coloured sweater with a deep V-neck. My hair is brushed out in loose waves cascading down my back.

I started wearing a little makeup. Kizzy gave me a tip. After I do my mascara and cat eyes, I apply bronzer to my cheeks, and, like magic, my face is transformed. It adds a touch of glamour without all the effort.

"Thank you."

Toby comes back with the menu, and I listen as the two men catch up.

After we finish eating, he invites Toby back with us. Markus helps me into my leather jacket and wraps my scarf around me. He reaches for my hand as we leave the restaurant, but I'm not ready to let him off the hook just yet, so I hold hands with Toby.

For the first time, Toby looks uncomfortable, so I let go of his hand and walk ahead of them instead.

Despite my annoyance with Markus, I enjoy having Toby around. I whip up scones in the oven, and we sit in the lounge, eating and drinking coffee.

Toby sits in the armchair. Markus and I sit on the

couch. Sometimes, I forget I'm supposed to be mad at him and touch his arm. Before long, we're sitting close to each other. I only notice because Toby tries to hide his smile.

"When are you flying out?"

"Next week, Saturday."

"You're planning to spend a week there? I thought you normally go for the weekend?" he asks, drinking his coffee.

"Toby, you approved my time off. Did you check before saying yes?"

"Jane takes care of that when I'm away."

"I'm off for the week. I'm having a small procedure done on Monday," Markus and I look at each other.

"Are you sick?"

Toby's face is alarmed, so I move closer and put my arm around him.

"No. I'm having a myomectomy."

"What's that?"

"Women's troubles."

He turns to Markus, but he's not looking at either of us. Toby is holding my hand very tight.

"Do you have to be in hospital?"

"No. I registered as an outpatient. Honestly, Toby, it's more like going to the dentist," I say, shrugging.

It isn't quite true, but he is visibly shaken. I'm touched. My Toby loves me. I give voice to this.

"Of course, I love you, Dylan."

I kiss him on the top of his hairless head.

"I love you too, Tobes. Like, forever."

Toby leaves soon after.

"I'll clear my calendar so we can have lunch," he says as I give him a hug.

He hugs Markus and says goodnight.

I'm packing the leftover scones away, when it occurs to me that if Toby is upset about my procedure, Markus must be upset, too.

Choosing Love

I made the booking and didn't think anything further about it. Markus had asked me for the information to take to his consultant a few weeks ago, but we never discussed it. I don't really want to think about it until the time comes. He's coming down the stairs, wearing different clothes. He notices me staring.

"What's wrong?"

"I just wondered how you feel about the myomectomy."

"You'll be fine."

"You know we won't be able to have sex for a while."

"I know," he nods.

"There's also the risk. I may not be able to conceive. I have seven of them, and it's highly probable they'll grow back."

He takes my hand and sits on the couch, pulling me on his lap.

"I read your file, Dylan, so I know all of that."

"I think that's why I went to see her. It might be your only chance to have a baby."

"Dylan, I do want to have children one day, *with you*. But if it's not in the cards, then that's also fine."

His voice is so sincere.

"I'm sorry I was upset with you."

"Don't be. You were right. I've behaved abominably, and I'm ashamed."

"I've also made sure that Stacey won't contact you again. I'm so sorry about that."

I draw circles on his shirt with my fingers.

"That sounds rather ominous. What did you do, have her put down?"

"No. I gave her back the photos and asked politely," he replies, sounding very grown up.

"You went to see her? Markus, that's exactly what she wants?"

"I know that. Maybe I should've done it sooner."

He takes my hand and puts it back on his chest,

and I smile and start touching him again right over his heart.

"What did you say?"

"Until the baby arrives, and I know for sure whether or not he is mine, she should back off."

"That sounds fair."

I lean into his chest and kiss him. I don't want to talk about her anymore. In fact, I'm done talking tonight.

D S Johnson - Mills

Going home

A light dusting of snow plots the wintery scene as the plane touches down at Logan International. This is Markus's first time coming to Boston. I am excited to be taking him home. I wish it was under better circumstances. I wait for him to go through Immigration and meet me on the other side.

"Hey," I smile at him.

He comes out faster than I was expecting.

"That was quick."

I look back at the other foreign passengers, and

the queue stretches for miles. I wonder how he sailed through so effortlessly, but that's my guy. He helps me into my jacket.

Kizzy sees us before we see her.

"Dilly!"

She looks amazing in her short puffer jacket with tight jeans and a white fur hat. It's so good to see her beautiful face.

"Hello, Kizzy."

"Welcome home, Dilly."

"Hey, Markus," she says, giving him a hug.

He bends to greet her with kisses on both cheeks. Between them both, the bags are packed into her brand-new, shiny SUV. Markus sits in the back, and I ride shotgun.

There's nothing in this world like coming home. Nostalgia wraps me in her loving arms as the familiar sites roll past my window.

"When did it snow?" I ask.

"Two days ago," she replies, focusing on the road

ahead as she waits to pull out.

Before long, Kizzy is in full road rage mode, so I leave her to get on with it. I glance back at Markus, and he smiles, clearly amused.

An hour and a half later, we arrive in Plymouth. Kizzy goes off the highway, drives down the main road and pulls up onto the paved driveway.

My father's beachside house is white with red shutters. The American flag flies on the front porch, and I notice Markus looking at it. He and Kizzy take the bags indoors while I follow at a slower pace.

My dad appears from the basement, and I run into his arms. No matter how old you are, hugging your dad never goes out of style.

"Dilly," he says, holding me close.

Daddy is looking good. He is five eleven with shockingly dark wavy hair. He's slim with a dark mocha skin tone. His face is heart-shaped, and neatly shaved with a dimple in his chin.

Kizzy and I both inherited our father's straight

nose. Our dad is an exceptionally handsome man, and when he smiles, he can light up any stage.

"Hey, daddy," I say, closing my eyes briefly and kissing his cheek.

He holds my face in his palms.

"My beautiful girl," he says, and I remember Markus.

"Daddy, this is Markus."

"Hello, Markus, I'm Brandon, Dilly's dad."

He smiles, and Markus shakes his hand.

"Nice to meet you."

I'm ten shades of embarrassed. I've never introduced any guys to my dad before. Sam, my ex-fiancé, was already a family friend.

"You kids must be tired from the flight. Let me take you up to your room," dad says, reaching for the bags.

"It's alright, daddy, I got it," Kizzy says, coming down the stairs.

She picks up another bag.

"Do you need some help with that, Kizzy?" Markus offers.

"No, I'm all set. I'll be right back."

"Do you kids want something warm to drink?" dad offers politely.

"I'll do it, daddy. Markus, would you like one?"

I take his hand, and we go to the kitchen. My dad follows behind. I tell them both to sit, and I make myself busy with the kettle.

It's a bit awkward at first, but before long, they're talking as I make the tea. I can hear Kizzy moving about upstairs. We sit at the large dining table. Markus is asking my dad about the snow.

It's much heavier on the ground here.

"I had no idea it was snowing. I've been in the studio for the past few days," he admits, and I laugh.

Kizzy finally comes to join us.

"Daddy lives in the studio."

"A photo studio?" Markus asks.

"A recording studio," Kizzy and I both say at the same time.

"Your room is ready," she says.

I offer her tea, and she sits next to me.

"Daddy is a recording producer," I say.

"I have a few projects to finish up before Christmas," daddy says.

Markus tells my father that some of his clients are in the music industry.

"Like whom?" I ask, intrigued.

He rattles off the names of a few famous singers.

"You've never mentioned this before," I say.

"These artists come to my firm to protect their brands and intellectual property," he replies.

"You're an IP lawyer?" my dad asks.

"I am," Markus says.

I can see the wheels in my dad's head turning.

"Dad, it's British law, not American," I say before he gets any ideas.

"I specialise in international law as well," Markus says.

I look at Kizzy, roll my eyes, and we laugh.

"How is it that I don't know any of this?"

"You work with American artists?" dad asks Markus.

He mentions the name of one famous rapper, and I stare at him. My dad smiles. Music is his life. Before I know what is happening, Markus goes down to the basement to see my dad's studio. Kizzy and I follow.

We used to joke that at least we always knew where to find daddy. The studio is massive, complete with a shower room and bedroom, it covers the entire width of the house.

After twenty minutes, I've seen enough.

"I want to shower and change."

"I'll come with you."

"I know the way, Kizzy."

"I've put your bags in my room," she says.

Dad has the entire basement. Kizzy's room spans the entire top floor. Dad had it completely done for her. I had to settle with a smaller room on the second floor.

"I thought you should stay in here as you're the guest, and you have Markus with you."

I'm touched.

"Are you sure?"

I enter the spacious room with white wooden furniture. She's even put a vase with winter berries on the windowsill. The ensuite is up the stairs, as the builders used some of the attic space for it.

I shower and dress, feeling refreshed. I give Kizzy her gift, and we sit on the small couch, catching up. It's just two thirty in the afternoon, so it's seven thirty p.m. in London.

"Markus looks amazing; you both do. I hope it won't be awkward between us. You know, because of what happened last time."

"Water under the bridge."

"You always do that, Dilly."

"Do what?"

"Forgive so easily. I wish I could be like you."

I hug her, and my tummy rumbles loudly.

"I'm going to cook," she says, and I offer to help.

Kizzy goes overboard, cooking everything from scratch. She is making Tagliatelle.

"I don't do that, Kizzy. I buy it already done."

"It tastes so much better when you make it fresh," she says.

"Daddy will have no idea he is eating vegan," she winks, and I laugh.

I take notes as I want to do this for Markus. She makes the sauce and asks me to taste it.

"Mm, that is heavenly."

"Kizzy, if medical school doesn't pan out, you have a future as a chef."

Choosing Love

She cracks up.

"Dinner is ready. Can you let them know?"

When I go downstairs, Markus is sitting next to dad with headphones on, listening to music. He gestures with his fingers for dad to wind back.

I tap him on the shoulder to get his attention, and he looks at me and smiles.

"Dylan."

"Sorry, Dilly, I'm keeping Markus from you."

"Dinner's ready."

"Markus, we better go up," dad says.

Markus nods and removes the headphones.

"Where can I wash up, Dylan?" Markus asks.

He's still in his travel clothes.

"Come with me," I sing song.

He changes into a thick green sweater and black jeans. The four of us sit down at the dinner table.

After dinner, Markus helps to load the dishwasher despite dad's protest.

"It's alright. I don't mind," he tells dad.

I give daddy his gift of finest mince pies. He lights the fire as it's quite cold, and we all sit in the lounge. He breaks out his best brandy and pours a glass neat for Markus.

He shares the mince pies, but Markus declines due to his diet.

"Daddy, he's allergic," Kizzy says.

"Isn't it just fruit and liquor?"

"Daddy, there are hidden ingredients like high fructose sugars."

"Alright," he says, putting them away.

"Why don't you just tell him I'm vegan?"

"Daddy won't understand."

Dad surprises us when he does not go back to the studio. He and Markus are chatting about copyright infringement. Dad is soaking up everything that he's saying. Kizzy goes for her hairbrush, and I'm lost in her strokes.

We dress warmly the next day in heavy coats,

hats, scarves, and gloves. Kizzy is taking us on a tour of Harvard Square. Markus is worried about me being out in the cold, as my surgery is scheduled for tomorrow morning.

"It'll do me good, the exercise," I reply, but he's not convinced.

His cracks started to show when we were in bed last night. He's trying to hold it together, but I know him too well now, so I know the signs.

He and daddy are both nervous. Kizzy and I are surprisingly calm. Markus is dressed smartly in his long, dark wool coat. He helps me into the car.

"He looks like a GQ model," Kizzy whispers.

We don't stay out too long, as the wind bites. The weather forecasts heavy snow in a few days. I'm excited. I loved storms as a child.

"That's because we lived with Grams, and she was always prepared," Kizzy says.

Back at home, we eat dinner, and everyone is subdued, even Kizzy. I wish they wouldn't be; It's making me nervous. I say this out loud. Daddy puts on the stereo and pulls me in for a dance.

Markus and Kizzy stand looking at us.

Later, in bed, I want Markus to make love to me, but he is reluctant.

"I won't scream or make any sounds."

"You should sleep, Dylan."

He kisses my forehead. His hands tremble, and I notice this happens when he is aroused, so I know he wants to. I reach for his hand and put it inside my shorts.

"I'm so wet and ready for you," I whisper, and he closes his eyes and moans softly.

"Dylan, I can't," he whispers, "I'm sorry."

He kisses me again on the forehead. He doesn't move his hand away from my wetness. Great fat tears roll down his face.

"Markus, it's okay," I say soothingly.

I kiss him and hold him close.

Choosing Love

"I love you."

"I love you, Dylan."

We leave early the next day. Markus is all business, focused. I try to stay in the zone with him. Daddy kisses me.

"See you soon," he says.

Markus had a rental car delivered. He tells Kizzy he needs to feel as though he's doing something. I kiss her goodbye, and Markus loads up the map and drives us to the Brigham Women's Hospital. A text message comes in from Toby wishing me good luck.

At the hospital reception, I tell them my name and their attention changes. I'm whisked away and prepped for surgery. I've never been in the hospital before, so I assume this is the norm.

The surgeon walks in, and everyone in the room looks at her. She talks to me in a friendly voice, as if we're at a social event. I'm completely at ease. The music is playing, and she asks me what my favourite song is. I tell her. Then she tells me to count down from ten.

"Ten, nine, eight, seven...."

* * *

I'm in excruciating pain; my body is burning from the inside out. I come to, but I can't move. Panic rises in me as the cool liquid fills my abdomen, but it brings instant relief. Slowly, I drift off. This cycle repeats itself a few times and then stops. This must be a dream.

I wake up for real in a large white room. Markus is asleep next to me. He sits in a chair and is holding my hand. A nurse comes into the room.

"You're awake," she says, and he stirs.

The nurse checks my drip and then goes back out.

"Dylan," Markus wakes up, rubbing his eyes.

"Hi," I am happy to see him.

"Did you sleep in that chair?"

It doesn't look very comfortable.

"How do you feel?"

Choosing Love

"Strange. How come I'm still here?"

"You were in pain, so they decided to keep you in for observation."

He kisses my hand, and my tummy muscles contract. He notices when I cringe.

"Sorry," he whispers.

"What time is it?" I ask.

"It's almost six a.m."

Closing my eyes briefly, I drift off again. This time, when I wake, Markus is not there. I stare at the vacant chair, wondering if I dreamt the whole thing.

"Hello, Dylan."

It's the same voice that asked me to count before I lost consciousness.

My heart rate spikes.

"I'm Dr Bernstein. I'm here to check on you. How are you feeling?"

She smiles at me, and I relax. Her voice is soothing.

"Fine," my voice croaks.

She checks my pulse and examines my tummy, then she listens to my heart with her stethoscope. Her hands are cool, and I close my eyes as she works.

She tells me the surgery went well and I open my eyes. There is a little swelling, which is normal, but she needs me to have a bowel movement and pass clear liquids before I can be discharged. She also tells me I need to walk around, and I exhale, preferring to lie here forever, as I drift off to sleep yet again.

When I come to, there is a nurse in the room. She helps me to the bathroom and asks if I'm hungry.

I tell her, "a little."

I wash up and change into my clothes. There is some blood, and I am a little light-headed. I dress in my comfy, bloated day pants and a fitted cotton turtleneck sweater.

Pulling my hair up in a ponytail and applying mascara makes me look human again. My tummy is hollow and bereft as I walk out of the bathroom.

Choosing Love

Now that I'm on my feet, the urge to be in bed disappears. I walk the length of the room back and forth until the nurse comes in with some food.

I sit at the small table and eat a horrible-tasting jelly-like yoghurt. I almost cry when it is finished. The nurse goes and brings me another one. It tastes better the second time. I eat slower so I don't finish it too quickly.

I'm wondering where everyone is when Markus and Kizzy appear, followed by dad.

"Dilly!" Kizzy comes over to me and sits at my table, rubbing my hand with her fingers.

Daddy moves closer and gives me a pat on my shoulder.

"Well done, Dilly," he says.

Markus brushes his hand along my hair and down my ponytail, and kisses my forehead. He offers the last chair to my dad and remains standing.

"I have to walk about the room."

I move to stand, and Markus reacts. He helps me

up, and I walk back and forth.

"Have you had a bowel movement yet?" Kizzy asks.

I look at Markus, but his face gives nothing away.

"No."

"You need to drink more fluids. I'll get you some water," she says, standing.

Dr Bernstein comes back into the room.

"Oh, hello," she says.

"Very good. Dylan, I see we have made progress. Have you eaten?"

"I had two yoghurts, but I'm still hungry."

"How about some chicken broth?"

My face falls. I'm famished. They've taken half of me away, and now they are feeding me baby food.

"If you can hold that down, we can introduce some solids," she says, smiling.

My hands fall to my tummy.

"Are you having any pain?"

"A little."

"We have started to wean you off the pain medication, so you might experience some discomfort from the swelling. The pain should be subsiding and not becoming more intense," she explains.

"If that happens, I need you to let us know. I will leave you to carry on with your exercise."

She smiles and leaves the room.

"Oh, my goodness," Kizzy gasps, grabbing my fingers.

"What's wrong?" I ask, alarmed.

"That was DR. Ingrid Bernstein."

"Oh," I reply, too hungry to care.

"Dilly?"

"What?"

"She's the top surgeon in the entire United States of America. How did you get her?"

"I don't know Kizzy. I'd prefer it if the food was

top-notch."

"Do you ever think of anything but food, Dilly?"

"You've just had surgery. They need to make sure you can hold down liquids first before anything heavier. I'll make you something nice for dinner tonight," she offers, and I hug her.

"You're the very best sister in the entire world," I say, and she rolls her eyes. I continue walking.

"I'll get you that water," Kizzy says as my broth arrives.

A different nurse brings it in and sets it on the table. I go over to eat. The nurse is eyeing Markus up. Kizzy notices, too, and grins at me.

"That's been happening all day," she whispers to me.

"We're in America," I reply.

"Exactly. When we see something looks good, we appreciate."

We both laugh, but this causes my stomach muscles to pull. I place my hand on the spot where I felt the sharp pain. Markus comes over and squats next to me. He puts his hand over mine.

"Is the pain getting worse?"

"Kizzy, don't make your sister laugh right now," daddy snaps.

Kizzy and I laugh some more.

I have a meeting with another consultant before I'm discharged. Kizzy and Markus sit in with me. It's good news, and I'm relieved.

He shares the ultrasound of my uterus before and after. Kizzy studies the pictures closely and asks all the medical questions. I don't even recognise my sister when she is talking. She is impressive.

I know she will translate all the jargon for me later, so I sit holding Markus's hand. He is so much more relaxed than yesterday.

I hear Kizzy ask about sex and I stare at her, then look at Markus.

He smiles.

"She is being thorough," he whispers, but I also

want to hear this.

"It would be up to you, Dylan. I recommend waiting until the four-week healing period is over. Have a check-up with your OBGYN in London before resuming sexual activity."

He sounds so clinical, but I suppose it's his job.

"How long until the pain stops?"

"The pain usually goes after a few hours of surgery. The pain you are experiencing now is the body healing. This is normal and should go away in a few days. If the pain persists, please seek medical advice. You should also have mild to moderate bleeding over the coming days. This should clear up after a few weeks," he explains.

The session takes over an hour before I can finally leave. Markus helps me into the car and buckles me in. The day is bitterly cold. He puts the car heater on full blast.

"How are you doing with driving on the right-hand side?" I ask.

Choosing Love

"It takes some getting used to," he admits.

Despite the cold, the sun is shining brightly, and he is wearing Ray-bans to deflect the glare. I close my eyes, feeling drained and tired.

When we arrive home, we all stay together. Daddy and Markus start a game of chess in the lounge.

I watch them play for a while then go to the kitchen to help Kizzy. She tells me I can wash the vegetables. Kizzy interprets the medical jargon. She is pleased with the outcome.

"I guess it's true what they say about the legendary Ingrid Bernstein. Dilly, I don't know how you ended up with her as your surgeon, but I don't think you will even have scar tissue. The incision was miniscule. You got the very best of modern medicine."

"If she's so good, she should be accessible to everyone who needs her," I say.

"You'd think. The world doesn't work like this, though, Dilly. Money talks, at the end of the day."

"She would have had to fly from her home in Malibu, where she works, to come to Boston to perform the surgery."

"She lives in Malibu?"

"Yes, she has a private practice there," Kizzy says.

"Wow," I reply, passing her the vegetables.

She's making lasagne.

"I have a theory. The hospital is linked to my college, so perhaps she was doing a teaching session. Harvard would have the clout to retain someone of her calibre, and you were the lucky patient."

"I was worried about the aftereffects," she stops and whispers, looking serious, "I'm sure you want to get pregnant someday. After I saw the ultrasound, I was relieved. She did an amazing job."

"I hope someday to be like Dr Bernstein. I want to be the kind of doctor who my patients trust implicitly. I don't want to be exclusive, either. I want to be accessible to everyone."

She resumes her cooking, and I smile.

Choosing Love

"The dream has evolved," I whisper, and we hold hands briefly.

Kizzy has talked about being a doctor since she was three years old. She wanted to be every type of doctor under the sun.

Kizzy is a testament to the fact that if you work hard, anything is possible. Her drive and determination will make this dream of hers a reality. It's always been that way with my sister. Daddy and I sit on the sidelines, cheering her on. She rolls over us sometimes, but we keep on cheering.

* * *

We spend the next few days preparing for Thanksgiving. I'm not sure if it's my going to the hospital, or Markus visiting, but daddy spends most of his time with us, only going to the studio for brief periods.

The storm is set to blow in on Friday, so Kizzy and daddy pick up the Christmas tree early. We would usually decorate the day after Thanksgiving, but due to the impending storm, we do it the night before.

Our traditions for Christmas come from Grams. Dad used to work overseas, but he would always call us on the day. Kizzy and I are nostalgic as they decorate the tree. Markus fills in for me.

I took a walk earlier, and now I sit by the fire wrapped in blankets. The chill seeped into my bones despite all my layers. Kizzy has saved the old baubles, whereas I always want to have a new theme every year. Usually, we argue over this, but this year, we decided it doesn't matter.

Markus is completely intrigued. In London, they do things differently. Kizzy gives instructions to Markus about where the tree should go. There is a hilarious moment when daddy makes eggnog and offers some to Markus.

"No, Markus," Kizzy says, as he puts the glass to his mouth, "It contains eggs."

She takes the glass from him and drinks it herself. Markus shudders.

"Sorry, Markus, are you allergic to eggs as well?"

Choosing Love

daddy asks, looking puzzled.

"Yes," Kizzy says, and we laugh.

Markus doesn't understand why we don't just tell daddy the truth.

"Daddy won't get it, and he'll lose sleep over it," I say, and he shakes his head.

I soften the blow now by telling daddy that Markus will have some more of his Courvoisier neat. He happily goes off to make Markus his beverage. He comes back with a large glass, and we laugh. Kizzy pours some into her eggnog.

"I can't have you getting liver failure on my watch," she winks at him.

We resume our work, playing Soca music, and the snow starts to fall outside. Daddy tells us the snowfall in Buffalo is already twenty-five inches deep. Markus goes outside, and I join him.

We are wrapped up, but the temperature is warmer. We huddle up on the porch bench and watch the snow come down. Kizzy brings us warm apple cider.

"Sit with us," I say, and she goes inside for daddy, who is watching from the window.

I'm sandwiched between dad and Markus, with Kizzy sitting next to daddy. We watch the snowfall for another twenty minutes. Then it starts to blow onto the porch, so we're forced to go back inside. Daddy stokes the fire, and we turn on the Christmas lights.

Markus lifts me onto his lap and pulls a blanket over us. I lean on his chest, cosy and content, as he runs his hand down my hair.

Thanksgiving morning, we wake up to a winter wonderland. I call my mom and Toby.

I won't be able to see my mother on this visit. I don't fancy sitting in a car for an eight-hour round trip. I know if I ask her, she will come, but I don't want to upset Kizzy.

I'm still bleeding a little. I dress in a form-fitting black dress with a boat neckline that I bought in London last week.

Choosing Love

It fits me perfectly and shows off my figure. I stand to the side and examine my tummy in the mirror. It had been swollen for the past few days, but today, it looks flatter than it has in years. I could get away with a smaller size dress. Kizzy pins my hair up.

"You look ravishing," she says.

She looks gorgeous in her yellow dress.

"Do you think the black is too morbid?" I ask, reconsidering.

"It's perfect," she says.

She does my eye makeup, exaggerating the lines and applying red lipstick. When I go downstairs, Markus exhales.

"You look so beautiful," he whispers, kissing me softly on my lips.

He's wearing a light green sweater over his shirt and tie. I go to greet daddy, and he has tears in his eyes.

"Daddy, what's wrong?"

"It's nothing."

He smiles sadly, and I adjust his tie.

I have no doubts that Kizzy made him wear it. She's in the dining room, adding last-minute touches. We eat in here once a year. The windows offer a view of the beach, covered in snow. She's worked so hard to make everything perfect. I'm lighting the candles when the doorbell rings.

"Are we expecting guests?"

"Sam mentioned he might pop over."

"Why didn't you say?"

"He wasn't sure which day he could come. I thought he might make it for tomorrow, to be honest, but he called last night."

I stare at her and wonder briefly if she's up to something.

"Kizzy?"

"Dilly, it'll be fine. We're all adults, and Markus can deal with a healthy dose of competition."

She smiles cheekily, and I exhale.

The last I heard, Sam had moved to Texas to play

Choosing Love

ball and was supposed to be dating an actress. But every Thanksgiving, when I came home, without fail, he would come to the house under the guise of visiting our father but then ask me to dinner. I would oblige. Occasionally, we would kiss.

Sam and I didn't part well, and I've always been a little guilty about the way I hurt him. Not so much anymore. Now, I understand that he wasn't the man for me. It was good that I listened to my heart.

Daddy only moans once about the absence of turkey. Kizzy tells him she wanted to try something new and winks at Markus. The food is delicious so there are no more complaints.

As predicted, Sam makes things a little awkward.

Kizzy sits him far away from me on the other side of dad at dinner, but he still stares at me with his puppy dog eyes.

He's very polite and speaks to Markus throughout the visit, but he is also very touchy-feely with me. When he first greets me, his hug lingers until I pull away.

He takes my hand at one point as I pass him a drink. I don't make a fuss; I simply remove my hand and pat him on the head, imploring him to get the message.

I know Markus has had enough when he excuses himself. He goes outside to the back porch. I grab my coat and scarf to join him. He wraps me in his arms. He does not hesitate.

"Who is he?"

"A family friend."

"Dylan, I'm used to guys staring at you, but why does he have to touch you?"

"I know Markus, I'm sorry."

"Don't apologise for him. He knows we're together; it's just rude to do it when I'm sitting right there."

"Sam is my ex-fiancé."

He gazes at me for a long time without speaking, then he finally says, "Perhaps he needs reminding you're no longer his, so he can keep his hands to himself."

"Markus, there's no harm. We've known each other all our lives."

He narrows his eyes at me.

I remind him that Sam did not make it to third base with me. It's my attempt to put a smile on his face.

"Am I supposed to feel better knowing this guy has seen you naked?"

He is so cute when he is jealous.

"No, but you know that he doesn't turn me on. He didn't get to have me. You did," I whisper softly, praying my dad is nowhere close by.

"Your hands are cold, Dylan. Let's get you inside."

* * *

I drive Markus to show him our childhood home. Another family lives there now. We walk along the beach; the waves are choppy. The snow lies on the sand like fine powder. Our swing is still there. We stand in the cold, looking at the house.

The next-door neighbour, Ms. Grimes, recognises me and invites us in. We sit in her warm kitchen, drinking apple cider. She tells me I look so grown up and beautiful and makes a fuss over my dashing English boyfriend. She must be in her eighties now, but she looks good. She tells us she sees my sister all the time.

"I love me some Kizzy," she says, chuckling, "That girl's a mover and a shaker. Ever projecting upwards."

"Yes, that's our Kizzy."

"And you, Dylan. You're Lily's daughter. The second prettiest girl I've ever laid eyes on."

"Who was the first?"

"Miss Lillian Rose Johnson still holds that title," she says.

"Who's that?" Markus asks.

"Her mother," she replies, "Do you still see Lily?"

Choosing Love

"I saw her in early March."

"How is she?"

"She's good."

She shakes her head.

"Such a shame. It just goes to show being pretty isn't everything. You've got to be ready for life."

* * *

Kizzy and I are heading out to visit our grandparents' grave. Today, the thermostat dips into minus. It is bitter, and the wind is biting. Markus is worried, but I tell him I must go.

"You're not resting enough. You look pale," he says, helping me with my fleecy hat.

I pull it down over my ears and put earmuffs on.

"We won't stay long," I promise him.

He kisses me and helps me with my jacket. He wraps my scarf around me and walks with me to the car. Kizzy has backed into the garage, and the engine is already running, so it's nice and warm.

She has a thermos of warm tea, blankets, and a hot water bottle. I smile at her; she has thought of everything.

When we arrive, it's a twenty-minute walk from the car park to the graveside. Kizzy carries the flowers and tries to support me as well. We go slowly. I am lethargic today. Markus is right; I'll rest once we return home. This is an annual event that I did not want to miss.

The trip to the cemetery tires me out, and I fall asleep sitting by the fire. I wake up, and Markus comes over to me. Kizzy curls up in the armchair, reading a huge textbook. Dad is in the kitchen at the dining table, working on his Mac. He looks over when I wake up.

Kizzy brings me a large glass of sarsaparilla root juice. Grams used to give us this when we were younger. I sit up and drink, and then Kizzy takes my glass away.

"Do you feel up to shopping tomorrow, Dilly?" Kizzy asks.

Choosing Love

It's the first year we've not gone out. The sales are always on over the Thanksgiving weekend. Markus and I are flying back to London tomorrow night.

"Yes, sure," I say.

Markus shifts next to me. I look at him, and he gives me a tight smile.

"We'll take it easy. We'll only go to the local mall."

"Is that okay, Kizzy?"

"Of course."

Daddy comes into the lounge.

"What are you doing for Christmas daddy?" I ask.

"We're going to Montserrat to play in the carnival," he replies.

He's in a strange mood today. He hovers as if he wants to say something to me. None of us have had to go to the hospital for any reason before, so I tell myself he must have been worried about me.

The pain is now a dull ache.

"Are you going as well, Kizzy?"

"I can't, Dilly, I have to work."

Her phone rings, and she looks at the caller ID and smiles. She goes off to take her call.

I laugh at her retreating back.

It must be a guy, I think to myself.

Markus says he will go up to start packing.

"I'll help you."

"No, Dylan. I can manage."

He kisses me on my lips, right there in front of my dad. I suddenly feel like this is a set-up as dad comes and sits next to me.

"Hey, daddy."

He puts his arms around me.

"Are you okay, dad?" I turn to look at him.

"I'm okay, Dilly."

My dad will be forty-two in a matter of weeks, but

sometimes he looks older. He walks around like he has the weight of the world on his shoulders. Only when you see him on stage playing in his band do we have a glimpse of the gorgeous, young eighteen-year-old guy that caught the eye of the prettiest girl in town.

Their story doesn't have a happy ending, but it did have a beautiful beginning.

"Are you happy with Markus?" he asks, completely derailing me.

"Don't you like him, daddy?"

"Yes. I like him very much. I'm asking you if he makes you happy."

"He does, daddy. I love him."

This is a tough conversation. I know my dad wanted me to be with Sam. I wait for him to tell me to take things slow.

"You know, Dilly, we sometimes have the best intentions, but things don't always work out how we plan," he sighs, and I wait.

"I never got a chance to say thank you to your grandmother. She never liked me; I wasn't good enough for her, Lily. Still, she did me the biggest favour, and I never got to say thanks."

It's true Grams never liked daddy, but she also never said anything negative about him to us. Whenever he wanted to take us away on his gigs in the summer holidays, she always let us go.

"Dad, why are you talking like this? You provided for us. Kizzy and I were happy. We loved living with Grams, and she loved us."

"Were you happy with me, Dilly?"

"This is why I'm asking if Markus makes you happy. You and I are so much alike. We make do with what we have. We may not be happy, but we don't complain. I don't want you to live like that."

"When you were younger, I would always put Kizzy before you, and you never complained. You should have."

"Daddy," I say, looking to see if Kizzy is close by.

Choosing Love

For the first time, Kizzy and I have had a drama-free visit, and I don't want to stir the pot on my last night.

"When you left to move to London, it broke my heart, but I was proud of you. I heard you loud and clear. I said to myself, Dilly is taking a stand. This is what Rose did. She transformed my girls into strong, brave women."

"What about Mom? Grams raised her, too. How come she wasn't strong and brave?"

"When Lily became unhappy, she didn't say anything to me or to her parents. We never knew until it was too late. Kizzy was born, and where was I? Halfway across the world when I should've been with her."

I ease off the couch and go to the kitchen. Kizzy is standing around the corner, crying. I hug her and grab our coats, and we go out to the back porch. Daddy comes out and lights the fire pit. I'm shooting daggers at him.

I briefly wonder where Markus is. I go inside to

get my hat, and when I go back outside, dad and Kizzy are sitting huddled together. The wind has died down, and the evening air is much more pleasant.

"Daddy," I whisper, "why do you have to bring this stuff up tonight?"

"It's okay, Dilly," Kizzy says, "We never talk about it, and we should."

"I don't want to discuss this when Markus is here."

"Doesn't he know about mom?"

"Yes, he knows. It doesn't mean I want to rehash this!"

I sit next to Kizzy and pull her close aggressively, and she laughs.

"The sarsaparilla is working, Dilly."

"I'm sorry, girls."

"Dilly, you, and Markus seem so in love. You're happy with him, so I'm happy for you," he reaches over Kizzy's shoulder to touch me.

"Although, how anyone could be happy and not

eat meat is beyond me," daddy adds, and we crack up.

"He does eat meat," I whisper in Kizzy's ear, and she screams into the night.

* * *

Kizzy fires up the barbeque, and I go inside to check on Markus. He is sitting in the lounge.

"Hey, I was worried about you."

"I didn't want to intrude."

"Sorry, daddy is being a bit emotional today. He's not usually like that. Kizzy thinks it's the meatless week, so she's fired up the grill and is cooking steak."

"I told you not to deceive him."

"You did. Come on out back. With the firepit and the barbeque, it's like a sunny day in London."

"Hey, Markus," Kizzy calls.

"Pull up a chair, Markus," daddy says.

We put on the Christmas tree lights and Markus helps us hang lights on the back porch.

"Kizzy, it's a shame you'll be working over Christmas," I say, "With Daddy away, you're more than welcome to come to London."

She flips the steak over and closes the lid of the grill so we don't get smoked out.

"It's fine, Dilly. Occupational hazard to work the major holidays."

"You'll be in this huge house all by yourself," I say, and she gives me a wistful look before jumping up to put daddy's steak on a plate.

Markus notices and chuckles, kissing my head. The phone call earlier was my first clue.

She's totally seeing someone.

Daddy enjoys his steak. Kizzy grabs him a beer from the fridge.

"Is it good, daddy?"

My father sighs and gives a thumbs up.

* * *

"Come on then, spill the beans," I say to Kizzy.

Choosing Love

We are in the drive-thru waiting to order coffee. We'd only been at the mall for an hour before I became tired with some tightness in my abdomen. I told her, and she said we should head home. We stayed up extremely late last night.

"He's in his final year at Harvard, so he graduates next spring. His name is Howie. He lives in upstate New York, but he is Canadian."

"Why didn't you bring him to the house?"

"He went home for Thanksgiving."

It's our turn in the queue, so she orders our drinks.

"I didn't know Canadians celebrated Thanksgiving?"

"Well, they've lived in America since he was five, so when in Rome and all that."

She passes me my coffee and I put it in the holder.

She does the same with hers, and we drive home. I try to imagine the guy Kizzy will end up with. She never had any serious boyfriends.

"Be careful," I say, being the overcautious big sister.

It's my role, and I like to play it well.

"I am," she assures me, giggling.

He must be cute.

Saying goodbye to my family is always tough. Markus packs our bags in the rental car. Daddy and Kizzy stand by the Christmas tree.

Kizzy wraps her arms around his waist, and daddy puts his hand over her shoulder. It's a perfect picture for me to take back to London. I kiss them both.

"Enjoy the Caribbean sunshine, daddy. Try not to fall into the volcano."

Kizzy releases him, and he hugs me.

"I love you, daddy," I whisper.

"I love you too, my darling Dilly."

He kisses both my cheeks, and I giggle.

"Daddy is trying to be European," Kizzy laughs,

Choosing Love

"I think he's been influenced by one suave English dude."

We laugh and touch foreheads. I love this girl something fierce. We hug, and I kiss her.

"Take care of yourself, Kizzy. Call me if you need anything. I love you."

The inevitable tears threaten to spill.

"I love you, Dilly."

She smiles, and her face lights up. She wipes away tears, and I do the same.

"Brandon, thank you for having me in your home. It was a pleasure to meet you."

Markus offers to shake daddy's hand, but dad pulls him in for a hug. Kizzy and I laugh.

"It was good to meet you, Markus. Take care of my precious Dilly."

"Always."

Kizzy gives Markus a hug, and I shake my head. They look like a postcard photo of the perfect couple.

Markus takes my hand, and we walk out to the car. It's frosty, and our boots crunch over the snow. It's dark outside, but daddy has put on the porch light so we can see. He buckles me in and kisses me quickly on the lips. Kizzy and daddy stand at the door, so Markus waves, and I do the same, blowing kisses.

"Ready?" he whispers.

"Yes," I say, and he backs out of the drive.

Healing

"Hey Beautiful, we're home."

I open my eyes. We're in the car parked outside our apartment.

"Did I fall asleep again?"

I don't recall much after the plane took off from Logan.

"You're tired. You need to rest."

"I want to walk for a bit."

He takes the bags upstairs while I do a loop to the security gate and back to the car.

The temperature is nice and pleasant. I remove my scarf.

He takes my hand, and we head upstairs. A stunning array of yellow roses is displayed on the dining table. Pleasantly surprised, I give him a hug.

"Wow. Did you do this?"

"No, these are from my family. Savannah dropped them off earlier."

He smiles, brushing my hair off my face.

"Why didn't she stay?" I say, smelling the sweet perfume and reading the card.

"They wanted to come and see you, but I said you'd be tired after the long flight."

"Roses in Winter. I love London."

"I'm sure you want to shower first. Let me help you."

I hunt for comfortable clothes, settling on cotton blue jeans and a red plaid shirt. I'm relieved the heavy winter clothes are no longer required.

The bleeding is heavier, and I'm lightheaded. I

haven't eaten much since Kizzy fed us yesterday.

I'm brushing my hair when I hear the doorbell ring. My hair is fluffy and soft. This always happens when I go home. The water is less harsh. Markus knocks on the door.

"Toby's here."

I hurry down the stairs. He is sitting on a stool at the kitchen island but stands as I rush into his arms.

"I know you're tired. I won't stay long."

"I've slept all the way home but can't seem to shake the fatigue."

I rub his back.

"I brought you some soup from Nate's. He asked after you."

"Thanks, Toby, I'm starving."

Markus is in the kitchen, and I turn to him, smiling.

"Do you know how to heat soup?"

Toby offers to help him.

"How did I end up with a man who can't boil water?"

"I have other talents."

As if to prove his point, he sets the table for three.

"Markus, I won't stay," Toby says.

"Have lunch with us. I need help convincing Dylan she shouldn't work next week."

Toby turns to look at me; his face registers shock.

"You're thinking of coming to the office?"

"I've never had a sick day. I don't want to ruin my record."

"Well, let's call it a recovery day," Toby replies.

He grabs a wooden spoon.

"Didn't your doctor sign you off?" he asks, stirring.

The aroma makes my mouth water. I know I won't win this one.

"Fine. I'm too hungry to argue," I reply, pouting.

Markus chuckles.

Choosing Love

"I could use your persuasive powers around here more often," he says to Toby.

Markus puts my soup in front of me, and I devour my bowl. Nate puts tiny little dumplings in. I usually give mine to Toby, but not today.

Toby also brought bread, vegetable soup for Markus, and various fruits and nuts. I listen as they chat. When Markus asks Toby what his plans are for the holidays, I perk up, hoping he'll give Toby an invite.

"I'm going to spend it in Munich this year," Toby replies and gives me a shy smile when I make kissing sounds.

"Mm, are you?"

Toby and I laugh, but Markus stares at me. He's sitting across from us, and I wonder if he realises he's staring.

"What?"

"Nothing," he replies.

Toby is trying not to look at Markus, so I know

he's noticed.

"What's for dessert?" I ask to dispel the awkward moment.

"I can make scones," Markus replies, and I open my eyes wide.

"I'm suddenly full," I say.

Having Toby here is like medicine for my soul. We move over to the couch and sit and chat, while Markus cleans up the kitchen. He stays another couple of hours and then tells us he will leave.

"Make sure you take it easy and rest," he says.

"Okay, boss. Will you come to visit me? I'll be bored out of my mind."

He sighs and gives me a kiss, and then Markus walks him to the door. I head up to clean my teeth and put on my Pyjamas, blue cotton shorts and a red camisole. I'm tired again, and it's only four-thirty.

It's already dark outside. I lay across the foot of the bed for a moment and stretch out my arms over my head.

Choosing Love

I come to hours later. The clock on the bedside table reads three a.m. Markus is asleep next to me, and my silk wrap covers my hair. I smile. He must have done it for me. He knows I hate to sleep with my hair open. He stirs.

"Are you alright?"

"Yes."

We lie facing each other. He pulls me close, and I touch his face, my fingers graze across a day-old stubble.

"Oh!" I gasp, "I like this," I say, kissing his lips lightly.

I deepen the kiss, and at first, he's in the moment with me; he moans softly but then pulls away. I kiss his neck.

"Dylan, stop."

"Sorry, I forgot," I whisper and close my eyes.

"Sleep now," he says, kissing my forehead, and I drift off again.

* * *

The shades are drawn, but the sunlight threatens to burst through. I groan, throwing off the covers. I hate to sleep the day away, but I feel refreshed and no longer dizzy, so I start my morning routine. I check out my tummy in the mirror; the swelling has gone completely, and I'm amazed.

My workouts must have contributed, but my tummy is back to how it was before I moved to London. I hunt for something nice to wear, settling on a long white dress with spaghetti straps.

The apartment is toasty warm, but I add a long, dusty pink blazer to the mix and brush my hair, leaving it loose. My tummy growls so I go hunting for breakfast.

I stop at the top of the stairs. Markus is at the dining table working on his laptop, and Sarah is on the balcony cleaning the windows. This is not what makes me stop. There is a large Christmas tree in the corner by the window leading out to the balcony.

He looks up and notices me.

"You're awake."

He stands, and I step gingerly down the stairs. He meets me at the bottom.

"Hi," I say, looking around.

"You look lovely. Did you have a nice sleep?"

He bends and kisses me. He still has the hair on his face.

"What did you do?" I gesture to the tree.

"I thought you'd like it."

"I love it."

I walk over to inspect the tree. Sarah comes inside and says hello.

"Can I clean the Master bedroom and Ensuite?" she asks.

"Yes. Please," I say shyly.

Feeling strange telling his staff what to do, I look at Markus, but he doesn't seem to mind.

He has been busy. The refrigerator is stocked with all my favourite foods. He tells me to sit and brings a smoothie from the fridge. I recognise the brand from one of the local cafés. It's lemon and ginger.

"That's good."

I take a long swig, and he smiles. He brings over my favourite salad. It has all the trimmings, so I dig in. He sits on the stool next to me.

"I thought you'd be at work," I say between bites.

"I wanted to stay with you."

"How can you have this much time off?"

"I can work without being in the office."

"With such high-profile clients, don't they demand a stellar service?"

He lifts my fork, putting more food into my mouth. I narrow my eyes at him. I know when he is being evasive.

"You look very sexy with the facial hair."

"Really? It looks messy."

"So, why'd you keep it?"

"Because you like it."

"I like this, yes. It adds drama to your face, but I prefer you smooth."

We spend the afternoon decorating our first Christmas tree together. He puts on Christmas music, saying it doesn't feel right otherwise. He has ordered all different baubles for the tree. I recognise the label of a top-end store on the boxed packages. The colour scheme is silver and white.

"When did you do this?"

"I had the idea when we were in Boston."

We go all out and hang lights around the apartment. Markus phones the building super for a handyman to help as we need a special ladder; the ceilings are high.

Sarah smiles when she comes down and notices us. She is heading to the laundry room with our dirty clothes.

It took me a while to become used to someone else doing my laundry. She even organises our dry cleaning. I add her to my Christmas list.

"Does she have children?"

"Who?"

This annoys me. It's like he does not even notice her.

"Sarah," I whisper.

"I don't actually know," he replies, and I give him a look but don't say anything more as she's still here.

I continue with my work. We turn on the Christmas lights and stand admiring our spectacular display.

"Our first Christmas together!" I say happily, with his arms around me, my head on his chest.

"The first of many," he whispers and leans in for a kiss.

* * *

Two weeks later, I visit Dr Amy's clinic for my first check-up. Markus offers me his car, but I go alone. I lay on her table as the nurse examines me, then sit in her office for the update.

"You are making excellent progress."

Choosing Love

"I feel good."

"You're young, and it is expected that you will recover quickly, but I won't discharge you until the four weeks have passed, just to be on the safe side."

"What would you recommend for contraception?"

She offers me brochures and explains the options.

"Have you thought about starting a family?"

Her question throws me, and my hand shakes slightly as I take the glossy pamphlets.

"I only mentioned it because the fibroids will most likely grow back."

"How long until they return?"

"Maybe three years or maybe ten. It's not an exact science, but, in my experience, they usually do."

I hurry home to Markus. My head is full of information, and I need one of his hugs but when I arrive home, he's on the phone. I head upstairs.

After the nurse's intrusive inspection, I'm desperate to feel clean.

I'm showered and dressed, and he has not come to see me to ask how it went, and though I am a little disappointed, I seek him out. When I arrive downstairs, he is deep in thought, staring out at the view, the phone in his hand.

"Markus?"

He comes out of his trance and turns to hug me. It feels divine, and I wrap my arms around him.

When he does not let go for a while, I catch onto his mood.

He sighs heavily, "Stacey is in labour."

I take his hand, sitting him on the barstool.

"Did you want to go to her?"

He seems conflicted.

"Would you be okay if I did?"

I shrug my shoulders, a little unsure, but then I offer him a small nod.

Choosing Love

"You should go."

He hesitates, but I smile encouragingly. He smoothes my hair off my face.

"It's just that...if he's mine, I would want to be there for his first few hours."

"Yes. Of course."

His eyes fill with tears.

"I'm sorry."

"There's no reason to be sorry."

"This is not what I want for you."

"Life doesn't always give us what we want."

"But sometimes it does. You are everything I've ever wanted."

* * *

The leaves have fallen from the trees in the sky garden. It's barren, but still beautiful. The naked shrubs with colourful stems catch the late afternoon sunlight. Tiny oranges blossom on a citrus plant I had bought back in the autumn.

An hour after he left, Toby arrived. He has enticed me to put up outdoor decorations. He is hanging fairy lights on the trees, precariously dangling off the ladder he found in the garden shed.

"Should we do them all?"

"No. Just the odd one. It will be more effective that way."

"Less is more. You have such an eye for the finer details, D. When I buy my new place, I would love your inputs."

He hums along to the tunes coming over the speakers. The radio stations have started to play Christmas songs. Toby does his best to distract me, but not even he can divert my attention.

I sit on the garden bench, a silver box of baubles and fairy lights on my lap. My mind is racing. I have not heard from Markus but its only been four hours.

Toby turns on the switch and beams at me.

"Viola!"

The lights flicker like tiny teardrops, turning

blurry. Dark clouds obscure the sun, and Toby complains that he is cold. The temperature has dropped below seven degrees. I don't feel it much. There is hardly any wind, but we head inside.

We cook and eat dinner in relative silence, which is unusual for us.

"Ah. I'm used to it. Gina's been giving me the silent treatment for the past three months," he says when I apologise for being a sullen hostess.

"Perhaps you should let her meet Nicolos. He's so charming. I bet he can make her come around."

He narrows his eyes at me.

"It's worth a try," he sighs, "I think I preferred it when she was just disappointed. Not talking to her feels weird."

I reach my hand out and he grabs it, bringing it to his lips.

"Thank you for being here," I say.

"I'm not really helping, though, am I?"

"If I was alone, it would be unbearable."

"Have you and Markus discussed what would happen if he's…"

"The father? No. He doesn't talk to me about any of it."

Toby reaches for my other hand.

"I knew Markus for a year, and he did not utter more than two words to me. I thought he didn't like me. After that bully, Simon, nearly caused me to drown, Markus beat him up. We've never discussed it, but I know he did it for me. You are the woman that he loves. Imagine what he'd do for you."

* * *

The waiting frazzles my nerves. After Toby leaves, the silence is loud. Sleep eludes me. Markus's pillow is cold. I wrap it in my arms and fight the tears threatening to escape. I close my eyes, and the next moment; the room is bathed in the glow of a new day.

My phone has remained silent all night.

By midday, I've decided to call Toby and take him up on his offer to accompany him to view a potential house.

The apartment door opens, and Markus comes inside, carrying a large bouquet of stunning blush pink roses with white winter berries.

My heart skips a beat. He is utterly heartbreakingly handsome in his long black winter coat and leather gloves. He is smiling as he walks towards me.

My fears tumble to the floor when he folds me in his arms. I decide then, whatever it is, we can face it together.

"Hello..."

"Hi."

"Did you sleep well?"

"Did you?"

"Not really. I missed you."

I'm tempted to say that it was his choice to go, but instead, I say, "I missed you too."

His lips press softly onto mine, and he hugs me close. I wait for him, not wanting to speak first.

"He's not my son."

A broken sob escapes, and the tension evaporates from both of us. When we break apart, my heart is fuller than ever before.

"Markus..." I begin, but my voice is heavy with tears, and I start crying my eyes out.

He lifts me in his arms, breaking the chains that bind me. It's like Scotland all over again; he is carrying me down the mountain with his unwavering love.

* * *

After dinner, I tidy up in the kitchen. Markus remains sitting at the dining table. He is quiet and a little pensive. Sensing he is looking at me, I walk over to him. His face is serious.

"I need to tell you something," he says.

I bend my head, kissing his lips.

"What is it?"

"I've decided to provide for the baby. His name is Zachary Markus St Cloud."

Choosing Love

My face must register my shock.

"You mean financial support?"

"Yes."

His hand moves to caress my back. I move away from his touch.

"Dylan, I want to know you're okay with this."

Stacey's confident words echo in my head, *"In the end, he will always come back to me."*

"Me? It's not my business what you do with your money."

He recoils as if I've stung him. I head up the stairs and out to the garden. The Christmas lights Toby hung are twinkling like diamonds. Daylight has faded to dusk, and the evening is cold. Sitting on the bench, I pull my cardigan close to ward off the chill.

His shadow falls across the doorway, but I don't look at him.

"You know what I'd like, Markus?"

He walks over and sits next to me.

"What would you like?"

He offers a small, tight smile. His eyes are burning.

"I'd like to not have any more drama to do with your ex-lover."

"This is what I'm trying to do."

"By supporting her son?"

I speak slowly so he can hear how that makes no sense.

"I'm just trying to make this right."

"Is this an attempt to stay close to her?"

"What? No. Dylan, haven't you been paying attention? I love you, only you. It hurts when you tell me that what I do is none of your business. Everything I do, it's for you."

"How is this for me?"

"My legal team is taking care of it, but she must agree never to come near you or contact you. In return, I'll provide for Zachary until he turns eighteen or leaves full-time education."

Choosing Love

He holds my hand as he speaks. I don't say anything in response. I lean forward and kiss him.

I sigh wearily, not wanting to give this woman any more of my time.

"I'm sorry I hurt you. In future, please tell me the full story instead of telling me in bits."

I smile and hold both of his hands in mine. He looks down at our fingers entwined.

"I thought you liked my storytelling."

New sensations

Savannah invites me to a spa day. She picks me up in her Jag, and we drive out of London and head to Stratford-upon-Avon.

The place is a sprawling country manor set in a beautiful English countryside. The day is cold but sunny.

My massage therapist works magic on my muscles, and my mind drifts into sensual thoughts. I'm ready to resume intimacy with Markus. On occasion, our kisses have led to heavy petting, but he always stops after a while.

Choosing Love

Things got heated yesterday. My shirt and cardigan were on the floor, and I was sitting astride him on the couch, but I had to work just for that to happen.

He was sitting at the dining table, tapping away at the keys on his laptop, while I sat in the armchair in the lounge looking at him. He noticed and looked over at me. I smiled. He smiled. Then he went back to work, his fingers moving on the keys.

Deciding it was unacceptable, I went upstairs and changed into tight, stretchy hot pants and a tiny fitted white shirt. I threw on my long, sheer cardigan and went back downstairs.

Markus was in the kitchen making coffee and topping up my lemon water. He looked up when I came back down the stairs. His eyes followed me as I sat on the couch and crossed my legs. He exhaled, but he came over and sat next to me.

"Dylan. Heading out?"

I laughed, and the kissing started in the next second.

"I love that sound."

"What sound?"

"The sound of you laughing," he replied, kissing me again.

Our tongues touched and triggered my nuclear charger. I removed my cardigan and pulled my shirt over my head, discarding them.

The girls were standing to attention, and he put his mouth on one. We both groaned at the same time. I leaned back and watched as he moved to the left.

"I miss you," he said, and I smiled.

Yesterday was only a teaser session. Today, I work on readying my body for action.

After hours of being waxed and plucked, I replenish my organic oils.

By the time I meet up with Savannah for lunch, I feel like a new woman. She convinces me to go shopping, and we stop off at a quaint village. Luxury boutiques line the street. I buy lingerie, a black sheer

Choosing Love

outfit held together with the cutest bow and matching thongs.

Savannah giggles throughout the shopping experience. It's infectious, and I enjoy my day. She drops me home with the promise to do this again soon.

Markus greets me at the door.

"Hello," he says, pulling me in for a kiss.

"You smell delicious."

"Did you miss me?"

"I did. What's in the bag?"

"I haven't tried it on yet. I wanted to get your opinion."

He opens the bag and holds up the underwear.

"Interesting," he says softly.

"Come with me."

I take his hand and lead him upstairs, then sit him on the Chaise Longue. I remove my clothes slowly. I have his undivided attention. His feverish eyes trail up my body and my confidence soars. I slip on the tiny underwear first, then pull on the sheer negligee and tie the little ribbon at the front. I check myself out, glancing at him in the floor-length mirror.

I turn around and walk over to him.

"Do you like it?"

"Very much."

"Make love to me?"

"Dylan. You haven't been discharged."

"A minor technicality," I point out, leaning down to kiss him, "I'm ready."

I sit on his lap, my thighs on either side of his and kiss him with urgency, wanting to devour him, but I know he will prefer to be cautious for our first time. He hesitates.

"Markus, touch me."

Desire pools in his eyes. He wants to. I undo his jeans and free him from the constraints. I smile at the sight that greets me. Touching the very tip, I bend over to kiss it.

When he doesn't stop me, I lick him with my tongue the way he does me. He throbs, growing impossibly larger before my very eyes.

"You want me," I whisper.

He runs his hands up the back of my legs. They're smooth and glistening from my afternoon at the spa.

"I always want you," he whispers.

"First, can I try this?" I say, indicating what I want.

Whenever the topic of me performing oral sex on him comes up, he's always reluctant. I'd love to do it for him the way he does for me.

He hesitates now.

"I don't want to see you in that way."

"Why not? You do it to me."

"Because I can't resist your scent. I can smell you now."

"Do you think I'll be rubbish at it? Is that why?"

He laughs.

"No. I prefer to please you. Your expressions when we make love are the sexiest thing I've ever seen. For me, that's always the goal."

"I'd love to please you like this. Let me. I want to."

Instinctively, I fall to my knees, lifting the top of my negligee, exposing my breasts, and rub the tip of his shaft against my already engorged nipples. He inhales sharply.

Tentatively, before he can say no, I lick the tip and all around the shaft. He pulsates in my hands, warm and rock-hard.

He tastes good.

"Mm, delicious."

A moan escapes as I explore him for the first time.

"Show me what to do."

He nods. Standing, he removes the rest of his clothes. I watch with my eyes wide. My man is a sight to behold. I move to the edge of the Longue and pull him towards me. He smiles down at me, watching my every move. Then, he removes my negligee top and bottoms, lifting me up in his arms. I feel a rush of excitement as he lays me gently on the bed. He lies next to me, on his side, facing me. I rub my hands over his chest, touching his hard body and revelling in his beauty.

Suddenly, he lies on his back and spins me around. I squeal, laughing. I'm on top of him with his head between my thighs and my face over his lower half.

I catch on quickly. I take him into my mouth, but at the same time, he licks me, pulling me down on his face, his hands splayed on the cheeks of my bottom, breathing deeply. He kneads my flesh, his moans vibrating my core, and I tremble.

I follow his lead, and soon, we are simultaneously pleasing each other. It doesn't take long, and before I know it, my body is locked in the most powerful orgasm. It's almost painful. I cry out, and he quickly turns me upright.

"Did I hurt you?"

He's breathless, and I'm at a loss for words, but I shake my head no. We're both dripping, so he cleans us up.

"Your body looks different."

"Different good, I hope."

"Curvier. It's very sexy."

"Curvier means fatter."

"Irresistibly so," he whispers.

He kisses me until I'm breathless, and then, ever so gently, carefully, he enters my body and proceeds to show me just how irresistible he finds me. He reaches my hands above my head and entwines our fingers.

His other hand lifts my thigh, caressing my flesh. My memory has not served me. I knew it was good between us, but nothing prepared me for this feeling of euphoria.

Being intimate with him again is like food for my soul.

Choosing Love

Tremors rock my body as I climax multiple times. This is my happy place when we're alone, and I'm loving him, and he's loving me, over and over, until even my bones cry out.

"Thank you."

"You're welcome."

I'm lying on his front, with my back to him, but I can hear the smile in his voice. I notice it has started to rain. It was a perfectly beautiful sunny day earlier.

"This English weather is so unpredictable," I remark.

"Very much like you," he replies.

"Do you find me difficult?"

"There's never a dull moment."

He plays with my hair, which has come loose from its bun.

I turn in his arms, and he rolls me onto my back. He then slides into me slowly; I close my eyes and moan. I feel stretched by the sheer size of him. He swears softly. I want him to go faster, deeper, harder, but I know he won't.

Today, he wants to go slow, and I let him. I did ask him to make love to me, and that's what he does. From the moment he enters my body, he loves me until I break into pieces in his arms, and then slowly, he puts me back together again.

* * *

I hang the phone up and growl in frustration just as he walks through the door. He is carrying takeout food from Nate's.

"What's wrong?"

"I've been on the phone for two hours with the insurance company," I reply.

I walk to the kitchen and top up my water.

"Is everything alright?"

"No. They sent me a letter saying they are closing my claim. I rang the billing department at Brigham, and they said my bill was settled privately. I want the insurance company to reimburse the payment, but they say they won't cover the extras."

"I asked them to send me the details, and I know there's been a huge mix-up. They're saying I requested a private room, a private surgeon. Her flights and her hotel are all added to my bill."

"Markus, this is daddy's insurance. I would never dream of doing such a thing. He'll think I've lost the plot."

I pack up the paperwork I'd printed earlier. Markus stands in the kitchen, looking at me.

"Dylan, I paid the bill."

"What? Why didn't you tell me?"

"If I'd asked, you would have said no."

"You did this behind my back?"

"I wanted you to have the best possible outcome."

I stare at his face and then sigh, "Thank you, Markus."

"You're welcome."

I switch on the shredder and destroy the documents. I'm too tired and hungry to argue, but the figures don't add up when I do the math in my head.

I know an IP lawyer has a good salary, but he would have to put in the hours. I never see him stress about work. He's sometimes home before I am. He went to Spain on business a few times in the early summer, but only for two days.

Toby has the top role at our firm. He works long hours, travels all the time, and is well paid, but still, there is a limit to what he can afford.

I'm famished, so I concentrate on eating. It's one of my favourites: chicken korma with Peshwari naan. Markus has dahl roti. He likes this dish. He makes polite conversation as we eat.

I want to ask him about the money, but I realise I'm afraid of what he will say after the baby drama with his ex. I just want to enjoy being with him. I'm not sure I want to know how he could possibly have this much money.

* * *

"Toby, do you think Markus could be involved

Choosing Love

in anything illicit?"

I ask the question slowly. Toby and I are standing outside the gates of St Paul's Cathedral. The enormous Christmas tree in the courtyard is lit with multicoloured lights. We attended the Christmas service. I love the choral carols.

"Like what?"

I lean closer to him; a small crowd is gathered in the courtyard.

"I don't know. Money laundering? Embezzlement?"

Toby waits for me to finish.

"Don't forget International Espionage?" he says.

I frown, and he starts to laugh. He is being overly extra, howling very loudly. A few people stop to look at him. He holds on to the railing and bends over laughing. I smile at him.

"I love you," he says.

Tears of mirth roll down his face, and I roll my eyes at him while he wipes his.

"Seriously, D, where do you come up with this stuff?"

"I know it sounds like I'm paranoid. Maybe I am. He can afford things that are just not reasonable, and he never explains."

"There has to be a logical explanation."

He takes my arm, and we start walking towards the Bank Station.

"That's what I keep telling myself, Toby, but I'm not sure if I'm trying to convince myself that all is well because I'm so happy."

He stops walking and looks at me.

"What's going on?"

I glance around and wait for a couple to go past us.

"This past week, he's been acting very strange. He was on the phone with someone, getting very irate about a package. He was in the spare room, so I couldn't hear all the conversation. Then he had to go out, so I assumed he was picking something up, but then he came home empty-handed."

Toby stares at me.

"You're going to have to give me more than that," he says.

"He paid for my surgery."

"Okay. That was nice of him," he replies.

"Toby, he paid to fly the surgeon from Malibu and for her hotel stay, and I'm sure she would've wanted a retainer as well."

"How do you know?"

"I saw the bill."

I fill him in, and he looks intrigued.

"Who needs watershed?" he replies, and I glare at him.

"Toby, this is serious to me. I'm in a relationship with him. The one you encouraged me to pursue. What do you have to say for your good friend now?"

"D, why don't you just ask Markus?"

"We just got over the baby drama and we're in

this sweet phase. I'm not ready for it to be over."

"You and Markus are meant to be together."

"Does that mean I have to be Bonnie to his Clyde?"

"You do have borderline paranoia. I'm sure if you ask him, he will explain, and it will all make sense."

He takes my hand, and we cross the street to the tube station.

We don't discuss it anymore as we're in the busy station. We stand on the DLR, weaving and bobbing as the train winds through its route. Toby holds on to the rail, and I hold on to him. He rolls his eyes but indulges me.

I'm happy to come out and share this special day with him. Toby and I never exchange gifts for Christmas. Instead, we donate to his favourite charity for underprivileged boys. It is the same charity that paved the way for a humble boy from Greenwich to attend the most prestigious boys' school in the country.

Choosing Love

I would have liked very much for him to spend the holidays with us, but I want to encourage his relationship with Nicolas, so I don't make a fuss.

I say goodbye to Toby when I disembark at Canary Wharf Station. He's leaving for Munich tomorrow, so I won't see him until the new year.

"Talk to Markus. I'm sure he'll tell you anything you want to know."

"Merry Christmas, Toby. I love you."

"Merry Christmas, D. Love you too."

I wave as the train pulls away.

The Christmas lights sparkle as I walk through the streets. The wind picks up slightly, but the weather is quite mild for mid-December, just two days until Christmas. I'm wearing a dark blue Mac over my dress. My Louboutin's have scuff marks, but I wanted to walk today. I make the short journey back home.

Markus is coming down the stairs as I walk in. He smiles and greets me with a kiss. This is what makes it so hard to ask.

My OBGYN discharged me officially on Monday. Markus and I are back on track. He has made love to me every day. Every day and every night, if I'm honest. I smile at him.

"How was it?" he asks, helping me out of my coat.

"It was beautiful."

I head upstairs to shower and change, then I cook, and we eat. I have an apple and blackberry crumble in the oven. Dishing up, I serve it with warm custard. He puts a spoonful into his mouth and closes his eyes.

"Hmm, that's good," he says, complimenting my cooking as usual.

His lips are moist as he chews, and this distracts me. He continues until his bowl is clean. It's been four hours since I arrived home, and I haven't plucked up the courage to ask him.

"What would you like to do tomorrow?" he asks.

"I'll call Kizzy," I reply.

Choosing Love

"Have you finished all your shopping?"

"Yes. My gifts are in the spare bedroom."

I didn't like the idea of leaving gifts under the tree.

"I have one for Sarah. Is she coming tomorrow?"

"That's very kind, Dylan, but you didn't have to."

"I wanted to. She does all our cleaning and laundry. It's the least we could do."

"She provides a service, and she is paid. I also give her a Christmas bonus. Same with the gardener."

"Well, with Sarah, it's personal. She cleans up after us."

I walk off in a huff and retrieve the gift from the bedroom. I use a biro to put her name on the label.

To Sarah, thanks for all you do for us.
Markus and Dylan.

I place her gift under the tree so I don't forget to

give it to her tomorrow. I sense he is watching me. He comes over and reads the card.

"What did we get her?"

"It's a silk scarf, blue. It'll match her eyes."

Markus is one of the kindest people I know, but he sometimes behaves arrogantly.

"Her eyes are blue?" he asks, "I hadn't noticed."

I exhale and stare out at the view. It never ceases to amaze me.

A large white boat is sailing by. I watch as it makes its way slowly down the river. He reaches for my hand and pulls me into his arms. We kiss and I forget I'm annoyed.

"You always know how to disarm me."

"I hope you don't think I'm insensitive."

"I hope you don't think I'm always annoyed at you."

"You're honest. I appreciate that. You call me out on the things I should do better."

Choosing Love

I put my arms around his waist and go in for a longer kiss.

* * *

On Christmas Eve, we walk down to the local ice rink. I used to love doing this in Boston Common with Kizzy. It's her birthday today, so before we leave, we ring her. It was five a.m. her time, but I knew she would be up.

She opened her gift while we were on the call and screamed excitedly. Tickets for two to Orlando. Kizzy loves Universal.

Markus was overly generous, but she deserved it.

The call was brief as she was leaving for the hospital to work. I felt a pang of guilt. I've been off work for six weeks. It's the longest hiatus since I got my first after-school job at thirteen. I say this to Markus after we hang up with Kizzy. We were sitting at the breakfast bar.

"If you didn't have to work, would that bother you?" he'd asked.

"Yes. I must always work; I wouldn't be happy otherwise."

He gazed into my eyes for a moment too long and then brushed his lips against mine.

"Let's go out," I said.

He's wearing a long-sleeved white cotton shirt and black jeans. He pulls a dark green sweater over his shirt and puts on his long dark wool coat, lacing up his boots by the door.

"We only have a couple of hours. If you want to catch Sarah; she'll come at midday."

The ice rink is lit up with multicoloured lights, and seasonal pop songs blast from the nearby speakers. It's early, so it's not yet crowded. We buy our own skates as I don't relish the idea of wearing used ones. He is surprised I'm good at skating.

"How do you think I got these thighs?"

"Kizzy and I spent our winters ice skating every chance we got."

I spin around for emphasis. I'm wearing tight

black jeans and a short leather jacket. My red scarf blows in the wind as I zoom around the small ice rink.

We buy take-out lunch at our favourite Japanese restaurant and eat at home. The surfaces are gleaming. Sarah is here working. I want Markus to do the talking since he is her employer, but he tells me to do it.

"Sarah," I call to her softly.

She looks up from watering the Christmas tree. I bend and pick up the box.

"Markus and I wanted to say thank you for the work you do. We appreciate it very much."

I smile shyly and pass her the box.

"Merry Christmas."

I give her a hug, and she laughs.

"Thank you, Dylan," she replies, "Thank you both, this is very kind."

She looks at Markus, and he smiles. She goes to put the gift in her bag and comes back to resume her work. We sit and have lunch. The dim sum is especially good.

"What do you normally do on Christmas Day?"

He seems reluctant to answer.

"Do you go to many parties?" I ask.

He didn't attend his firm's Christmas party, and I didn't go to ours as I'm on sick leave.

"Some," he replies, shrugging.

I almost ask who with, but I stop myself in time.

"Have you decided if we will join Savannah in Switzerland?"

"I'm not sure. It all depends."

His response is rather cryptic.

"On what?" I ask.

"You're still recovering. Let's take it easy."

His eyes don't meet mine.

I'm suspicious, but Sarah is still here cleaning, so I won't go into it now. Later, when his mouth is on mine, I don't think of it then, either.

Choosing Love

* * *

"Merry Christmas!"

I open my eyes and glance at the clock. It's ten a.m.

"Merry Christmas!" I reply, smiling.

His mouth on mine is urgent, and it's a while before I catch up to where he is. His hands move under my powder blue negligee to fondle my breasts. My body is awake before my brain can react. My negligee falls to the floor, and my matching undies follow. He trails kisses down my body.

My eyes follow his path of desire, sucking, licking his way down. It's rare that we make love first thing in the morning, but I don't have time to think about it now. My magician works on me. I bow to his will, running my fingers through his hair as his tongue touches my centre, consuming me until all my juices spill from my body. I climax, screaming his name, and he enters me.

He waits for me to float back to Earth. I open my eyes and stare into his.

"My delicious Christmas Angel."

He starts to move inside me, reacting to the sound of my moans. His muscles ripple, and I stare in fascination as the wonder of him unfolds. I match his rhythm, wanting him to go deeper still.

He touches the very edge of my soul as he grants my wish, and yet I want more. We detonate in unison, calling out to each other. He wraps me in his arms. I can feel his heart racing, and I put his hand over mine.

"I love you, Dylan."

"I know," I say drowsily.

When my eyes open again, it's midday. Groaning, I crawl out of bed and head for the shower, dressing for the day in a black strapless jumpsuit with a monochrome silver belt. I slip on black velvet stilettos, apply minimal makeup and brush out my hair.

A nice necklace would go beautifully with this outfit, but I never buy jewellery.

Choosing Love

Markus often offers me his card to go shopping, but I always end up purchasing sexy lingerie instead.

His Christmas presents are in the spare room, so I collect them on my way downstairs.

He surprises me for the second time today. He's made breakfast. The table is set.

"What's this?" I say, approaching him.

He's in the kitchen pouring a smoothie into my glass. He looks very handsome in a crisp white shirt and dark jeans.

"I thought I would make breakfast for a change," he says, smiling.

"Try this," he offers, and I take a sip.

Kiwi and lime with a hint of ginger.

"It's good," I say, beaming when I notice my little recipe book on the counter.

I put the presents under the tree and freeze. There are three tiny gift boxes already there, wrapped in exquisite paper. Mine look lack-lustre next to them.

"Santa has been!" I laugh and join him to eat.

We have homemade granola. He warms up my milk just the way I like it. The smoothie is sweet and refreshing. I thank him for breakfast.

"You're welcome," he smiles.

"You look very handsome."

He smiles shyly, and I reach over and kiss him on his lips.

"Thank you for this morning," I whisper.

"My pleasure."

Kissing him again quickly, I stand to take the dishes away. He helps me. There is much to do, so I want to start cooking and baking.

When Markus said we would spend Christmas just the two of us, I was surprised. I thought we would go to his parents or his sisters.

"Do you want to exchange gifts?" his voice breaks into my thoughts.

"Sure. I'll go first."

Choosing Love

I grab my boxes and place them on the kitchen counter. He sits on the bar stool.

"Pick one," I say.

The boxes are of varying sizes. He picks the big one first, unwraps it and laughs.

"Well, this is more a gift for the apartment."

It's a coffee machine.

"Thank you," he says, and I move the machine into the position I've already decided will work.

"Pick again."

They are sunglasses for Skiing.

"Last one."

This one is special. It's a copy of Robert Frost's *The Road Not Taken*.

He stares at me with unreadable eyes.

"I hope you like it."

"I do," he whispers with emotion, "Very much."

"My turn," he says, smiling.

We exchange positions so that I'm sitting on the stool he vacates. The sun's rays light up the apartment. It's a beautiful sunny day, and I hope we can go out for a walk. He places the boxes in front of me.

"Pick one," he says, copying me.

"Did you wrap these yourself?"

He doesn't speak; his face is suddenly so serious. He shakes his head no.

"This one," I say, indicating the box in the middle.

The wrapping paper is exquisitely beautiful. I remove it carefully, admiring the intricate attention to detail. The cream paper is thick and heavy, and it takes a while to remove it.

Underneath is a little white pearlescent box. I lift the lid, and my heart stops.

Nestled in the centre is a sparkling, emerald cut, yellow diamond, set on a thin gold band. Minutes must have passed, but I'm frozen, suspended in time.

Choosing Love

Yellow Diamond

"Dylan, will you marry me?"

"Yes."

The next second, his mouth is on mine, and his groan is a strangled cry. I break the kiss to stare in wonder at my gorgeous ring. He removes it from the box, his fingers trembling as he slips it onto my finger. It fits perfectly.

The gold band and yellow rock are beautiful against my skin. The sunlight catches the brilliant diamond, and it glitters and sparkles. The light reflects off the both of us.

"Markus, it's beautiful. I've never seen anything like it before."

"Now you know how I feel when I look at you," he replies.

I kiss him again, softly and slowly, and he hugs me close.

"Thank you for saying yes," he whispers in my hair.

"Did you doubt that I would?" I run my fingers over his full lips.

"You always surprise me, so yes, I thought you might say no."

"I love you," I remind him.

"I know, but I thought you might think it was too soon," his voice breaks with emotion. "Brandon told me you would say yes."

"You told my dad?"

"Yes."

"When?"

"The day you went to visit the cemetery."

"That's why Daddy was being weird."

"He was very emotional when I asked for his blessing."

"Thank you for asking. You're the man of my dreams."

The moment is suddenly overwhelming. I start to shake, and my tears flow.

"Are you going to pick again?" he gestures to the other boxes.

"I hit the jackpot the first time, so I'm good," I reply, grinning.

"Go on," he urges softly.

The second box has a key card inside.

"There is a tag at the bottom," he says, and I remove the key.

It has the address for the Canary apartment printed on a tiny tag inside.

"Is this a key for this place?"

"No, this is the key to *your* apartment," he says, and my eyes widen, "I bought the penthouse for you."

"What?"

"Why?"

If he wants us to marry, why buy me the apartment?

My confusion must show on my face.

"I didn't know if you'd say yes. You love it here, and I wanted you to know that whatever happens, you made this place your own, and I want you to be happy."

My tears start to flow again. I throw my arms around him.

"Happiness, for me, is wherever you are," my voice breaks.

I speak through my tears. We kiss, but I need more; I throw my arms around his neck and press my body against him. His response is instant. I can't believe this is happening right now.

Choosing Love

"I want you," I barely whisper the words.

* * *

Hunger breaks up the afternoon of love making. After three hours, I'm so famished I have the shakes. I shower in the spare bathroom to escape, dressing casually in black jeans and a white T-shirt.

Markus goes to the laundry room with our soiled sheets while I hunt for starters, preparing a salad and garlic bread. I'm making coconut bean curry for dinner.

It's four-thirty, and we went upstairs at one. I smile to myself, deliciously sore but it was so worth it

The last remaining gift sits on the marble top, and I wonder what it could be, but food is more urgent. Markus appears, freshly washed in baggy jeans and a long-sleeved white T-shirt.

I serve up his starter and place some nuts on the table, then start prepping the ingredients for the berry crumble.

"Come and eat, Dylan," Markus calls to me.

I place the candles in the tall silver candle holders, lighting them and adding a bottle of white wine to the table. These are gifts from his family. Savannah brought a case of wine all the way back from South Africa.

"Mm," I moan after the first taste.

He laughs as he pours himself wine.

"Let's toast," he suggests, refilling my lemon water.

"To the happiest day of my life so far."

His eyes sparkle, and I smile.

He picks up the final box and passes it to me. A smaller box is inside. My fingers refuse to move as excitement courses through my veins.

"You better tell me what it is. I don't have another three-hour sex session left in me."

"There's always tomorrow," he replies, and my heart flutters.

"I bought the diamond uncut, but I didn't think

Choosing Love

it was you once the ring was finished. It was rather ostentatious, so I had them redo it, and what was left they fitted into a necklace."

I open the box and there it sits. A beautiful golden necklace with my yellow diamond.

He fastens it around my neck. It nestles in the hollow just above my cleavage. My hand, already heavy with my ring, reaches up to touch it.

"Thank you. It's beautiful," I say, my voice thick with unshed tears.

The significance of the day suddenly hits me, and I'm so happy, it leaves me breathless. He soothes me, rubbing my back.

Tomorrow, I think to myself, *I'll ask him about the money.*

He helps tidy up, and I start our Christmas meal. We don't sit down to eat until just after seven, but my curry is cooked to perfection. I scrub the kitchen down, discarding the rubbish. I love curry, but I hate the smell it leaves behind.

I light my fragrance candles and watch as Markus makes his first homemade cappuccino. He offers me one.

"Oh, why not?"

Happy and content, we curl up on the couch, and he reads me poetry from his new book. He stops reading.

"We should probably tell our families," he says.

I have three people to tell, so I go first.

We ring together using my phone. Toby and Kizzy cry; only daddy is dry-eyed, but he already had the heads up. Markus' family are also happy. Savannah, Helen, and Becca cry over the phone. Matthew is composed, but Markus tells me later that his dad already knew.

After the calls, I run upstairs to put my necklace away and hurry back downstairs to him. It has started to rain. Markus is staring out the blackened windows as water cascades down the pane. I slip my arms around him, and he pulls me in. We stand together like this for a while. He exhales.

Choosing Love

"What's wrong?" I ask.

"Not wrong. Everything is perfect."

He sighs and takes my hand, and we move around the back of the kitchen to the dining table. He gestures for me to sit, then seats himself opposite me. We're facing each other.

"There's something I'd like to share with you. I want you to know my reluctance to tell you was not because I don't trust you. I do."

"Is this about the money?"

"Yes. I know you probably worked out that I'm more than just a city lawyer."

"It worried me, but I could never pluck up the courage to ask about it."

"Mama's father died when I was three and he bequeathed his entire estate to me. I inherited money and his assets. Most of which were sold off, but we retained the pharmaceutical company. It was started by her great grandmother and so mama wanted to keep her legacy going."

"It wasn't a great deal of money at the time after converting it from South African Rand to Sterling. My grandfather was a staunch patriot and he lived in his country all his life. My father took over running the business and turned it all around. He already had his property business, and we also own a vineyard just outside of Cape Town."

"The three entities are controlled by a holding company of which I'm a shareholder, along with my parents. When I turn thirty, I'm expected to take full ownership."

"Mama and Daddy didn't tell me until I was eighteen. As you know, I had dreams of being an athlete. I'd put everything into my training but in my final year of sixth form, my father told me I had to give it up. He expected me to work in the family business. I was devastated. It was the first time in my life I truly hated him."

"I first appealed to Mama. I didn't understand why she would side with him. I wasn't going to bend. Then Becca came to see me. She told me it was what Grandpa Joe had wanted so I went into Law."

"The next year, they told me about the inheritance."

He is quiet for a while, gazing into my eyes.

"Three years?" I whisper.

"Yes. It's one of the reasons I have so much free time now. I've started to scale back the workload at my firm. My team takes care of my division. I'm still involved but not as much as I was two years ago."

He reaches over to fondle my fingers.

"I was always worried about you taking so much time off work. I thought you'd be fired for sure."

He laughs.

"There are places where the boss can be fired, but I'm the generous and rewarding type."

"What will happen with your law firm?"

"I'm not sure what I'll do yet. I have a few years to plan. It'll be hard to walk away. It was important for me to be successful. I didn't like the idea of just having money handed to me that I hadn't earned."

"I thought you said it wasn't a lot of money."

"I receive annual dividends from my sixty percent share of Eirith Holdings, and as an equity partner I own forty percent of my law firm."

My head is swimming with the influx of information.

"What does all of this mean for us?"

"This is the bit I struggled with. Your life will change. I don't advertise my wealth or draw unnecessary attention to myself, but I'll have to protect you. I might become overbearing sometimes."

He smiles at me when he says this. The wheels are turning in my brain. Now that I know this, so much about him makes sense, why he's so guarded and secretive. I ask the loaded question.

"What will change?"

A sliver of fear jolts through me.

"Having access to that kind of money creates possibilities that one can only dream about, but I've also learned it can be destructive. If it's handed to

Choosing Love

you like a gift, then very soon it can feel like a curse, a noose around your neck. I found my ways to escape, but now with you, I'm terrified. I never want you to become anything other than who you are."

"It would be easy to become targets for unsavoury characters. Think about your life now. You travel around London freely. Imagine if that is taken away."

"I remember the first time I saw you dancing. You were so beautiful and happy. I couldn't take my eyes off you. I worry that I will lose that carefree, happy girl I met in the spring. When you and Toby are together, she appears."

His voice is so sad it pulls at my heart strings.

"As long as you are with me. If you always love me the way you do now, I will survive anything. You make me happy. I hope you know that."

Changes

I go back to work on the second of January. My yellow diamond ring is like a homing beacon. Everyone congratulates me.

"When is the big day?" a lady from the HR asks.

"We are planning for some time in March," I reply.

"That soon! Are you sure there isn't a bun in the oven?"

I smile to myself, imagining if that were true. Everything in good time, I think to myself. I have other distractions.

"Earth to Dylan!"

Toby taps into my reverie. We're in Islington, walking along the canal. The gloomy day occasionally threatens brightness. A slight wind is coming off the water, but I'm warm under my brown fedora and scarf.

"Sorry, I didn't catch that," I apologise, turning to look at my bestie.

"You haven't caught much of anything I've said today."

"I'm feeling overwhelmed," I admit to my buddy.

"That's understandable, but surely you feel other things too, like excitement for one. You're getting married!"

A few passers-by stop to congratulate me.

"It does feel unreal. Markus' family are generating enough excitement. I'm nervous about my family and how to explain why my mom won't be attending."

"What? I was hoping to meet her," he says, dreamily, "Send her an invitation. She might surprise you."

"She'll come if I ask her to."

"Then, why don't you ask her?"

I look away as hot tears escape releasing the pent-up emotions.

He wraps his arms around me, rubbing my back soothingly as I cry on his shoulder.

"There, there," he says, but it makes me laugh.

He buys hot chocolate from a stall. I lean against the railing, watching the ducks as they swim closer, waiting as he pays for our drinks, and then we walk on.

"Kizzy refuses to be in the same room with our mother. She hates her. As a girl, seeing my mom, was the only thing I ever truly wanted. I thought about her every single day. When I was fourteen, my Papa Kit dropped me at the bus station, and I took the Peter Pan all the way to New York to see her. It was the best day of my life. It still is."

"I remember the driver asking me if I was meeting someone, and I told her I was meeting my mom. I walked down the steps of the bus, and she was there, waiting for me."

"When she put her arms around me, I felt such warmth. I knew without a doubt that she loved me."

"You know what's crazy? The first time I spent the night with Markus, I had the same feeling when he put his arms around me. I didn't understand how someone I'd only just met could evoke such feelings in me."

I smile now, remembering.

Toby is quiet and when I glance up, he has tears in his eyes. I put my arm around him. It's not often I render him speechless. He kisses my hat and I laugh.

"You should talk to your sister."

"What would I say to her? It's the reason for the resentment between us. She was always upset when I came back from visiting Lily. She felt betrayed. I love Kizzy, and I don't want to hurt her. I think the only solution is to elope."

"Weddings have a way of bringing families closer together. These two women love you, so this might be your golden opportunity to finally heal the rift."

"Do you really think so?"

"I do."

"Toby?"

"Yes, D."

"It's such a pleasure to know you."

"Ditto."

We sip our beverages in silence. Mine has gone cold and Toby makes a face. I bravely finish mine, but he tosses his into a bin. He takes my empty cup, discarding it and we walk further into the market. The stalls are heaving with an assortment of fruit and vegetables.

I shake a coconut to see if there is enough water inside. Toby browses at the green vegetable stall. The

Choosing Love

fruit is a little too dry for my taste. I decide to stock up on nuts for Markus, and that is when I notice the window display.

"Would you like some okra?" Toby is asking, but I'm transfixed.

Across the road directly in front of me is a tiny blue shop. There's nothing spectacular about this shop, except one thing.

"Toby!"

I call him and start across the busy market. I don't know if he's following. I stare at the mannequin in the window. The shop is called *All things Vintage*. I notice Toby's reflection in the window. He's on the same page as me.

"Can you believe this?" I ask.

"You have a knack for finding good things when you're not even looking for them."

"Let's go in!"

He grabs my hand and pulls me into the shop.

* * *

I arrive home, walk through the door and exhale. I've missed the rain by a few seconds.

"Sorry, I'm late."

I don't bother showering. I change out of my suit and go downstairs to eat. I'm famished.

"How was your day?"

"Awful. After being off work so long, I'm still trying to play catchup."

"Didn't they arrange a cover?"

"Yes, but that makes things worse. Everything is not how I left it."

He smiles at me. He bought pearl barley soup from Nate's. I could kiss him.

"I was wondering. Can we postpone our honeymoon until later in the year? I just need to find my rhythm at work again."

"No. Dylan, when I marry you, we're having a honeymoon. The day we wed, I take you away."

"I suppose a couple of weeks won't hurt much," I say, resigned.

I know this tone of his. There's no point arguing.

"Things are not finalised yet, but it will be more than two weeks."

"Please be reasonable Markus, this is my career."

"I happen to know your boss."

"Fine. My colleagues already talk behind my back. If Toby keeps approving all this time off for me, he will have to do the same for the others."

"You were off sick."

I sigh. Deciding to tell him what is really on my mind.

"I've been thinking, maybe I should be my own boss, like you and Savannah. I'm selling my apartment and I have some savings. I could start out on my own. Do something that defines me."

"That's a great idea."

"You really think I could do it."

"Of course, I do. You won't have to use your savings. I'll help you."

"Thank you. I'll start on my plan, and then maybe next year, I'll make my move."

I'm resolved. I finish my meal dreaming about the possibilities.

* * *

I drive to pick up Toby. We have an appointment with the seamstress to check the progress of my dress.

He comes out of his town house, having recently moved. He's still living in his beloved Greenwich.

"How was it?" he asks, kissing my cheek in greeting.

"It was sad to say farewell to my place, but she valued it double what I paid. I mean, how is that even possible?"

"House prices have gone nuts D, now is the time to sell."

It's slow going in the car, and I'm anxious.

"Traffic is slow."

"It's murder. We could've taken the tube," Toby

Choosing Love

replies.

He checks the navigator. I haven't been on the tube for a while; I've been taking the car.

"The wedding planner is coming to the apartment at six this evening."

"According to this it should be smooth sailing after these lights up ahead."

We're not moving so I ask him about Nicolos.

"He's away at the moment, working," he replies.

"I'm planning to invite him to the wedding. Is that okay?"

"Are you sure about that? I don't want to offend anyone."

"It's my wedding, I think I can invite who I want."

"Discuss it with Markus and if he is okay with having gays at his wedding then let me know."

He grins when he says this.

"Markus adores you. He wouldn't want to be

married without you there."

I crane my neck to look up ahead.

"I know but it doesn't mean he wants me to show up with my gay lover."

"It's not like you two will be snogging on the dance floor. You could just be two friends attending a wedding!"

"Are you inviting Jack Daniels?"

His voice drips with his usual sarcasm and I laugh.

"You know when Jack shows up at a party, anything can happen."

We're finally on the move. I park outside the shop. We're in Primrose Hill, and it's lovely. Gale the seamstress comes out to greet us. She ushers us in and tells us to go upstairs.

Toby gestures for me to go first. I'm excited. It's three weeks since we first saw the dress in the shop window. It's made of ivory silk with pearl beaded lace trimmings along the neckline and top of the gown.

Choosing Love

It has intricate designs on the sheer lace and three-quarter-length sleeves, and the asymmetric skirt is cinched in at the waist with a train at the back. It needs a considerable amount of work.

Toby found Gale through word of mouth. She first told us there was no way she could fit us in, so two days later, when she agreed to see us, I was surprised.

"How did you pull this off?" I questioned him at the time.

"D, I have my secret ways," he replied, winking at me.

"Did you sleep with her?"

He doesn't laugh. I was joking.

"Toby!"

The dress suddenly didn't seem so vintage anymore.

"I didn't have to resort to such measures. Though that did cross my mind!"

"How then?"

"Never mind how. It's done. Anything for my girl."

When we walk into the large spacious room there are two dresses hanging up.

The dress we bought in the vintage store and another one. I assume she must have another client and walk over to see what she has done.

"Gale, you're a genius," Toby says.

He took the words out of my mouth. The dress three weeks ago was a fading beauty; age was not kind to it. Toby assured me it just needed some love and new beading, and it would be restored to its former glory. He was not wrong.

"I've removed the old beads and ordered new ones. They will be arriving sometime next week. The alterations are based on your measurements, so I need you try on the dress so we can see how it fits."

Her voice brims over with excitement.

I take the dress into her changing room. The silk lace is soft against my skin. I spend a few moments

Choosing Love

staring at my reflection. In my family photo album is a picture of Grams on her wedding day. It is the image I see in the mirror.

Gale knocks on the door.

"How are we doing?"

"I need help with the fasteners," I say, "It must have taken the groom ages to remove her dress."

"I'm going to replace all of this with ivory pearl buttons," Gale says.

"That'll be beautiful."

"Have you considered a veil?" she asks, her fingers working.

"I think a veil would take away from the dress," I reply.

Gale smiles at me.

"Wait right there."

She is shorter than me, and in my heels, I tower over her. Makes a nice change.

"My waist looks so small."

"When you are wearing your corset underneath, it will be even smaller. Your fiancée will be bowled over when he sees you. You have an envious figure."

She stands on a small stool and slides an ivory comb into my hair. It's attached to a long ivory veil.

"You could wear your hair up on the day, and the veil would add a nice touch,"

I turn and look at the veil. I am not sure.

"Let's see what Toby thinks," she suggests.

I smile and go out to him. He sits on a small couch but stands as I walk into the room.

"Dylan," he whispers, and he has tears in his eyes.

"You like it then?"

"I love it. You look like a goddess. The veil. It's perfect."

I walk around the room, and Gale instructs me to try sitting in the dress, crossing my legs, and lifting my arms.

"Is this to practice throwing the bouquet?" I ask, and she turns to Toby.

Choosing Love

"You didn't tell her?"

I turn to my bestie.

"Tell me what?"

"This is the dress you will walk down the aisle and marry in, but when you throw the bouquet later on, *this* is the dress you will wear."

Gale points to the other dress in the room.

My eyes take in the masterpiece; a beaded chiffon halter-neck gown with an open back, hook and eye on the neck. It's vintage Versace and kicks my first dress out of the park. Even on the hanger, it sparkles.

"Try it on," Toby says.

It takes a while, but with Gale's help, I showcase the halter-neck gown to Toby. His smile says everything. He reaches for my hand and kisses it.

"We'll take it in around the waist and adjust the length a fraction so you don't trip."

 "To work on a dress like this is a seamstress' dream come true, but I have to say, seeing you in it, you'll be dazzling."

On the way home, Toby is subdued, deep in thought. I glance over at him occasionally. He sits on the passenger side wearing his green beanie and aviator sunglasses. He is such a beautiful man; it's unreal. I tell him to try to make him laugh.

"I was just thinking the same thing about you," he replies softly.

"Hey, you're not going all weird on me, are you?" I joke.

"Because you know it would just be incestuous, right?"

He sighs.

"I'm just happy to have you in my life."

"Ditto," I whisper.

"Tell me where you found the halter-neck?"

"Nicolos. He's working in Milan. I told him about our dilemma, and he came up with the idea," Toby smiles.

"Then, he's definitely invited to my wedding. He saved the day."

Choosing Love

I can't seem to pull him out of his funk, so I leave him alone.

I take him back to his place and go in with him. His town house is a new build. It's just around the corner from his old place, but it's like we are in a different world. It suits him. It has a retro decor with a modern twist.

Toby is minimalistic with his design taste. He makes me tea in his spacious kitchen. Everything is white and immaculate. I sip and spot where his new cappuccino machine will go. It's his birthday on Wednesday, and he is having a combined house warming and birthday celebration right here next Saturday. I can't wait.

"Gina will be here next week," he says.

"That's wonderful," I say, "Is Nicolos coming as well?" I ask excitedly.

"Yes. It'll be interesting having them both here together."

He drinks his tea, and I reach for his hand.

"Nicolos can stay with Markus and me if it's easier for you."

He fondles my ring and stares at it.

"I want him to stay here with me. If it gets awkward, I'll put her in a hotel."

"I have to go."

I hate leaving like this when he's obviously upset about something. I don't move, and we stand in his kitchen, staring at each other.

"Market tomorrow?" I ask, smiling.

"Greenwich?" he asks, and I nod.

I reach up to kiss him.

"Ok. See you tomorrow."

He walks me to the door.

* * *

The heavens have opened, adding drama to a dull and overcast morning. Markus wants to see Toby, so he comes with me. I text Toby to let him know.

I park the car at his new house and the three of

us walk together, with me sandwiched in the middle and Markus holds a large umbrella over us. The market is indoors, so Toby and I stock up on our weekly fruit and vegetables in relative comfort.

Markus is over by the meat stand, staring at the chunks of meat hanging from the stalls. I nudge Toby, and we both look at him. He notices us looking, and we crack up. He walks over to us.

"This is your side. Why are you over there?" I ask.

"Was that an actual pig's face?" he shudders.

"Pig snout is a delicacy," I reply.

"The poor animal," he says softly.

"Let's take him somewhere else. He looks green," Toby suggests.

We move to the posh end and order coffee. A young girl approaches, asking to do my nails. I keep my fingernails short and natural as I'm always cooking, but I agree to have a pedicure.

I leave Toby and Markus having their coffee. I

can see them from the shop window.

Toby is in better spirits than when I left him yesterday. Markus coming along today was a good call.

At midday, we head back home with our spoils. The rain is coming down heavier now. We put our shopping in the car, and Markus and I follow Toby up the stairs and into the kitchen leaving our wet shoes on a mat by his radiator.

Toby hangs our wet coats to dry, and I wash up and start cooking. Toby has requested pumpkin soup.

While I cook, the men talk. They are sitting at an oval dining table in the corner of the kitchen. There's a view out onto the terraced balcony and the river. Once the soup is cooking, I go to join them. Markus instinctively pulls me on to his lap and kisses me.

"Markus, can you please tell Toby there is no issue for him to invite Nicolos to our wedding?"

"Ah. There may be one small problem with that," Markus replies.

Choosing Love

"What?" I say, giving him a dirty look.

He smiles.

"I'm planning on asking Toby to be my Best Man, so we'll need to find someone for Nicolos to sit with."

Tears return to Toby's eyes, and I go to him.

"Hey, Toby."

I put my arm around him.

"Markus, he's already my Best Man, so go find someone else."

"I thought Kizzy was your maid of honour," Markus says.

"Yes, but she's miles away studying for finals, and Toby has already helped me pick out my dresses. There's lots to do."

"What do you say? Will you be my best man?"

"Yes," Toby replies, and I kiss him on the head.

I'm pleased.

"Thanks, mate."

I check on the soup. The aroma fills the kitchen. It would be ultra-tasty with chicken, but Markus is eating with us. I cut up some bread and slip it in the oven.

"Have you decided on the venue?" Toby asks.

"We're finalising the plans, but it will most likely be in the Cotswolds. My family has a place there, and it is large enough to accommodate everyone. You and Nicolos will be welcome to stay with us. The other guests will stay at hotels nearby."

"Dylan and I will be there for two weeks prior to the wedding, so hopefully, the weather will be nice."

He smiles when he says this, and I glance at Toby to gauge his reaction. I've been putting it off, but there's no time like the present, so I explain my plans.

"I was hoping to at least stay for another year, but the honeymoon will be for a month, which is a long time to be off work. I just don't think it's fair to the team for me to be away for so long, and I feel like it's time for a change. I've no idea what I'm going to do yet, but I hope I can have your support."

"Of course," Toby says, giving me a small smile.

I am suddenly overcome with sadness. It's the end of an era.

* * *

The next day, I hand in my notice. I sit at my desk, writing the letter and crying. In the ladies' room, I freshen up my mascara and pull on my suit jacket before knocking on my boss's door.

"Come in."

I hear the voice I know so well. My heart is racing. He smiles as I enter. The last time I wore this red tweed suit, he complimented me, telling me red was my colour. I imagine that is what he's thinking now.

I give him the letter; he reads it and nods.

"Thank you."

As my boss, he's supposed to say so much more: the firm will be sad to see you go, Is there anything we can do to convince you to stay? He doesn't say any of this.

I stand and walk out of his office. I rush to the toilets and cry my eyes out.

* * *

Pockets of sunshine cast a luminous glow onto an otherwise cloudy, dismal day. The little park across from the office is deserted. It's cold, but I don't feel it much as I sit and reminisce. Working for this firm was my dream job. I remember seeing Toby on my first day.

My flirtatious hello when I first laid eyes on him walking towards me. He was wearing a dark blue suit and yellow tie. I couldn't believe he was real.

He came to join me at my lunch table. I fell in love with his British accent. The first time we went out for drinks, he was like a different man and so much fun.

The way he reacted when he realised I never touch alcohol. And he always made sure that no matter where we ended up, I would get home safely.

Choosing Love

This is how he finds me. He sits next to me and takes my hand. When he was promoted, things changed, but apart from when he's travelling, I still see him at work. Even when we can't have lunch together, he is still there, inside his office. I can always go in.

"I'll still see you, right?" I whisper.

"Of course you will."

"That's what people usually say, and then they never meet up again. I was very popular in high school. Now I have no clue where half those people are, and I'm okay with that, but I'm not okay with you not being in my life," I say, looking at him.

I'm sad about leaving work, but I'm looking forward to a new challenge. I cannot lose my friend; he is irreplaceable.

"When I saw you in your wedding dress on Saturday, it suddenly dawned on me that things are going to change," he admits, "But change doesn't always have to be a bad thing, we adapt to it. The fact that Markus has invited me to be with your family means a lot."

I smile.

"Yes. He thinks of you like family, and so do I."

Silver linings, I think to myself. *I'm not losing anything; I'm gaining, as my family has now been extended.*

Traction

Every waking moment, I'm busy planning my next move. The days are rolling by so fast, and my twenty-fourth birthday is approaching. Markus tells me to take the day off work, but I say no. He doesn't push me on it, so I end up working on my birthday.

I arrive late, of course, as he insisted that we must keep traditions going. The first thing on my agenda is a handover meeting with my replacement in Toby's office. I walk in fifteen minutes late. He looks at me, and I don't dare make eye contact.

He introduces my successor.

"I'm really sorry I'm late, and on my birthday, too."

It breaks the ice. The day goes by quickly after that. I receive a message from my mother, and I call her during my lunch break. I don't mention the engagement. She asks when I will visit next, but I have no answer.

The disappointment in her voice pulls at my heart strings. She tells me to come when I have time as she knows I'm busy, and guilt eats away at me.

There's no time to dwell on this, as I'm distracted with the handover.

Toby gifts me an assortment of spices. The team presents me with a box of Godiva's. Markus sends me twenty-four red roses and a message to meet him out the front at four. Toby and I walk out together.

"Good job today, Ms Weekes."

"Thank you. I'm so sorry about this morning."

"You know it was written all over your face,

right?"

"I've no idea what you are talking about, Mr. Smith,"

He laughs and suddenly stops.

"Wow!" he says softly, looking towards the revolving doors.

Markus is standing outside, waiting for me.

"Happy Birthday. Have fun!"

Toby kisses me on my cheek, but I pull him along, and we go out to meet Markus.

"Do you want to drive home, birthday girl?" Markus says, his eyes sparkling.

He passes me the keys he's holding. I press the button, and a shiny, silver-grey Audi TT lights up.

"Is this for me?" I ask excitedly, and he nods.

"Hey Toby, would you like a lift home?" I ask, flashing my keys.

We end up in a swanky London bar, drinking cocktails. Mine are non-alcoholic, but far too sweet, and I'm buzzing, so I push the glass to one side.

"You have a strategy meeting first thing tomorrow," I remind Toby.

He's on his third cocktail, and they're strong. Markus' eyes are glazed over. This is his 'I have had too much alcohol' look. He switches to drinking water.

"Last one," Toby says.

"Has Gina left yet?"

"Thank heavens, yes."

"Was she putting a kink in your sex life?"

"Hey, we didn't talk about sex before, and we're definitely not going to talk about it now," he replies, throwing back his drink.

"I'm old enough now."

"Not to mention experienced," Markus whispers in my ear, and I giggle.

"You've had enough, Tobes."

The ladies in the bar are eyeing him up. We head

out soon after and I drop him home. I enjoy driving my new car through the deserted streets of London.

"Do you like it?" he asks softly.

"Yes. I do. Very much," I say, smiling.

His eyes smoulder, and I step on the gas.

"Where do I park?" I ask, pulling into the security gates.

"Pull up in front of my car," he replies.

"Did you get me a new spot?"

"Technically, since the apartment is in your name, this spot is yours," he says.

"Where will we live after we marry?"

"Anywhere you like," he replies.

Once we arrive inside the apartment, he takes my coat and bag and I hold my shoes in my hand. I'm not ready to leave my happy city.

"Do you have a house in London?"

"No."

He sits on the bar stool and spins to look at me.

I walk over to him. It's quite late, but I am buzzing.

"I don't own any residential properties."

"How is that possible?"

"I never stayed in one place for long enough, I suppose."

He shrugs.

"What about when you lived with Stacey?"

"She owns that property," he replies, not looking at me, and I'm suspicious.

"Did you buy it for her?"

He doesn't answer, and I sigh.

"What about the villa in Spain?"

He goes quiet, so I suspect he doesn't like these questions.

"You bought that for her as well?"

"I'm going to bed!" I say, angrily turning to walk away, and he grabs me.

"Hey, it's your birthday. Why do you want to pick a fight with me?"

"I'm not picking a fight. My birthday is a perfect day to find out how generous my man is."

"Is that a bad thing, Dylan?"

"It doesn't make me feel very special," I say, immediately regretting it.

I see in his eyes that I have wounded him. I want to take it back, but then my phone rings. It's Kizzy. I answer quickly.

"Happy birthday, Dilly!"

"Thank you, Kizzy."

I watch as Markus walks up the stairs, and I spend some time catching up with her.

"Did you get your birthday gift from me and daddy?"

"No. It will be at the front desk if it arrived, so I'll pick it up tomorrow. We went out for cocktails after work with Toby."

"Daddy wants to say hi."

My dad and I talk for a bit. He tells me he is off to Brazil in a few days. He asks about Markus, and I remember that I upset him. After I end the call, sending them both love, I hurry up the stairs.

He's in the shower, so I go to the other bathroom to clean up.

As a peace offering, I dress in my new red negligee with the straps knotted at the top. I don't bother with underwear. He's at the window looking out at the moon, deep in thought.

I go to him and put my arms around his waist. He smells so clean. This is the number one thing I love about him. He takes care of himself, so I know he will take care of me. I kiss his back.

"Sorry, Markus. I didn't mean to say that. I do feel special."

I put my cheek on his back, and he turns around.

"I love you."

"And I love you," he replies.

"Material things don't matter, not to me. I'm fortunate to be able to afford those things, but what I want with you is so much more than all that."

Choosing Love

His fingers trace my lips.

"I want to know that you'd still love me if I had nothing at all. That's why I fell in love with you because I think that's who you are," he whispers the last part.

"The women in my past, they all said they loved me, but you're the only one I believe, and that's what makes you special."

He kisses me softly on the lips, and I feel awful.

"Look what I have."

I put his hand on the right strap of my negligee. I help him pull the string loose, and it falls, exposing my breast. I pull the other one, and my other breast pops out.

I slide the top down my body, and I press myself to him. I want to show him how much I love him. The feel of his skin on mine is exquisite. I take him to our bed and push him back onto the fresh, crisp sheets.

This morning, we had a birthday session, and he

was in full control. Now it's my turn. He smiles as if he can read my mind. I remove his pants, and he springs to attention.

My mind drifts into a dark territory, wondering if he was like this with his other women or if this is exclusively for me. The errant thought spurs me into action.

I want to make him forget them all. I kiss him with fervour; his mouth is hot and so delicious. He reaches his hand out to touch my breast, but I push it away.

My hair is in the way, so I braid it quickly, wrapping it up. His eyes feast on me as I do this. He sits up to kiss my nipple, and I push him back down. I just want him to lie there and enjoy the show.

On impulse, I touch and fondle my breasts, and he groans. Grazing his fingers across my tummy, closing his eyes briefly. I'm saturated with wanting him. I lift my negligee and expose my legs, then I slide onto him slowly, and he exhales. I enjoy the sensation of him filling me up to breaking point. He grabs my hips and thrusts hard.

I take his hands and move them over his head, holding them there. It would be so easy for him to push mine away, but I know he won't.

I start moving slowly at first, but then the deeper strokes push me over the edge, and it becomes a feverish grind. He moans, but I press down on his hands so they stay put. This drives him wild.

"I want to touch you," he whispers incoherently, and I'm heady with this power.

I gyrate my hips, squeezing him tightly, and he shouts my name.

I lean forward and put my nipple in his mouth, and he sucks. His full lips cover each one at a time. I move my hips faster, and his pleasurable moans send vibrations through my swollen breasts. The sensations rock to my very centre and take me closer to the edge.

I always want to prolong our love-making, but the inevitable approaches fast. He explodes, calling out to me, telling me he loves me, and I follow soon after, falling on his chest. After some time, I move to clean us up. He's asleep.

I slip his pants back on and pull the covers over him.

"I love you," I whisper.

I hope he can hear me in his dreams and know that despite the things I say in my hot temper, he has always made me feel special.

* * *

I'm up early for my morning Pilates class. The clock reads five-thirty. I don't have far to go, thankfully, as it is held in the indoor gym in my building. I prepare Markus' breakfast smoothie. I'm heading out the door when he appears at the top of the stairs.

"Good morning."

His eyes shine as he kisses me.

"You're up early."

In the winter months, he is usually up at seven to go out for his run.

Choosing Love

"You can take your car today. The car park next to the Barbican is prepaid," he says.

"That's great. Then I can leave at seven thirty, so I'll see you later," I reply, smiling.

"You were amazing last night."

He kisses me again.

"Thanks to my Pilates."

I head to my forty-minute session and then rush downstairs to collect my package from Kizzy. I don't have time to open it, so I will do it later. I'm dressed and out the door in record time, heading to the office.

I toy with the idea of opening an accountancy firm. I notice a vacant building with a for-lease sign, and I run away with the idea.

Later in the day, Toby and I head out for lunch.

"I'm thinking I'll start my own firm to rival this one," I tease to gauge his response.

"That's not a bad idea," he says.

"I'm joking."

I laugh and poke him.

"Did you have a nice birthday?"

I blush, remembering the grand finale.

"Don't you remember what you got up to last night? I monitored and made sure you only had three cocktails," I say.

"You did good. I'm just enquiring if you enjoyed the day. It must be a bummer having to work on your birthday."

He holds the door for me, and I go in.

"I had a nice time with my two favourite guys," I say, and he laughs.

We sit and order lunch.

"If I do start my firm, will you come and join me?"

"Can you afford me?"

"Probably not, but you could do it for love," I sing song, sipping my water.

"Love won't pay my bills," he quips, and we crack

up.

My phone vibrates, and I check it.

"It's Savannah. She wants to meet up on Saturday," I say and send her a quick reply.

Toby smiles.

"It's good that you're expanding your circle," he replies as our lunch arrives.

"I suppose. I mean she's his sister, but I do like her. She's really good fun."

"You should have more women around you. D. Variety is the spice of life."

He winks and digs into his meal. He doesn't ask about my mom and sister.

"I could say the same to you, Toby. You don't seem to have many friends, and you keep Nicolos on a very loose string. At your party, I got the impression that he wants this relationship more than you do," I say, tentatively taking a bite of my warm chicken salad.

"I have all the friends I need. I'm taking things

slow with Nicolos."

"You've been saying that for the past nine months," I say, "I just don't want you to break his heart, and I want you to be happy."

"You know what Markus and I have in common? It takes us a long time to trust the people we meet. You're the exception to that rule. If Nicolos and I are meant to be together, it will happen. I don't sweat it."

"I don't know how I got so lucky to have you both in my life. I'm such a nervous wreck half the time, especially with Markus. I always say things that upset him."

"You're passionate. It's the most irresistible thing to a man."

"Impulsive and reckless is more on target."

"Let that impulsive and reckless nature lead you to your next project, D. It'll be epic."

I think about this for the rest of the day, and by the time I pull into my drive and head upstairs, I have a million ideas bouncing around in my head. I start dinner and open my gifts. The bigger box is from Kizzy, so I open that one first.

Inside is a pair of gold satin designer shoes that will go perfectly with my wedding dresses. There is a note saying, *break us in*. I grin and slip them on. They're soft like butter. Kizzy and I wear the same-sized shoes, so it's easy for her to shop for me.

The search is over. I walk around the lounge, trying them out. I'm wearing a long-sleeved white mini-dress, and the heels make my legs look amazing.

Next, I open daddy's gift. It's a golden locket. I unclasp the clip and gasp in surprise.

On one side is a picture of me and Kizzy, aged twelve and ten, with Grams, all dressed up for church. On the other side is a picture I have never seen before. It's my mother and father, and they look young, happy, and very much in love.

I sit staring at the picture. It is hard to fathom that this beautiful, happy union ended in heartache.

I'm so deep in thought I don't hear Markus arrive home.

"I might have to put this in the prenup. This is what I want to come home to every day."

He smiles and walks over to greet me with a kiss.

"They're from Kizzy. I'm breaking them in."

He notices the locket, so I show him the photographs.

"May I?" he asks politely, and I nod.

He removes the locket and looks at the pictures.

"Is this before they had you?" he asks.

"Yes."

"They look so happy."

He puts the locket back over my neck and kisses me.

He heads up to change and wash up for dinner while I finish up. Markus wanted to have a party for my birthday, but I didn't want one. We're having a wedding, and I've seen the extensive planning that's going on behind the scenes.

His parents are giving him a proper send-off. He jokes that they want to make sure he doesn't return. I'm happy to keep him forever.

I'm distracted by him all evening, and it takes my mind off things.

"I'm meeting Savannah on Saturday. She wants to go shopping," I say.

We've just finished dinner, and he is cleaning up the kitchen. He nods.

"Do you have plans?" I am hoping he can come with us.

Savannah's idea of shopping is very upmarket, and my one and only Visa card trembles when I bring her out to those exclusive shops. As if he can read my mind, Markus heads upstairs. I think he is getting his magic card, and I smile to myself, but it's even better.

"I went to collect this at the bank today."

He passes me a tiny black card with my name on

it.

"It's only temporary, of course. The next one will say Mrs Dylan Francine Mills," he says, smiling.

His phone vibrates, and he answers. It's his mother, and I can work out the gist of what she is asking from his responses. She wants a final guest list from my side of the family.

Moving away, I walk up the stairs and down again to continue breaking my shoes in. He hangs up and looks at me as I walk.

"I could watch you do that all night," he says.

"I can make it more interesting for you," I say, hiking my dress up to my mid-thigh and shaking my hips.

"Your legs are incredible," he says.

I smile. He exhales.

"Will it just be Brandon and Kizzy coming over next month?" he asks cautiously.

"Yes," I say, still walking.

I know where this conversation is going. I stop

and sigh.

The ache starts deep in my heart and then spreads out to the rest of my limbs. I hold on to the locket, close my eyes and think of Lily. The image of her face that day ten years ago when I stepped off the bus.

In the photo inside the locket, she looks like me. It could be me at this very moment in my life. The irony is not lost on me. I'm also young, happy, and in love.

I squat in my heels and the sobs take over. Markus does not come near me. It's how I realise that he knows. He must have pieced it together, but I'm not sure when. He pays attention to the details. I guess I don't fool him.

He comes to me eventually. Lifting me up in his arms, sitting on the couch, and holding on to me as I sob, the locket clutched to my chest. The cold metal sends warmth into my heart. I cry until I'm spent, but I feel better afterwards. I stand and go to the downstairs bathroom to clean my face.

When I return to the lounge, Markus is sitting at the breakfast bar, watching me. I sit on the stairs. We've discussed this several times. It's the only topic he and I have disagreed on since the engagement. It's as if daddy knows and has sent me this locket to add fuel to the fire.

Markus sighs and comes to sit next to me.

"Dylan, I'd like to meet her."

"I'd like that. I was thinking we could go after the wedding."

"You'd deny her the chance to see her eldest daughter marry?"

"Weddings are supposed to be a happy affair. I'll not have Kizzy upset."

"This is your wedding day. You should have what you want."

He brushes my hair back off my face.

"Don't ask me to choose between them, as I'll always choose my sister," I whisper, breathless, but I don't want to cry again.

Choosing Love

I'm exhausted.

"Of course, I know that. I can't meet your grandmother, so I'd like to meet your mother. I'm marrying her daughter; I think this is the right thing to do."

"I still haven't told her," I admit, putting my elbows on my knees.

"Why not?" he asks.

"It would be awkward if I tell her, but don't invite her."

I chew my nail bed. He removes my finger from my mouth and holds my hand.

"You once told me you always choose for you," he reminds me.

He is right. I can't wait to introduce Markus to Lily. The thought makes me happy.

"Maybe we can have a weekend in New York, and then you can meet her. Do we have time to squeeze that in?"

I turn my head to look at him, my hands on his

legs.

"You're the bride; you can demand whatever you want, and everyone will do it."

He bends down to press his lips against mine.

"What about the groom?" I ask.

"Is he allowed to make demands, too?" I giggle as he presses his nose against mine.

"I have one for tonight. Come to bed wearing only your golden heels."

* * *

"Dylan," Markus calls to me softly.

I'm standing at the window looking out. The fully waxed moon is high in the sky, spewing rays of melancholy over my naked body. I go to him, and he opens his arms.

"What's wrong?" he whispers softly.

He is so warm I snuggle closer. He pulls the fleecy blanket from the foot of the bed and wraps it around me.

"I can't sleep," I say.

"I've lost my touch. There was a time when you would fall asleep after I made love to you," he says, kissing me softly.

"I've a lot on my mind," I exhale.

"Tell me," he coaxes, giving me his kisses.

"I'm feeling stressed trying to work out what to do next. I've decided to make a change, but now I'm struggling to think what I should do. Maybe I'll ask Toby for my job back."

"There's no pressure. You have time to come up with something that will make you happy," he encourages, "I'm here to help and support you in any way, and once we are married, you'll also have my team. They'll support you," he says.

"I know that you'll help me, and I value that, but I think it will be more rewarding if I can do it on my own."

"What about your plan A?" he asks.

"When I first met you, you said you were settling

for plan C. Maybe you can finally work on the first plan."

I stop breathing.

I'd forgotten about that. It was an idea I'd forged with Grams. She'd encouraged me to do it, but after I dropped out of Yale, I became discouraged and moved on.

"Yes. That's it," I say, and he smiles.

I feel like a great big weight has been lifted off my chest.

"Markus," I whisper and kiss him with sudden passion.

I love this man so much.

He kisses me back, and I'm revved up. He pulls the blanket away and sucks on my nipples. I moan my pleasure with free abandonment. I'm always this way.

When I have a problem, it can consume me, and I will function at sixty per cent depending on the issue, but once it is resolved, I'll bounce back, firing

Choosing Love

on all cylinders. It's the feeling I have now.

I make love to him with wild freedom, and he revels in it. He enters me slowly, and I moan as the sweet feeling spreads from my core and out to the end of my being. Our movements mirror each other. I want to please him; he wants to please me.

This makes for a perfect dance. He grabs my thighs and spreads me wider, going deeper still. I run my fingers through his hair and pull his forehead onto mine as we move to this rhythm of our hearts. He moans and calls my name, and I know he, too, feels this.

The honey runs thick and fast, threatening to spill over at any moment. We kiss, we grind, and when the release comes, he whispers my name.

"Sleep now," he says.

I drift away on a cloud of love.

* * *

"I can spare a few days next week. We can go shopping in New York!" Markus says.

"Dylan?" he calls when I don't respond.

I look up from my Mac book, and he smiles at me.

"Sorry, Markus. Did you say something?"

My fingers are flying over the keys. I can feel his eyes on me, so I stop.

"Usually, the words 'shopping' and 'New York' are enough to get a girl's attention," he says, and I groan.

"Yes. Of course, we can."

I flip open my Blackberry to check the dates.

"Its spring break and Kizzy will be in Orlando, so it's perfect."

"It'll only be for a few days as we leave for the Cotswold next Saturday," he replies, and I nod in agreement.

That is the tenth of March. I have it highlighted in red on my calendar.

I carry on with my task. It's been this way for the past three weeks. I'm working on my new venture

Choosing Love

and want to finalise it before we are off.

When we are back from our honeymoon, I want to hit the ground running. I realise that luck is on my side. I have not one but two brilliant men in my life, and I bombard them with questions.

They offer suggestions, and by the end of the first week, my business idea is generated.

Now, I'm working on how it will be executed. It looks good on paper, but how to turn this into a real entity is what consumes my every waking thought.

Savannah offers her insights about properties, and I make enquiries about the for-lease sign I saw a few weeks back. Markus offers his legal team for advice, but I stick to my guns and do the research myself.

It's fun, as I spend time at the library. Some days, I'm there so long I barely make it home to cook dinner, so on those nights, we eat out.

The wedding planner calls and asks about flowers and place settings. I'm surprised as Markus' parents are paying for her services, so I think she should ask them, but she tells me they want to make sure I'm happy with everything. I eventually tell her to call my sister.

She seems taken aback at my abrupt manner, but the next time I see her, all is forgotten, so Kizzy must be giving her the right level of enthusiasm.

During my excursions to the library, I meet Monica Jade Lewis. This is how she introduces herself; a young attorney at law. She heard me enquire about the building and gave me advice free of charge. She qualified a year ago and is already a bit disillusioned with the law.

She works at a legal aid office and lives in Tower Hamlets, which is not too far from my area. We had coffee and talked. She has been helping me ever since, but I insisted that she bills me for her time. She looked at my ring, smiled, and we shook on it.

"Your ring is so unique," she says, admiring it.

Monica has a beautiful smile. She wears her hair in long braids. She is tall and slender with beautiful long fingers.

"Thank you."

"When is the big day?"

"Twenty-fourth March."

"Dylan, that's in three weeks! You must file some of these petitions soon. Have you already hired legal representation?"

"No. I'm not back from my honeymoon until after easter. Do you know anyone who could help me?"

"You should go to a reputable law firm. They'll have experience."

I smile and pull the contract from my folder. Markus had helped me to draft it. She takes it and reads.

"I really appreciate this, but why me?"

"You graduated top of your class. Why not?"

"I don't have the experience. What if I make a mistake and do something wrong?"

"Monica, I don't have the experience either. My speciality is finance, and you know the law, so the only thing I can promise is we won't run out of money or end up in jail."

She laughs then, and I know I have her. I've hired my first employee.

It's the best move I've made so far, as I met up with her earlier today, and she has already found us an office space within walking distance of my place.

She will work for me on Fridays until she works her notice from her current employers, but I can already see that once she is working full-time, she will be great at her job.

I tick that box and tell Markus to add two more to the guest list.

Choosing Love

Mirror

We arrive at JFK Monday at midday. It's unseasonably cold for March, but there's a car waiting to take us to our Manhattan hotel. I snuggle up in my brilliant white coat and hat as the car speeds through the streets towards our destination.

Our hotel is on the exclusive upper east side, overlooking Central Park. The sun shines deceptively, and one could be lulled into believing this is the perfect summer's day. The view is from a post-card.

There is a lady in our suite. She greets us and asks if everything is to our liking.

Markus glances at me. The rooms are spacious, light and airy, all decked out in monochrome colours, spotless.

I tell him all is fine, but he kisses me and smiles, so I say it to her. She asks if she should light the fire, and Markus turns to me again, so I tell her, "Yes, please."

Before I'm asked to check the floral decorations, I excuse myself to shower and change. I sigh.

I have the Alice in Wonderland sensation from staying in this luxury hotel. My body feels suspended in a time warp as if I'm dreaming. I'm almost afraid to touch the shiny chrome shower dial. My tummy growls angrily, reminding me it's dinner time in London.

Back in the bedroom, my clothes hang neatly in the walk-in closet, causing me to wonder idly when this task was carried out and by whom. I remind myself this is only a short trip; we don't usually live

Choosing Love

in this type of excess. My anxiety probably has more to do with the nature of the trip than the handmade soaps and silk bathrobes.

Markus has showered and changed into jeans and a camel sweater.

"Hungry?" he asks.

"Can I ask you something?"

It's bugging me, so I better get it off my chest.

"Sure," he replies.

"Why did you look to me? If the room was fine, why didn't *you* tell her?" I ask, and he laughs.

"It's just something I picked up from my father. He always makes sure my mother is happy first. She's the woman of the house, so it's what we all do," he replies in a soft voice, "If it annoys you, I won't do it."

"No, It's okay. It's not annoying. I just didn't know that's what you were doing."

I give him a kiss and tell myself to trust my man and stop moaning. He smiles.

"Yes, I'm hungry."

We eat in the restaurant, both of us having vegan lasagne.

"I really enjoyed that."

"Yes, it was good," he agrees.

"Do you want to go for a walk?" I suggest.

"Baby, it's cold outside. It won't do for you to catch a chill," he quips, and I laugh.

"I was hoping to go downtown to shop."

"Have you already spoken to your mother?" he asks softly, and I shake my head.

"I'll ring her once we are back in the room."

I sigh.

"I'm ready when you are," he says, and I stand.

Then, he takes my hand, and we head back up to the room.

The New York ladies are so well-dressed I can't stop looking at them.

"They're so fabulous; it's giving me whiplash

trying to look at every woman I see," I tell Markus, and he laughs.

"Now, if I said that, I'd be in trouble."

"Look all you like, as long as you don't touch."

"I'm already quite content with my view," he assures me, kissing the back of my neck.

I blush; *he is so sweet.*

I call my mother. Her husband, Patrick, answers the phone. Lily is at work, but I tell him we will be at their place tomorrow at ten a.m.

"Have you hired the car?" I fidget nervously as I hang up the phone.

"Yes. It'll be here in the morning."

I'm starting to feel despondent about the whole affair. I would rather be home working on my start-up.

Firing up my Mac, I check my emails and start going through the to-do list. There's a gentle knock at the door, and Markus goes to answer it.

"Hello, Dylan!"

Two fashionably dressed ladies greet me as they wheel numerous racks of clothes, bags, and shoes into our hotel lounge. Markus moves the coffee table out of the way, and I stand to greet them.

"I'm Debra, and this is Cassandra from Saks Fifth Avenue. We're your personal shoppers. We'd very much like to show you our Spring Summer 2001 collection!"

I'm speechless. Spinning around, I walk straight into Markus' arms.

"Have fun, baby," he whispers and leaves me to it.

* * *

At ten a.m. I pull up outside my mother's brownstone. My heart is racing. We were caught up in the Tuesday morning traffic coming over the Brooklyn Bridge, but we still made it in good time. Markus smiles encouragingly. We walk up the steps holding hands.

It dawns on me; I was last here exactly one year ago. Patrick answers the door.

Choosing Love

"Dylan, look at you, so grown up, so beautiful."

"Hello, Patrick. Thank you. This is Markus."

Markus says hello, and Patrick invites us in. He takes us into the lounge. It's beautifully decorated in shades of warm walnut and mahogany. The chairs have white cushions. My mother has impeccable taste, and it shows in her interior design style.

Lily enters the room, and Markus' eyes nearly leave his head. My mother, in all her glory.

"Dilly," she greets me in her soft voice, and I go to her.

"Hello, Mom."

I close my eyes briefly as her warmth surrounds me.

She smells like heaven, as always.

I introduce Markus, and she greets him warmly. He is smitten.

"Hello, Lily. It's nice to meet you."

"Please sit. Would you like some refreshments?" Lily offers, but we say no.

She does not let go of my hand, and I happily sit next to her on the couch. Markus sits across from us. He cannot take his eyes off her, but neither can I. My mother is simply the most beautiful woman I have ever seen.

She is the same height as Kizzy but has the same body shape as mine. Her skin is very fair; she has large almond-shaped eyes, which are light brown. Her hair is naturally straight and thick. She wears it shorter these days. It frames her face, falling just past her shoulders.

"Dilly, you're so beautiful," she says, and I smile as she always makes such a fuss about my looks.

"The apple didn't fall far from the tree," Patrick quips.

"You're a lucky man," he says.

"I know," Markus replies.

This is the moment when Lily notices my ring.

"You're engaged?" she gasps.

"Yes, Mom. Markus and I are getting married."

Choosing Love

Markus takes an invitation from his jacket pocket and gives it to me. I pass it to her.

Her hands tremble as she reads it. Her fingers are beautiful, slender, and smooth. Her nails are perfectly manicured with French tips.

"How lovely," she whispers and passes it to Patrick.

"The Cotswolds," he says.

"That is supposed to be a place of exceptional beauty."

Patrick asks Markus what he does. Mom is looking at me. She smooths my hair from my face.

"I take it Brandon and Kizzy will be coming to the wedding."

"Kizzy is my Maid of Honour, and daddy will give me away."

"Are they well?"

"Yes. Thank you."

She smiles, but it doesn't reach her eyes, so I change the topic to keep things light.

"You look amazing, Mom. What's your secret?"

"Yoga. I opened my studio a few months ago."

"Wow, that's great. I've been doing a lot of Pilates and weights with a bit of cardio lately, but I better add yoga to the list."

"Weights? Dilly, you are so tiny."

"I've been on this diet trying to make sure I fit into my wedding dress."

"Don't diet too much, Dilly. You'll lose all your lovely curves."

She turns to Markus.

"What part of England is your family from?"

"My dad was born in Wimbledon, but my mother is South African," he replies.

This helps steer the conversation onto neutral ground, and I'm relieved.

Patrick and Lily are intrigued and ask him more questions about his life. He is such an expert. He keeps things light, and soon, they're both laughing. I start to relax, telling myself this could be a pleasant visit.

"Dilly, I'm sorry that Mama will miss this. She would've loved to be there."

"I know, and I would love for you to come. I just don't want things to be awkward for you."

"Thank you, Dilly. I would love to come, but I want you to have a great day with your sister."

Patrick asks how we met. Markus tells them he met me in a gay nightclub. My mom lets off peals of laughter.

"I couldn't believe my eyes. It was like she was glowing from the inside out. She was the most beautiful woman I'd ever seen. Still is."

His eyes blaze as he gazes at me, and my cheeks heat up.

My mom has tears in her eyes. She moves towards him, and Markus stands. She goes into his arms and kisses him.

"You're perfect for my Dilly."

"This is a surprise for us. Dilly always tells us that

none of the London guys have caught her eye," Patrick tells Markus.

"She was waiting for him," Lily replies.

My mom reaches for me, and I take her hand. She is also holding on to Markus, and we face each other. His eyes have that burning look. He takes my hand and kisses me on the lips right there in front of Lily and Pat.

I'm not sure what he is doing, but it works, and I'm so grateful to him. My mom is in her element.

"Paddy. We have to celebrate."

"I know just the place," he replies.

Markus and I sit on the couch, waiting, as Lily and Patrick dress to go out.

"To think I was worried about you and Kizzy, but you and Lily are the cause for concern," I say, and he laughs.

"Is it obvious?"

"Yes, embarrassingly so."

"The thing is, I do find her attractive; she looks

Choosing Love

so much like you, and I think this is what you'll look like when you're older. How old is she?" he whispers.

"She'll be forty-two next month."

"Wow. She's so much younger than Mama."

"I'll have to call off the wedding. The groom fancies his mother-in-law."

He laughs.

We head to a swanky Brooklyn restaurant. It has a young crowd and plays upbeat music. Lily holds my hand, and we turn heads as we walk in.

My mother and I may look alike, but she is an extrovert like Kizzy. She flirts with the waiter, telling him I'm her daughter.

He tells her we look like sisters. I want to roll my eyes, but I'm afraid they might become stuck. She entices the entire restaurant to sing Happy Birthday to me, even though my birthday was three weeks ago.

"It's no harm, Dylan," Markus whispers to me.

He can read my face. He sings along, his face

lighting up and it makes me smile.

It's almost five when we arrive back at the house. Lily breaks out her most cherished possession: her photo album.

Dad has been sending her photos of us over the years. We sit at her dining table, having coffee, and she shows Markus the album. I sit on the other side of her, looking, but I have seen these so many times. Every time I visit, she brings them out.

"Do you have a favourite?" she asks him, and he goes back a few pages to one where I'm glaring at the camera, annoyed. I remember I didn't want to have my picture taken. It was the year before I had my first trip to London, so I must have been eighteen.

We were at the beach, and I was wearing a light blue shirt tied at the front with cut-off jeans.

My figure looks stunning, but I'm pouting. I'm surprised he likes that one, and I'm even more surprised when she removes it and gives it to him. The last photo is of Kizzy at the junior prom. She wears a green off-the-shoulder dress that shows off

Choosing Love

her beautiful figure.

I took that picture. Lily runs her finger down her face. I rub her arm. The inevitable happens. Lily begins to cry. Markus puts his arm around her, and I do the same. He gives me a pointed look, and I say it.

"Mom, I want you to come to my wedding."

"It's okay, Dilly. I don't want to upset Kizzy. I understand how she feels."

"What about me, Mom? Don't I matter, too?"

I've been caught up in this drama with her and Kizzy for so long, and my nerves are stretched, always accommodating.

It's suffocating.

"Of course, Dilly. You came to find me, you forgave me, you're my heart."

"Well, I want to have my family there when I marry. Just for once, we can be together, all four of us."

As soon as the words leave my mouth, I know this

is what I want.

"Anything for you, Dilly."

Markus releases her and comes to stand behind my chair; Lily hugs me.

"I love you, my darling Dilly," she whispers in my hair, "I'm sorry I was not strong enough to take care of you and your sister. I regret it every day, but I hope one day you'll both understand. I hope Kizzy will forgive me."

She cries on my shoulder.

Patrick takes her in his arms. He has a small case of pills on the table, and he opens the pouch and gives her one with some water. I stand back, horrified, and Markus reaches for me.

"What are those pills for?"

"They don't hurt me, Dilly. They help me to stay calm."

I'm suddenly so stressed my head hurts. This always happens when I come to see her. I don't know what will stop this vicious cycle. I walk out of the

Choosing Love

room, and Markus follows. I want to lash out at him for making us come here. I turn to give him a piece of my mind, but his eyes stop me. He is crying. I hug him.

"We'll have to talk to Kizzy, Dylan. This is wrong."

I did not expect him to say that.

"She broke daddy's heart. Kizzy will not budge."

"Do you know how hard it is to give up something you love? It's the bravest thing anyone can do," he says.

"You think what she did was brave?"

"Yes," he says, and I recoil from him.

"She was obviously unwell; it was by no means deliberate."

"Lily just told you she was not strong enough. She loves her daughters; that much is clear. She stayed away to keep you both safe. You were with her mother, and it was the best place for you to be."

He takes my hand.

"Dylan, you know this. Isn't this what your plan A is all about? Making sure that mothers who need help can find it, so they don't have to be separated from their children?"

"An eight-year-old girl does not think of such things. Lily is the inspiration behind that dream."

I am hooked on every word he speaks.

"I will never forget this moment."

"Why?" he asks tentatively.

"Because in this moment you helped me realise that my mother is the bravest woman I know."

Choosing Love

Eirith manor

I'd done my research, but still, nothing prepared me for the breathtaking landscape before my eyes. Markus and I have arrived in Tetbury in the Cotswolds. When he first mentioned the plan to me back in early January to stay for two weeks before the wedding, I thought he was nuts.

Now, I need this more than ever. The past three weeks have been very stressful. I glance over at him and sigh. He has been my rock through it all, ever calm, ever patient, completely the opposite of me. But I have heard that opposites attract, and I'm thankful for him.

He pulls off the main road and drives down a long, winding country lane. I become alarmed at some points, as I think there is no way this is a two-way road. He smiles at my discomfort. At the end of the road, he pulls off onto a bridleway.

He drives through large security gates and continues for another mile until we pull up to a large manor-style house with a pristine front lawn. The walkway is lined with blossoming spring flowers, and perfectly sculpted evergreen trees are dotted along the path up to the front door.

"Wow," I gasp.

"Welcome to Eirith Manor," he smiles.

He opens my door, and I fumble with my seatbelt. The front door opens, and Savannah comes to greet us.

"Darlings!"

"You've arrived. Let the party commence," she says.

"Dylan. You look lovely as always."

Choosing Love

She leads me into the house, calling to her brother, "Daddy wants all the cars hidden away."

He returns to the car and reverses before driving back down the lane. I watch him go.

"He's just parking the car in the garages. He'll be back. Let's get you inside," she says.

"I thought he was making a run for it," I say, and she cracks up.

She takes me into the house, and I'm floored by the grandeur of the foyer. Spacious and wide, the sunshine floods through the windows.

"Look who I found outside," Savannah sings.

"Dylan!" Helen exclaims.

"Welcome to your party, Dylan!" says Matthew, giving me a hug and kissing my cheeks.

"Your bags arrived early this morning," he says.

He glances at the door expectantly.

"Is Markus about?"

"He went to the garages, daddy."

"Why does he not let the staff do it?" Matthew says, shaking his head.

"You know Markus, daddy," she replies, going to the small bar on the side.

"Do you want a drink, Dylan?"

"Can I have a lemon water, please?"

She smiles and brings me my drink.

"Sit down, darling," Helen tells me.

I sit on the fancy Chaise Longue by the window. I'm a little nervous, so I am grateful when Savannah sits next to me.

"I love your top," she says.

"I bought it in New York."

"That's right. You and Markus went for a mini trip. How was it?"

"It was very short, but I got some shopping done," I reply, sipping my lemon water.

"I love New York," Helen says dreamily.

"Is it really as good as they say?" Savannah asks.

Choosing Love

She tends to do Europe and Africa for holidays.

"It is. I'll take you one day. You'll be amazed," I say, smiling.

"You have such an angelic smile," Helen says.

"It runs in her family. Wait 'till you see her sister," Savannah says.

"When does the rest of your family arrive?" Helen asks.

"They'll be here next week," I reply, hoping my nerves don't show.

Matthew is looking out of the window. He moves to the sidebar, pouring a glass of wine, just as Markus comes to join us.

"There you are, old boy," he greets Markus with a hug and a kiss, passing him the glass of wine, "I was starting to think you'd left me alone with the ladies."

"Sorry, dad."

"Hello, mama."

"Darling. How are you?" she kisses his cheek.

"Very well," he replies, taking her hand and kissing it.

"Let's toast," Matthew says, refilling my glass with water.

"To Markus and Dylan. For being brave enough to embark on this wonderful journey together."

"Here, here!" Savannah agrees and hiccups.

She refills her wine glass.

"Vana, how many glasses have you had?" Markus asks her, and she glares at him.

He asks if I'm hungry, and I tell him yes. Helen jumps up.

"I'll see what the kitchen has prepared for lunch," she says and hurries away.

"Do you want a tour of the grounds after lunch?" Markus asks.

"How big is this place?"

"The grounds are about eighty-six acres. The house has ten bedrooms and nine bathrooms. I haven't been here in ages, but I think there is an indoor pool, right, Vana?"

"Yes. There is an indoor gym as well, but that's really for rainy days. We go walking or kayaking, horse riding. Mama has the stables. There's so much to do. We will have fun," she says.

"We've had some renovations done to the rooms," Matthew says.

"Did you? When did you do that?" Markus asks.

"We had the work done over the past few months. We needed to modernise the old place. You and Savannah never bother with this house, and we may need to sell one day."

Becca comes into the room.

"Dylan," she says, "You're here. The party can finally start."

"Hello, Becca," I say shyly.

We have lunch out on the terrace. It overlooks a large swimming pool and side views of the property. There is a wide, flat lawn on the other side of the pool, surrounded by flower beds and tall hedges. It is pleasantly mild in the sunshine. A young lady serves us a hot meal, and I am curious about who she is.

"Who's that?" I ask Markus as he sits next to me.

"There are serving staff here," he says.

"How many?"

Matthew tells us there are five staff members in the house and another three take care of the grounds.

It all sounds so grand and very old-fashioned.

After lunch, Markus excuses us and takes me for a walk around the grounds. He holds my hand. We walk until we come to a small pond. There's a lake further along in the distance.

"Where do the staff members live?"

"In the village. I didn't realise there were so many. The house is empty most of the year. They manage the upkeep of the place. I know this may make you uncomfortable, but they all work for Becca, and she only hires the best."

"It's fine. I wasn't expecting it, that's all. You

don't have staff in the house in Wimbledon."

"We did, but the number has been reduced over the years. Becca will do most of the cooking, but she does have help to clean the house. There are a lot of people working behind the scenes keeping this family going."

"Is this what's expected from me? To have a house with staff and all the grandeur?"

"We will always need people to work for us; that will be a necessity."

"How long have they owned this place?"

"It was a wedding gift from Phineas to my mother and father, so since way before I was born."

"Phineas?"

"Mama's father."

As we walk along, we notice a small patch of yellow tête-à-tête flowers. Markus picks one and puts it in my hair.

We don't walk very far, but what I've seen so far is inviting, and I can't wait to discover more of this place.

"Your grandfather bought such a lovely place. He obviously had a soft spot and was very generous like his grandson."

"A soft spot for my mother. He adored her. When she left with his wife, he was devastated. I can't imagine what it must have been like for him when he lost his family."

"Where's his wife?" I completely forgot to ask about her.

"She lives on the vineyard back in South Africa. She went home after Mama and my father married. You'll meet her; she arrives next week."

"What's she like?"

"She speaks her mind."

"Sounds like my kind of woman."

The sun is obscured behind the clouds, so the temperature drops. Markus drapes his jacket over my shoulders, and we walk back towards the house. We run into the groundskeeper, Mr Bradley.

Choosing Love

Markus says hello and introduces me. He seems a jolly sort of fellow.

I say this to him, and he tells me it's an occupational hazard when you have the second-best job in the world. I ask him which job has the number one spot, and he tells me it must be Santa Claus delivering gifts to all the children at Christmas. Markus laughs, and I smile politely, thinking too much fresh air will turn you balmy.

Everything in moderation.

* * *

Becca shows me to my room and my eyes open wide. It's like a small apartment with French doors that lead out to a balcony.

The queen-sized bed has a canopy. There is a small sofa with a coffee table and a large cream-coloured vanity with mirrors. I stare at the small log-burning fireplace with a guardrail around it.

My ensuite is the same size as my old bathroom in Essex. It's all white with mirrors all around and a window.

I walk out to the balcony, which overlooks the courtyard. There is a smaller cottage at the end, and Becca tells me that it is the Annexe. I breathe out. This place is unbelievable. There is a knock on the door. Becca introduces me to Naomi; she will be taking care of me during my stay.

I remember quickly to adjust my face; this is too much. Naomi looks to be the same age as me, and I smile politely as she makes herself busy. She lights the fire and offers to make tea. Becca tells me she must see to dinner, but I'm to give her a shout if anything is not to my liking. I look inside the enormous walk-in wardrobe. My clothes are already hanging up, and my shoes are neatly displayed.

"Do you know if my wedding dresses have arrived?" I turn, looking at Naomi.

"Yes. They arrived this morning. I've put them in this closet for you."

She smiles, opening a small door I hadn't noticed before. I thank her and check to make sure my dresses are all okay. They're still in the bags with a handwritten note.

I show her the dresses. She gasps, and I smile. She has the cutest dimple on her left cheek. Wedding dresses always make people happy. I relax a little with her, but I still don't like being waited on. When Markus comes up to check on me, I take him to the balcony and close the doors.

"Is this really necessary?"

"Don't you like her?"

"Yes, I do. She's nice, but that's not the point. I don't need to be waited on hand and foot."

"You didn't realise what you were signing up for when you said yes."

"No. I certainly did not. Is it too late to back out now?"

"It's because you're the bride. It's mama's way of honouring you. She is African and when they have weddings, it's more like a royal affair." He touches my face and presses his lips to mine lightly.

"Am I the only one who has a personal assistant?"

I try to be diplomatic, and he laughs.

"Yes, Savannah would throw a tantrum, and I would go sleep out in the woods."

"Where's your room?"

He indicates his head and then points to the Annexe.

"I'm staying over there. Mine is the room on the left. I can look up and see you if you come to the balcony. I'll climb up and visit you at midnight. Will you be my Juliet?"

I look down.

"It's a long way to fall, Romeo."

"I'll miss sleeping in your arms," I say, moving closer.

"I know, but the build-up, the sexual tension, will make the wedding night even sweeter. I look forward to that."

He kisses me properly then, and I cling to him. We're both panting when the kiss is over.

The drought begins. This is going to be a long

Choosing Love

two weeks.

* * *

Despite my protests, having a second opinion on what to wear and how to style my hair turns out to be invaluable. Markus' parents are throwing me my first official party tonight.

No doubt I'll be the centre of attention, so I'm having a mini moment of panic. Naomi is having fun; before long, I'm having a good time, too.

She picks out a red strapless dress with a mermaid tail, but I'm not sure.

"No way. It shows far too much cleavage."

"Yes, but that's fine if it's the only thing on show. You have a beautiful figure. Show it off."

She opens a tube of matching lip colour.

"Let's do it," I say.

My name is announced by the smartly dressed gentleman standing at the entrance. The room goes quiet, and I search for a pair of burning green eyes.

"You're perfect," he kisses me.

Everyone in the room claps, and I blush. Markus makes the introductions, taking me around the room. We are a party of sixteen in total. He explains that the people in the room all work for the family in some capacity.

There are so many names to remember, but he tells me I will come to know everyone in time, as they are like our extended family.

"This is Jess and Andy. They are our legal masterminds. Richard and Janet, financial advisers. Mike and Nora are our medical doctors, and last but certainly not least, our security team: Bowes, Ginny, Smithy, and our recent recruit, O'Neil. Have you got all of that?"

I notice he does not introduce me to a tall black guy in the room, so I assume he must be one of the servants. He catches my eye because his look is imposing. The way he is standing at the back of the security team looking at me, dressed in all black, makes the hairs on the back of my neck stand up.

Markus' family help to put me at ease. I'm soon

caught up in mingling and having a great time. Savannah is like a supermodel, wearing a midnight blue dress that clings to her slender frame. She is laughing gaily, and her arresting eyes sparkle.

She flirts shamelessly with the security guy called Bowes. I must admit, he is quite handsome. I notice none of the security team members are drinking alcohol.

I also notice the man in black has disappeared but no one else seems alarmed by this. I glance over at Markus, and he is completely relaxed in his dinner jacket and green tie, so I decide to forget about it.

We are treated to a four-course sit-down meal. A live band starts to play. Savannah is already up and throwing shades. The dancing has started.

"You ready?" Markus asks me softly.

I take his hand.

"Always."

* * *

It's almost eleven a.m. when I wake up the next

day. Slivers of white light stream through the tops of the window. Naomi must have pulled my shades. I open the French doors and walk out to my balcony, staring longingly towards Markus' bedroom window.

After a light breakfast, I find Savannah sitting by the pool. I entice her to go for a walk, and Helen joins us. She informs me that Markus is with his dad.

We're out for almost four hours, and I'm famished when we arrive back at the house.

We're sitting in the orangery having refreshments when Markus and Matthew appear. The daylight is slowly fading. Markus heads to the Annexe to clean up.

Helen tells us we will have an informal dinner this evening, so I change into black jeans and my red plaid shirt. There is a light knock on my door, and I smile. I even recognise the way he knocks. I'm doomed.

He stands outside my door, freshly washed, wearing jeans and a T-shirt. I pull him into my room, and we spend several minutes reacquainting. We sit

Choosing Love

on the small couch, and I tuck my feet under my legs and rest my head on his chest.

It's Sunday evening, and Naomi has already left for the day, so we are alone.

"What did you do today?" he asks.

"Savannah and Helen took me to the lake."

"That's a long walk. I thought you'd be tired after the dancing last night."

He plays with my hair.

"You're forgetting. I once danced all night and ran a marathon the next day."

"I'll never forget that day. It was the first time we kissed," he whispers.

His words spark my flame, and I turn to kiss him. When we make out in this way, the next part is inevitable.

"Stay with me tonight?"

"Dylan. I want us to wait until we're married."

"Is it because your parents will object?"

My need is urgent.

"No, they won't mind. We live together, but I want us to wait," he says, and I pull away from him.

"It was my idea to stay in the Annexe, if we were sleeping in the same house, the temptation would be too much."

"You're coping much better than I am," I pout.

"It helps to stay busy. They're watching a film tonight in the theatre room. We can join them," he says.

"You hate watching TV."

"Any distraction helps a lot."

"Is that why you were gone first thing this morning?"

"Yes. Your red dress last night. I almost came to help you out of it."

"I have Naomi for that, thank you. But I'm glad you liked it."

"Ready for dinner?" he asks and stands.

Choosing Love

He tries to adjust himself.

"Look what you've done. I can't go down to my mother like this."

I reach up and touch his bulge with my fingers, and he exhales.

"I'll go first. Maybe stand on the balcony for a while, and that might help."

I kiss him and head out of the door.

Distractions. That's what I need.

* * *

I keep myself busy with activities every day. The weather is dry and sunny, so we spend most days outside.

Matthew is in such good spirits. Helen tells me he loves spending time with Markus.

We're so caught up in our everyday lives that we hardly visit Markus' family, and I make a mental note to make sure we visit them more often. I have seen them only three times since Markus and I moved in together.

Paul is coming to do my hair on Friday. My second party is planned for tomorrow. There will be at least fifty guests. A white marquee goes up on the grounds.

I'm with Naomi in my room, trying to work out what to wear, when Markus calls me on my phone and tells me to come to the balcony. I go out to see what he wants, my phone still to my ear, and scream.

Standing below in the courtyard is one Mr. Tobias Smith. I run down to greet my buddy, jumping into his arms.

* * *

Tonight, I wear white. The party is in full swing under the stars. The family has invited friends from the local village, and some of the servants have brought their families.

I like that we all socialise together. Naomi is here with her sister. They look like twins. I don't let go of Toby's hand. Everyone thinks he is my brother.

Becca and Savannah are hilarious. When Toby greets them, Savannah goes beetroot red. I never

Choosing Love

imagined her to be the shy type, but my guy has rendered her speechless. Becca is not so subtle.

She tells him he is a tall glass of the finest merlot, and she would happily drink every day. Toby takes it all in good spirits. He gives her a kiss on the cheek. He is easily the most good-looking person in this entire party, and I tell him so.

"D, clearly you don't see yourself. You look like a queen in your white dress."

It's white chiffon with glistening sequins and a plunging neckline. The bracelet sleeves help to keep me comfortable. The evening is not freezing cold, but there's a chill in the air.

With so many of us under the marquee, it's not unbearable. There are heaters dotted around outside, and some of the guests have spilt around talking and laughing. The makeshift floor is impressive, and I plan to dance the night away. The band is playing funky tunes, and my feet are already tapping.

I constantly check the room for my number one

guy. Every time I catch his eye, we smile at each other. He occasionally brings someone over to introduce to me and Toby.

People are friendly; they talk to us as if we've been coming to these parts for ages.

One guy got extremely tipsy, though the night was young. Toby reckons he arrived drunk. He became a little too over-friendly, trying to hug me, but with Toby at my side, I wasn't worried. The security team is here tonight and looking very serious.

When the drunk man reached his arm around me, Ginny escorted him out. I don't see him again all evening. I shudder, wondering what she has done to him. Ginny is very pretty, but when her game face is on, it gives me the chills.

Speaking of which, I look around for the man in black, and sure enough, he is there in the corner, dressed from head to toe in a black suit. As I look over, I notice he is talking to Markus, his hand resting on his shoulder. Markus is relaxed, so I decide he must be alright.

Choosing Love

I keep forgetting to ask who he is. I check for the rest of the team. Bowes and Ginny are positioned at each entrance but I don't see O'Neil and Smithy.

I'm surprised I remember their names, but when your fiancé reveals he is extremely wealthy and that we could be potential targets, the security team are my new best friends.

I'm not overly anxious. I feel safer knowing they are here.

Savannah approaches, giving me an evil look.

"You're being far too greedy. You already have my brother; leave this one to me," she whispers in my ear.

"I'm sorry. You're right. He's all yours. I'm going to find my number one."

I head off, leaving Toby with Savannah. As I do, the band stops playing, and a giant cake is wheeled out. Markus puts his arms around me.

"Having fun?" he asks.

"Yes," I say, giving him my best smile.

Silence falls amongst the crowds, and Matthew takes to the microphone.

"I know that dads all over the world and right here tonight will say the same thing. But I have a son of whom I'm immensely proud. He has brought me joy from the moment I first held him in my arms. Even when he falls by the wayside, my boy finds his way back on the path."

"Tonight, Helen and I invite you here to celebrate as our son has found his perfect match. A young Bostonian lady blessed with not only beauty but grace and charm. We toast their good fortune. Congratulations, Dylan and Markus. We love you both."

The cheers go up, and Markus kisses me on my lips.

We take turns to kiss Matthew. His words touched me. Helen slips her arm around my waist, and we admire the cake. A young man takes to the mic as the band strikes up, and he sings his heart out.

Markus and I glide across the dance floor, and I

lose myself in a sea of green.

Of all the things he does to me when we are alone together, the way he looks at me takes the top spot.

"This was a tough week. Watching you and not being able to be with you," I confess.

"You've done good. Six more days."

"More like seven more nights," I groan, and he laughs.

"I love you. This dress is my favourite."

"Any reason, in particular?"

"I like the way it accentuates your curves, especially from the back."

I knew it. I did tell Naomi that my butt looked large in this dress, but she told me no. I couldn't be bothered to change. It had taken us ages to agree on this one.

Earlier, I asked Toby as well, but he told me my butt looked like Mount St Helens, and everyone would want to climb it. It took us both a few moments to recover from that one. I giggle, now remembering.

"What?" Markus smiles.

"Nothing."

"I see Savannah has snared Toby in her web," Markus says.

I look over at them and laugh.

"Do you think I should go and rescue him?" I ask as he pulls me closer.

"Probably," he replies, but I don't move an inch.

I'm right where I want to be, caught up in our own web of love.

Choosing Love

Kizzy's choice

Kizzy and daddy are on their way. I'm so excited to see them. Markus went to collect them from the airport, but I stayed back, as he probably needs the room for Kizzy and all her bags. Toby and I are sitting in the orangery, waiting for them to arrive. I sip hot lemon and ginger tea, and he is having coffee and freshly made scones.

The weather is not the best today. There's a light drizzle, and rain is expected later.

The others went to the indoor pool to swim, but I didn't want to risk ruining my hair, so Toby stayed to keep me company.

I saw him swim for the first time yesterday in the outdoor pool. Markus and I were having lunch on the terrace with his family. Toby had slept in after the late-night shenanigans, but then he came out of the Annexe and dove into the pool doing a series of breaststrokes. It was awesome. We were on our feet watching him go.

"He's still so fast," Markus said to Matthew in awe.

"Yes, he's a natural," his dad agreed.

"He sure has grown up," Savannah replied suggestively and in front of her dad, too.

How I wish I'd known them back when they were swimmers.

I hear the wheels on the gravel and jump up out of my seat, rushing inside the main house to open the front door. My sister emerges from the car looking every inch a glamorous movie star. I shake my head and laugh.

"Kizzy!" I call, and she turns, sashaying up the drive and entering the house.

Choosing Love

I pull her into my arms. She smells divine.

"How do you always look so fresh after a long-haul flight?"

"Travelling first class. I slept all the way. It was so comfy."

Daddy and Markus enter the foyer.

Poor daddy. He already looks out of place.

My all-American dad, in his jeans and tweed jacket that I know Kizzy made him wear.

"Hey, daddy," I say, going into his open arms.

He relaxes when he sees me. My dad and I have this in common. If we're comfortable, we are the happiest people in the world. I kiss Markus and thank him for picking them up.

One of the staff members —I think his name is Brian— brings the bags inside. Markus asks him to take my dad's case to the Annexe.

"Daddy, this is my friend, Toby."

"Toby. Thank you for looking out for my Dilly," daddy says, brushing his hand aside and giving him a hug.

"Kizzy, I'll help you unpack."

I take Kizzy up to her room. It is smaller than mine but quite charming. The large bay windows overlook a beautiful rose garden, but there is no balcony.

I listen to her chatter and talk excitedly. She wants to shower and change, so I hang her outfits up in the wardrobe while she does that. As predicted, Kizzy doesn't travel light. I seek out Naomi to help us. Kizzy has two Maid of Honour dresses, and I roll my eyes.

"I wasn't sure which style you'd like best," she says.

My wedding party is made up of Kizzy, Savannah, and Holly. I've left it up to them to pick whatever dresses they like; Navy for Kizzy, forest green for Savannah and wine for Holly. It's the only thing I had to think about.

I indulge my sister. I sit on the small armchair.

Choosing Love

"Alright. Go on. Try them on," I say.

Naomi laughs and helps her. Of course, both dresses look fabulous. The first dress has spaghetti straps and floats around her elegant frame; it is very lady-like. But the second dress fits her figure in an extremely flattering way. Her slim shoulders are on display. She is breathtaking, striking her pose and putting on a show for us.

"I like them both, but it's definitely this one," I say.

"I think the first dress. This one will bring too much attention to you. The focus should be on the bride," Naomi says.

I shrug. Kizzy has been upstaging me all my life; it doesn't bug me anymore.

"I agree with you, Naomi," Kizzy replies.

"Have you got your gold heels?" I ask.

She digs them out and slips them on.

"You girls are so beautiful. I can't wait to see your mother," Naomi says.

That's my cue. She helps Kizzy out of the dress and hangs it in the wardrobe. I thank her and take Kizzy to see my room.

The rain has started to fall. Becca brings us tea, and I introduce Kizzy. She tells her about the time she first saw us in Grenada.

"I met your dad downstairs. He's a legend!"

She leaves us to catch up, informing us that dinner is at six in the dining room and we are expected to dress formally. I wonder to myself who else will be coming to dine with us this evening.

"How fabulous is this, Dilly?"

She pours the tea, sits crossing her legs, and nibbles on a dainty cake.

"I used to tell my friends at school that my sister was a fairy princess."

"Did they believe you?" I smile, sipping my tea.

"The way you used to glide through the halls with your long pigtails, of course, they did. No one looked like you did, Dilly, and now the fairy tale has come

Choosing Love

true."

"Kizzy, this is not a fairy tale. Yes, Eirith Manor is amazing, but it's the way the people in this family love each other that makes this place magical."

She looks at me, no longer smiling. I place my teacup on the coffee table.

"I've invited Lily."

Kizzy has the same almond-shaped eyes, and they are light brown, exactly like our mother's. She nods her head.

"I knew you would."

"Really? I wasn't planning on inviting her."

"I know you wanted to, and you should. It's your wedding, Dilly."

"It's more important for my sister to be happy."

She exhales.

"Dilly, I completed my medical degree in three years instead of four. I'm so determined to become a doctor, but since I started working in the hospital, in the delivery room, I've seen things that I can't even talk about."

"Strong, healthy women reduced to babies themselves. Some survive, and some just don't, and there is no rhyme or reason. I don't hate Lily. She somehow found the strength to give me life, and I'm grateful."

"The way I behaved at Gram's funeral was wrong. To be honest, that had more to do with grief and guilt. Because you all wanted her back, and I wouldn't allow it. I made you feel guilty for wanting to have a relationship with your own mother, and I know that's why you left. Dilly, I'm sorry."

I did not expect her to say this. It's a moment before I react. I fold her into a tight embrace, never wanting to let go.

"Kizzy, I'm sorry, too, for how it happened to you. But she left both of us, not just you. I forgive her because when I think of the alternative, a life with no mother at all, for me, it's worse."

"I can be civil, you know, Dilly. I'm not ready for forgiveness, but for you, I'll do anything."

Choosing Love

"Do you not enjoy working at the hospital?"

"The days are mostly good, then one bad day happens, and it's soul-crushing, but I can never do anything else. It's my calling."

My sister has grown up. We both have. Another magical year. Since meeting Markus and falling in love, it's only today, sitting here with my sister, that I realise how much I've grown.

"Do you think you will finish in three years again?"

"No way. This is not to be rushed. I have so much to learn."

I tell her about the company that I want to start. She is so excited, her eyes light up.

"How amazing. Dilly, I've some ideas I could share with you. I'm on the front line every weekend, and I've seen the battle scars. What you want to do is very important. I'm so proud of you."

She hugs me. I close my eyes, breathing her warmth.

"I'm going to name the company Lily Rose Inc."

"It's perfect."

* * *

There is a lot of commotion downstairs when Kizzy and I arrive for dinner. The family are congregated in the lounge, and I introduce my sister to Matthew and Helen.

"My word, you are lovely," Matthew tells Kizzy.

She does look like a dream in her red oriental-style dress. Her short bob has grown out, and she wears it straight, falling to her collarbone. Her make-up is on point, as usual.

"Beauty obviously runs in this family," Helen says as Kizzy bends to give her kisses on her cheeks.

Daddy, Markus, and Toby are already here having drinks. Markus gazes lovingly at me.

"You're glowing," he whispers in my ear.

I'm wearing a yellow strapless top over dark dressy pants. Kizzy has styled my hair in a loose ponytail that falls over my shoulder.

Choosing Love

"Is dinner delayed?"

"Yes. Semi has arrived. Her flight was late and it's raining. She is rather put out."

"Who's Semi?" I don't recall hearing that name before.

"My grandmother," he replies, grinning.

I roll my eyes. Why he doesn't call her 'grandma' is a mystery to be solved another day. I'm hungry. I check on my father.

"Hey, daddy. How're you holding up?"

"Markus is taking care of me. This place is something, huh?"

"It is."

"You look lovely, Dilly."

"Thanks, daddy. You look nice in your dinner jacket."

I pull him over gently for a quiet word.

"Daddy, I don't know if Markus has mentioned it, but Lily is coming to the wedding."

He instinctively glances over at Kizzy.

"Dilly, is that a good idea?"

"I already spoke to Kizzy. She's okay about this, daddy, and I want so much for us all to be together. For once, like a real family. Lily is not bringing Patrick."

He stares at me, not saying anything.

"Are you okay, daddy?"

"I'm okay, Dilly. That's good for you. I'm pleased."

I was worried about telling Kizzy but did not expect this reaction from him. I don't have time to process this now, as Matthew calls me over. I hurry to Markus's side.

I'm not sure what is happening, but I assume we're going in for dinner now. Savannah appears at the door holding the hand of a stately-looking woman. She is tall and slender and does not look like a typical grandmother.

Her long hair is styled in a simple braid down her

back. It's shockingly white. She wears a heavy cardigan over her long green dress. Markus greets her first.

"Semi, you look well," he says, kissing her.

"Markus, you look more and more like Phin every time I see you. If it wasn't for those green eyes, I would swear he had come back from the grave to torment me," she says, and he laughs boyishly.

"Semi, this is my Dylan," he says.

She takes my hand.

"Hello, Semi," I say softly.

"You are a beauty. Markus, you've done well," she says, and he moves me along.

Savannah continues the introductions. First Kizzy, then daddy and finally Toby. Markus and I giggle as Semi speaks to Toby.

"You're the most beautiful man I've ever laid eyes on, and I'm eighty-three. Savannah, I need a brandy!"

Savannah goes to indulge her grandmother's

wishes.

"Mama, we are heading in for dinner now," Helen says.

"Are we? Alright then. I'll have one later, Savannah," she says, and we go in.

It's just past seven, and Becca appears flustered. I imagine it must have been a challenge to keep the food warm. My soup is lukewarm, and the vegetables are cold, but I eat every morsel.

The staff are busy catering to one woman in the room. The rest of us must settle, but no one complains. There is crumble afterwards, and Becca tells me mine has been specially made with less sugar and fat, so I enjoy it with warm custard.

Semi stands, and Savannah helps her up. We all follow suit. I glance over at daddy and Kizzy, but they're standing as well.

"To my grandson and his beautiful bride. May you have many happy years together," she raises her glass, and everyone drinks.

Choosing Love

Markus gazes at me and smiles.

* * *

I watch from my balcony window as Markus, daddy, and Toby emerge from the Annexe early the next day. My clock shows six fifteen a.m. The morning is grey and overcast. Last night, I couldn't sleep, so I stayed up listening to the sound of the rain.

It was a tough night. I wanted Markus so badly that I almost went to his room. I know he would not have sent me away. Four more nights, I say to myself.

I go back to bed and fall asleep. Naomi wakes me up and helps me dress. She brings me my morning smoothie. It's almost eleven-thirty a.m., and I am well rested. She tells me Semi wants to see me.

I follow Naomi down the stairs and along a corridor, and then she stops outside a set of cream-coloured double doors and knocks.

"Come in," calls a voice, and Naomi turns the door knob.

Semi is sitting facing the rose garden. She ushers me in, and I smile and enter the room.

The fire is lit, and she sits with a blanket draped over her knees. Her hair is loose and falls around her shoulders like a bridal veil. It softens her look, and she is not as formidable and scary as I thought she was last night. Her eyes are chocolate brown, just like her daughter's.

I greet her, kissing both of her cheeks, and she gestures for me to sit in the armchair facing her.

"I'm coming from the heat of South Africa, and the rain goes straight to my bones," she says, but I tell her I don't mind.

Her room must be beneath Kizzy's, as the same rose garden is outside her window.

She offers me tea and as I take the cup, she notices my ring.

"How fitting of my grandson to give you a rare South African diamond."

She takes my hand, examining the stone. Her

hands are soft, her nails perfectly manicured.

"He's rather sweet like that."

"Is he? Well, I suppose Joe got his hooks into him from the start. If Phin had his wish, he would have taken Markus under his wing. And then, who knows? Things could've been very different."

She reaches for a photograph and shows it to me. I look at the man in the photo and immediately see the resemblance between him and Markus.

"How old is your husband in this picture?"

"Twenty-seven. Those were the good days. My father hated Phin. I suppose that made me want him even more. He wouldn't give him one penny of his fortune, but Phin showed him. At the time of his death, Phin was sixty-two and the wealthiest man in South Africa. He left it all to his grandson."

Her gaze falls on me, and I fight the urge to look away. Since Markus mentioned the inheritance to me, I have been feeling a little overwhelmed. I now wonder if Semi has doubts about my motives for marrying her grandson.

"I can see that you two are very much in love."

"Yes. I love Markus."

"When Phin died, I could not mourn him. We were broken."

She takes another photo and shows it to me. It's a photo of a baby. Skipton Phineas Markus Delport is written on the back.

"He lived for only two days. It destroyed us. I lived only for Eirith. I brought her to England to save her, and when she married Matthew, I told her the same thing I'm telling you. It takes more than love to make a marriage work."

"I'm sorry for your loss, Semi. I imagine this could not have been easy. Markus and I will need our family's guidance and support more than ever."

She smiles at me then, as if I have given her a gift. Her eyes are like pools of wisdom. She is quiet for some time, staring into the fire. There is a knock on the door, and Helen comes in. I stand to greet her the way Markus always does. She tells me I can go.

"Mama will have a nap. The sun is out now, so make sure you get outside."

She kisses me, and I say goodbye to Semi.

I'm itching to be outside. I was housebound yesterday because of the rain. I find Kizzy and Savannah by the pool. Helen did not exaggerate. The sun is out in full force.

Kizzy dives into the water. Savannah is applying sunblock to her already glistening skin.

"Do you know where Markus went?" I ask.

"That's a mystery, darling. I've no idea."

Speaking of mysteries, I remember the man in black and ask Savannah who he is. She lets off peals of laughter.

"Are you speaking in riddles, darling?"

I realise how I'd phrased it.

"Sorry. When I met the security team, there was a tall black guy. Markus didn't introduce me to him. He was dressed in black."

"His name is Mason. He works for Markus."

"Why did he not introduce me to him?"

"Trust me, darling. That's a good thing. Meeting Mason is not a pleasurable experience. Take it from me."

I'm not sure what she sees on my face, but she leans forward, touching my hand reassuringly.

"Don't worry, you'll meet him in good time. Mason handles Phineas' estate. He is rather important as he takes care of all of us, in effect, but he is more of a serious type. I don't think that man has ever cracked a smile, not once."

I try to relax, but this conversation stresses me slightly. I say this to her.

"You see what I mean. Just talking about him is giving you the shivers."

She laughs in her sultry way.

Kizzy climbs out of the pool, dripping wet, with a huge grin on her face.

"I've not been swimming in ages. It's so nice."

"I would love to go in the water."

Choosing Love

"You can, Dilly. I'll take care of your hair. Come in. The water is warm."

I sprint up the stairs, hunting for a swimming costume. Settling on a powder blue two-piece that looks rather salacious, but they all do. Shrugging, I wrap my robe around me and fly down the stairs, taking two at a time.

I dive into the pool, mirroring the moves of Toby. My pristine, shiny hair now hangs in wiry tendrils. My face splits into a huge grin.

I swim until my limbs are about to fall off. We put music on and dance on the patio.

Naomi brings us lunch, so we don't have to go inside. When the sun disappears, there is a mild spring chill in the air, but the warm water helps.

Kizzy and I are racing in the pool when Markus and Toby appear. Kizzy wins easily. I'm holding on to the side of the pool, panting. Markus comes to me.

"Hello," he says, helping me out of the pool.

"Hey. Where did you go?"

He offers me a towel. I walk into it, and he wraps me tight, kissing me.

"You could've easily won that race. Kizzy has longer limbs, but you swim faster, so next time, make sure you have a better start."

"Okay, coach," I reply and hear Toby's chuckle.

"He's right, you know."

I roll my eyes.

Savannah is suddenly walking around the pool, show-casing her fabulous legs. I laugh. Toby should just tell her he's gay and save her the trouble.

"Why don't you two have a race?" I suggest.

"Show us amateurs how it's done."

They size each other up. Toby starts to undress. Markus shrugs and pulls off his polo shirt. His muscles are rippling. Kizzy's eyes go wide.

"Wow," she mouths to me.

"Daddy!" Savannah calls, running inside through the patio doors.

Choosing Love

Toby is already in the pool, swimming lengths effortlessly.

"We're going to warm up first. Can I have a good luck kiss?" Markus asks.

"Good luck. You're going to need it," I whisper against his lips.

Everyone comes out to watch the race, including members of the staff. Someone starts a bet. I have a feeling Toby will win after seeing him swim on Sunday, but I've seen Markus swimming on holiday, and it is equally impressive.

I decide, win or lose, I'm going with Markus. Matthew and I are the only ones, so we split up on different sides of the pool. Markus looks over at Savannah and Helen, shaking his head. Toby sees the funny side, but Markus is focused and ready.

"Heads, you do the freestyle, tails, for the breaststroke," Matthew calls to them.

He tosses the coin, and they're doing the freestyle.

"Ready, set, go!" Matthew shouts, and they're off.

Markus flies into the pool in a smooth, elegant dive. I scream for him to move faster. Toby is in the lead by a fraction, but Markus inches ahead, going faster. He touches the wall first. Matthew and I hold hands and celebrate, jumping in the air. Markus pants on the side. Toby is laughing. I take him some water and a fresh towel.

"Hey, did you slow down on purpose?"

"No, he just used a better technique. He waited for me to die first and then kicked. I thought he had nothing left," Toby replies, breathless.

"Hmm, so there is something to this technique business," I reply.

Markus walks over to us, and I reach up to hug him.

"Dylan, you should dry your hair. It's getting cold," he says.

"Well done," I kiss him.

He wraps another towel around my hair. Kizzy

and I head indoors, and that's when we notice Lily. She's standing inside the door with daddy. They must have been watching the race.

"Hi Mom, when did you arrive?" I'm so happy to see her.

I don't hug her as I'm wet, but she comes closer and hugs me.

"You were having so much fun. I didn't want to break it up."

I breathe her in. I never tire of her smell. She smiles at me happily.

"I have to wash my hair," I say.

I glance at Kizzy. She stares at our mother. Daddy has his arm around her.

"Hello, Kizzy," Lily says.

"Hello," Kizzy replies.

"You girls go get dried up," daddy says.

"Dilly, you don't want to have a cold on your wedding day."

That sends me into action. I run up the stairs, and Kizzy follows close behind me.

"Are you okay?" I ask.

She nods.

"We should do your hair," she says, offering me a small smile.

It takes us a few hours, but when we're done, my hair is glossy and shiny again. Kizzy puts large rollers in and tells me to sit still. The water from the pool has dried my skin, so I moisturise my entire body several times before I'm satisfied.

Naomi has laid out a white camisole dress with square straps and a tie at the back. Kizzy returns a while later, wearing a flowing green top over dark jeans. Her hair is styled back in her straight bob. She looks very glamorous.

"You look great, Kizzy."

"Thanks, Dilly. Let's see how your hair is doing."

"How come yours is done so quickly?"

"You're going to be a bride in a few days, so yours

Choosing Love

needs more love."

"What time is dinner?" she asks, but I don't know.

I assume six tonight because the mother of the bride has arrived. There is a gentle knock at the door, and I know it's Markus.

"Come in," I call to him.

He enters, looking very dapper.

"We thought we would go out to eat tonight," he says.

"Yes!"

"You'll need to dress warm," he says.

"I'll change and be right down."

He kisses me and heads off. I search my wardrobe for a warm sweater and jeans, and I change as quickly as I can, excited about breaking free.

"I think I'll stay here for dinner," Kizzy says softly.

"What? No, Kizzy, come with us."

"I'll stay with daddy and Lily."

"Okay, I'll stay as well."

"No, Dilly, you should go, be with Markus. I know you want a change of scenery. You've been saying it all day. I'll be fine. Daddy will be here, and I promise no drama; this is *your* party."

She grabs a multicoloured scarf and wraps it around my hair and neck, Audrey Hepburn style, and applies red lipstick to my lips.

She helps me into my jacket, and we walk slowly downstairs.

We drive to a local pub. Toby and Savannah are in the back of the Mercedes. It feels good to be out, away from the decadence, but much too soon, the evening is over.

We arrive back well past midnight. The house is quiet. Savannah pours Toby a large glass of wine. Her intentions are very clear. I turn to Markus.

"Come to my room."

He wavers. I move in, kissing him, despite the

audience.

Markus excuses us, and we move into the orangery. The stars are visible in the black sky. He pulls me down onto a loveseat. I sit astride him, grinding my hips slowly.

He groans. Encouraged, I don't back down. I take his hand and slip it under my sweater. His fingers graze where my skin is exposed.

"Dylan, no," he whispers.

He moves his hand away and adjusts my clothes. He lifts me with ease, and I gaze down at him, offering him my sultriest pout. He stands, leading me back into the foyer.

"I'll wait for you," I say before leaving him at the foot of the stairs, deliberately giving him an enticing view.

In my room, I shower and slip on my nightgown. I moisturise again and touch myself.

It's not enough.

I sigh in frustration, resigned that he is not

coming, when there is a soft knock on my door. I let him in, and he locks the door.

"The room is not soundproof. You'll have to be quiet," he whispers, and my heart rate spikes.

Now that he's here, I don't move a muscle. He undresses, never taking his eyes off me. I reach out to touch his face, and he kisses my hand. He pulls the straps of my nightgown down, revealing my breasts. My nipples throb painfully. His finger caresses one erect bud, pulsing with need. I whimper.

"No sound," he mouths to me, and I bite down on my lip.

He sucks on one engorged nipple, and I grip his hair, pulling him closer still. As he moves to the next one, the relief is instant. He uses his expertise to unravel my chords.

The rest of my nightgown falls away. His potent kisses trail slowly, working his way down my torso, and I tremble with anticipation.

His fingers spread my swollen centre and he licks

me with his tongue. My legs shake uncontrollably, so he lifts me in his arms, deposits me on the edge of my bed and kneels in front of me, pupils dilated, hurrying back to the matter at hand.

"Markus," my voice is hoarse.

He stops, holding his finger against his swollen lips.

"Baby, be quiet," he whispers.

This is sweet agony. I'm as quiet as a church mouse when he resumes the feast. The first wave hits, drowning me in a sea of pleasure, but I don't utter one word.

"Good girl."

He rewards me by easing himself inside my overheated core, and his mouth on mine stifles my exhilaration. My scent on his lips is heady. I taste my sex, and a few moans escape.

He loses control, thrusting harder into my slippery softness. The bed moves, but at this point, I don't care. I want it, and it's good. I wrap my legs around him, and he plunges deeper until the fiery end comes for both of us. Afterwards, we lay, panting.

"Thank you," I whisper as he crawls back beside me.

"Do you feel better?"

He rolls to the side and lies facing me.

"Mm," I say.

"Good," he replies, kissing me.

I run my fingers along his collarbone.

"What made you change your mind?"

He chuckles.

"I thought you might combust."

"I'm sorry, it was harder than I expected. I'm a little overwhelmed."

"I would've preferred to whisk you off to Scotland and have a small ceremony there. Spend a few days camping for our honeymoon."

I stare at him with horror, but he doesn't keep his

straight face for long. I can imagine what he sees on my face.

"That would be going from one extreme to the other."

"All this is for the wedding. We decide how we live our lives once we are man and wife."

I like the sound of that.

"Can I ask you something?"

I might as well get it all off my chest.

"Of course, you can."

"Why haven't I met Mason?"

He groans and sighs.

"It's the way he wants it. Once you and I are official, he'll do the formalities."

His eyes look shifty; there is more, but he does not say.

"Markus, I'm going to be your wife. Stop being so secretive. Just tell me."

"Mason wants you to sign a prenuptial

agreement."

"I don't mind. I can sign it."

It is a while before he responds. He gazes into my eyes, and then he inches forward to kiss me.

"It's not what I want for us."

"Does he think I'm only with you because of the money? Because it's not, I'm only with you for the sex. I hope you remembered to put that in the agreement."

"You've given me more than I can ever give you," he says.

"I just want to spend the rest of my life loving you. I've found my purpose, my reason for living. You've unlocked feelings inside me that I didn't know I possessed. Before you, I was going through the motions, barely sentient, merely surviving. Now, I'm alive. All that I own, I want to share with you."

He kisses me, and I return his kiss with fire. We don't talk for a while.

Afterwards, I lie in his arms, feeling incredibly

Choosing Love

loved. I cannot imagine it might not be this way forever. I reflect on the locket, the picture of Lily and daddy. A small voice in the back of my head reminds me that love is sometimes only fleeting.

"Semi wanted to talk to me today."

"How was it?"

"Did you know they lost their son?"

"Mama has mentioned it."

It seems in life, something always happens to distort the course. The idea of Love and commitment trampled in its path.

"Hey. Are you getting cold feet?" he asks.

I shrug.

"Aren't you?"

"No. I can't wait to marry you," he replies.

"A wedding is not a marriage."

"It's the beginning of the rest of our lives. From here on end, I will be devoted to you no matter what."

***

In the morning, we make love before he sneaks back to the Annexe. He offers to come again tonight, but I'm resolved to wait. Our heart-to-heart has helped to calm my nerves. I have a full itinerary today, so I head downstairs early. I'm famished after my extracurricular activities.

Lily sits alone in the orangery, dressed casually in denim jeans and a button-down top, with a bright yellow knitted sweater thrown over her shoulders. She fits the setting to perfection. I greet her with a kiss.

We sit on the couch, and I rest my head on her shoulders, her arms around me. The early morning mist on the trees glistens and sparkles when the sun shines. It must have rained again last night.

"Have you got much planned today?"

"You go off, darling. I know you're busy."

It's a while before I move. The house bustles around us as the staff prepares breakfast. Daddy and Kizzy come into the room and sit across from us. A

Choosing Love

distant memory comes back to me. I'm seven years old, and Lily comes to visit. We both sat in the room, just like today. Daddy was coercing Kizzy to come over and say hello, but she screamed and became so upset Lily had to leave, and then I started to scream. Today, the room is silent.

* * *

I spend the afternoon at a spa with Savannah and Kizzy. We pull up to the wedding party venue, but we are stopped at the gate.

"Hello, Dylan. Ladies," O'Neil says.

"Hi, O'Neil."

"We're just taking a look at the venue. Is that alright?" Savannah says, and he waves us through.

"Wow, security is tight," Kizzy says.

D S Johnson - Mills

At the entrance of the hotel, there is a notice:

Mathew Henry Joseph Mills $ Eirith Grace Helen

Mills

With

Brandon Everton Weekes & Lilian Rose Johnson-

Mayor

Invite you to attend the wedding celebration

of

Mr Markus Anthony Mathew Mills & Miss Dylan

Francine Weekes

Saturday 24th March, 2001

Choosing Love

"Dilly, how exciting! Your name in lights."

It is a wonderful feeling. The hotel is luxury at its finest.

I wander away, trying to visualise how it will look on the day. Elegantly curved French doors back out onto a vast outdoor space with breathtaking views of a wide lake. Kizzy puts her arm around me.

"How was it with Lily last night?"

"Don't worry. I was on my best behaviour," she says.

I reach for her hand and bring it to my lips.

"Lily certainly charmed Markus' folks. Semi was so smitten. It was a lovely evening."

"And how was daddy?"

"Staring at Lily with his puppy dog eyes, of course," she says, laughing, "I could tell he was anxious. I think at one point he broke into a British accent."

We both chuckle.

"Is Lily always this way?" Kizzy asks.

"How do you mean?"

"Soft-spoken, polite and sweet-natured," she says, and I laugh.

"Yes. That is our mother, Kizzy."

"It makes you wonder...." she starts.

"...how she produced not one but two feisty and highly opinionated women?" I finish.

"Exactly," she says, and we laugh.

"Daddy called it at Thanksgiving last year. Grams, in her infinite wisdom, raised us to be strong women. She knew that to survive life, her granddaughters had to be warriors."

* * *

Holly arrives the next day with her parents and brother. We have all gathered outside to greet the newcomers. Joshua says hello and blushes furiously.

A red Ferrari roars up the drive, making me wonder if the security has been breached.

Markus had informed me that guests can only have access if they have an invitation and can only come to the house if they're in the wedding party or a close family member.

A tall man emerges from the car. His bright red, shaggy beard matches his long hair and his awful maroon jumper.

"If you're going to drive a Ferrari, shouldn't you look the part?" Kizzy whispers to me.

"Aristotle!" Markus shouts and runs over to greet the stranger.

"Oh no. Not that idiot!" Savannah says and walks off.

She's never been anything but gracious, so I watch her retreating with curiosity.

"New addition to the clan?" Toby asks.

"It's unlikely with his ginger looks, but you never know," I say.

A beaming Markus brings him over to me.

"Dylan, I want you to meet my good mate, Tim. We were at Cambridge together."

"Pleased to meet you, Dylan."

Tim pulls me in for a hug, and my feet leave the ground. When he does the same to Toby, I decide I like him. Then, he's introduced to Kizzy. He picks a flower from the path and gives it to her, kissing her hand.

Now that all my ladies are here, I want to see them in their dresses. The rehearsal is tomorrow at the chapel. Kizzy takes over, and what starts out as trying on dresses turns into a fully-fledged fashion show.

We're in Helen's dance studio. It's easy to wheel the clothes from Savannah's bedroom as it's on the same level. The mirrors all around make a nice backdrop. The loud music attracts everyone, even Semi.

Helen and Lily join me on the judge's panel. We score the outfits, and Kizzy gets a ten every time. Daddy and I smile at each other. We know all about Kizzy and her fashion shows.

* * *

The ladies and I are having our nails done. I

Choosing Love

choose a neutral shade. I ask Savannah about Tim, as she is sitting next to me in the nail bar.

"He's Markus' friend from Uni," she says, but I already know this.

"You don't think much of him then?"

"Forget about him. What's the deal with Toby?"

"Why? Do you like him?"

"What's not to like?" she huffs, and I smile. "Does he have someone else?" she asks.

"Yes," I say.

"Is it serious?"

She looks at me with familiar green eyes.

"I'm not sure," I shrug my shoulders.

"In any case, you're Markus' sister. I don't think he would go there."

She purses her lips but lets it go.

Our next stop is the reception venue. Holly wants to see it. I'm pleasantly surprised to find Markus at the hotel.

"Dylan," he calls, and I go to him.

"Look who's here!" he says, grinning.

"Hello, Dylan. I see your ankle is all patched up," the coarse voice says.

"Cameron!" I say happily.

He pulls me in for a hug.

"Are Fiona and Benjamin here with you?" I ask excitedly.

"They should be down shortly. We drove all the way, and Fe is tired. Maggie is here. You'll get to meet her."

I call Kizzy over to meet Cameron. The guests are arriving, so I spend the rest of the afternoon meeting people.

"Hallo, Dylan."

I would recognise that German accent anywhere.

"Nicolos!"

He looks handsome with his long locks up in a ponytail.

Choosing Love

He doesn't ask where Toby is. I'm not sure what's going on with the two of them, and obviously, my loyalties will always lie with my best friend, but I like Nicolos. I only think of it this minute, but I tell him I have an important job for him.

"Anything I can do to help," he replies, smiling.

Later, back at the house, everyone is in good spirits. We eat dinner and socialise until quite late. I don't notice when daddy and Lily leave the lounge. I'm looking for Lily when Markus comes up and hugs me from behind.

"Hey," he whispers in my hair.

We slip into the orangery, and he pulls me in for a kiss.

"I was looking for Lily."

"I was looking for you," he whispers and kisses me again.

We spend a few minutes communicating without words. I never grow tired of his lips.

"I've asked Nicolos to be her escort at the

wedding," I say between kisses.

"I'll take care of it," he says.

I show him my gratitude. He chuckles, breaking the kiss.

"We're heading out to the hotel tonight," he says.

"How come?"

"The lads are throwing me a bachelor party."

"What are you going to do?"

"Do you want to come?"

"No, thank you. Have fun."

I kiss him, and he closes his eyes, pulling me closer, his hands in my hair. We're breathless when we pull apart.

"See you tomorrow," he whispers and kisses me softly on my lips.

* * *

We meet at the chapel for a final walk-through. The church is perched on a hill overlooking open fields of green. The ladies and I stop to take in the magnificent view: an English garden of exceptional beauty.

Familiar hands surround me, and I smile.

"You survived then."

I giggle as he nuzzles my neck.

"Just barely," he groans.

It must have been a heavy night. He takes my hand, and we walk inside. Ginny and Bowes are standing outside the entrance. The wedding planner is here, with the florists, giving instructions. The church is small, and the aroma of fresh flowers perfumes the air.

"I brought my groomsmen."

Benjamin, Joshua, and Timothy are inside the chapel with Toby, chatting animatedly.

We spend a few minutes organising the procession. They look to me, so I decide. Joshua will walk with Kizzy as he doesn't want to walk with his sister.

"It's just weird," he says, and I indulge him.

He seems smitten with Kizzy. Ben will walk with Savannah because when I suggest Tim, she shoots daggers at me. Tim and Holly will walk together.

Holly is wearing a wine-coloured dress, and it will be a nice combination with Tim's ginger looks. The wedding planner's daughter, Daisy, will be the flower girl. She's four and very sweet. Her blonde hair spills down her back like fine wheat.

She offers me a yellow rose. I stoop and give her a hug, and then it's time to start. We take our positions. I find daddy in the hallway.

"Daddy!" I call, "Where have you been hiding? I feel like I haven't seen you for days."

"I'm here, Dilly. Enjoying the lovely English countryside," he replies.

His eyes are distracted, but he kisses my cheek.

"Are you nervous, daddy?"

"No. I'm proud."

* * *

I choose a gorgeous designer outfit, midnight

Choosing Love

blue with long chiffon sleeves. The dress falls to my mid-thigh but doesn't look scandalous. My yellow diamond necklace is the showpiece tonight. Slipping on my new, velvet, blue Jimmy Choo's and grabbing my small, beaded bag, I'm ready for the night. Naomi compliments me.

"Are you coming to the party tonight?" I ask, hugging her.

"Tonight is only for immediate family and those taking part in the wedding," she replies, smiling.

"You're taking part. You've been helping the bride to look her best."

"The bride is a natural. She certainly doesn't need any help to look beautiful."

She touches my necklace.

"Thank you," I whisper, giving her another hug.

"Have a wonderful time," she says, just as there is a knock at my door.

I rush to open it for my guy. He's standing on the other side, smiling. He gives me a yellow rose and I laugh. He is dashing in his navy blue suit and yellow tie. I wave bye to Naomi, and he offers me his arm.

"You look radiant," he says.

"So do you."

Sometimes, I still can't believe he's mine. He lifts me in his arms and carries me down the stairs. The house is eerily quiet.

"Where is everyone?"

"They've already left."

He barely finishes speaking when I throw my arms around his neck and kiss him.

"I wanted to come for you myself, but we'd better go. Don't want to be too late for your party."

We walk hand in hand down the drive. The night air is cool and pleasant. He opens the door for me, and I slide in, still clutching my yellow rose.

He walks over to his side, glancing at my legs appreciatively and buckles me in. We gaze lovingly at each other, and he presses his lips lightly to mine.

"I can't wait to marry you," he whispers.

Choosing Love

His kisses are more urgent, his hands caressing my neck. This is not a good idea right now; I'm starting to fire up. I break away, and he groans.

"We'd better go."

It's almost six thirty, and the hotel is a twenty-minute drive. He starts the engine and smiles at me. I think back to our very first car journey together. We were talking about choices, and I remember telling him that I always chose for me.

Will that still apply when I'm his wife? I'm not sure.

"Do you remember that night we first met?"

"It was a year ago today," he says.

"Yes, it is. I forgot."

This was the reason he picked the date for our wedding. I wanted to get married in June.

"Thank you for choosing me," he whispers so softly I almost don't hear it.

I did choose him, but only to take my virginity. I never expected what came next.

I think about when I met Toby. That was also in March two years ago. I said hello to him, and it sparked a close bond that led me to Markus and an even deeper bond of love.

We walk into our party and the band starts to play, my second surprise of the evening.

It's my dad's band, and he's there on the keyboards. He smiles at me, and I beam. I wave hello to his bandmates.

Lily is seated next to me, in her place of honour, as mother of the bride. She is breath-taking in an off-shoulder cream-coloured dress. Kizzy and Toby are sitting across from us.

I smile and wave to the others sitting at the table. I gasp in surprise when I notice Tim. He is sitting two seats down from Toby and is like a new man. His facial hair is gone, and his ginger hair is pulled back in a ponytail. He is gorgeous.

"Tim looks fabulous," I tell Markus, and he laughs.

"He does scrub up well when he makes the

Choosing Love

effort."

Dinner is about to be served, so the band takes a break. Daddy sits on the other side of Lily. His bandmates come to greet me. I'm so excited to see them.

"It's the last night of you being a free woman," Markus whispers, "Are you ready?"

He gives me his burning look.

"Yes. When do we leave?"

"Tomorrow," he replies.

"So soon? I thought we would stay until Sunday."

I'm looking forward to our first night together when he is legally mine.

"Nope, tomorrow we ride out after sunset."

He has not revealed where we are going. He'd only instructed me to pack for warm weather. I wonder if he is taking me to Africa.

The past few weeks have been so wonderful. Now that they are coming to an end, I feel an unexpected tinge of sadness.

Markus was so right. This is such an important part of the transition. Spending time with the people you love and seeing everyone so happy. I'll cherish these memories forever.

It's time for the speeches. My beautiful Maid of Honour, regal in her red fitted dress, goes first.

"Growing up with my sister was the best. For me, not so much for her. Anything Dilly had, I wanted. Daddy would go out and buy the biggest and the best to appease me, but I didn't want my own. I wanted Dilly's. Poor daddy."

"The amazing thing is, she would always let me have it, even if it was something she really loved. Markus, I want you to know just how lucky you are, not only because my sister is beautiful, but because once Dilly loves you, she'll never stop, no matter what."

She takes her seat, and I smile at her.

"Thanks, Kizzy," Markus says.

Toby stands next. He's gorgeous in his white shirt and red tie, his Armani jacket draped over his chair.

Choosing Love

"I first met Markus when I was thirteen years old. He is simply the best man that I know. Imagine how I felt when I introduced him to Dylan, a notorious heartbreaker, and he could not take his eyes off her. I had to be the one to tell him he wouldn't stand a chance. I obviously underestimated him."

"Watching two people I care about fall in love is an unbelievable experience. Dylan, Markus, thank you for allowing me a front row seat. I never take sides because I'm rooting for you both."

Leap of faith

Heavy footfall in the hall outside my room rouses me from a deep sleep.

"It's snowing!"

I must be dreaming, so I roll over and go back to sleep. When I open my eyes again, Naomi is lighting my fire. She greets me cheerily. A pang of sadness comes over me as today is my last day with her.

"I dreamt that it snowed."

She opens the blinds.

"Come and take a look."

I jump out of bed, and sure enough, there's a light

Choosing Love

dusting of snow on the ground.

"It's a sign of good luck," she assures me.

"I don't have a coat for my dress."

"It's quite mild outside. The sun will be out soon, and the snow will be gone by the time you're on your way to the church."

She runs me a bath, and I move in a dreamlike state through the motions. Too nervous to eat, I sip hot lemon tea. She helps me with my corset and undergarments. There's a knock on the door at around ten thirty. She opens the door and my ladies file into the room. Their presence helps to banish my anxieties. I sit on the couch, as instructed, and they surround me.

"Dilly, as traditions go, we wanted to present you with tokens that will hopefully bring you good luck. I'll go first, something old."

Kizzy brushes my hair off my face and passes me a box.

"It's from Lily."

Inside, wrapped in tissue paper, is a fine pair of sheer lace long vintage ivory gloves.

"Kizzy, are they Grams?" I'm already tearing up.

"Yes," she says, reaching out to touch them.

Part of the inspiration for my dress was the one she wore in her wedding photo. I never knew Lily had these.

Kizzy takes the box and puts it on my dresser.

Holly smiles at me and exchanges seats with Kizzy. I smooth her hair from her face.

"I go next with something new."

She gives me a tiny box.

"This is from Markus."

My fingers tremble slightly as I recall the last time he gave me a box like this.

Inside is a diamond clasp bracelet.

"Oh, wow."

"That's perfect," Kizzy says.

There's a note inside, and Holly reads it aloud.

Choosing Love

"Dylan, something new because your love is true, meet me at the altar today at two."

Kizzy takes the bracelet and puts it on the dresser. Holly moves down on the couch, and Savannah slides next to me. I exhale, and she laughs.

"Firstly, let me tell you how happy I am that you will be my sister. I was inspired by Kizzy's speech last night. This was Semi's, and she passed it on to me when I turned eighteen, as a hint, I think. I'd like you to borrow it, and maybe one day, I will finally have my chance to wear it."

She puts a square box on my lap. I lift the lid, and nestled inside is a diamond tiara, dainty and slim, with a brilliant emerald at the head. I'm lost for words.

"Something borrowed," she whispers, and I hug her.

"Thank you. It's exquisite."

I'm touched beyond words. Kizzy takes the tiara, her eyes sparkling.

"Now, tell me you're not a fairy princess. You'll be decked out in jewels today," she says.

"I already have something blue."

I open my robe, flashing my leg and showing the garter belt, where it sits proudly on my thigh. The ladies squeal with delight.

The wedding photographer arrives as Paul and Kizzy are doing my hair and makeup. Kizzy knows what works best, and Paul's the expert who can create the look. I sit in the chair for over an hour. Paul is in a flutter.

He tells me the tiara changes everything.

I'm finally relaxed, and I manage to eat some food. By one-fifteen, I'm fully dressed, and there are no dry eyes in the room.

"Thank goodness for waterproof mascara," Kizzy says.

Gail has done an amazing job. The new pearls add glamour, and my dress shimmers and glows, cascading over my curves like water. I feel beautiful.

Choosing Love

Savannah's tiara sets the whole look off.

"When my brother sees you, he's going to think he's dreaming."

She can barely say the words. There's a knock on the door, and my heart flips over.

Daddy comes in wearing his suit. As if on cue, everyone leaves the room, and I'm alone with my dad.

"Dilly," he whispers, tears in his eyes.

"Daddy, I don't want to ruin my makeup. Hold it together," I plead, and he nods.

He looks at me, and we laugh at the same time.

"Can you believe it snowed in spring on my wedding day?"

"It's mostly melted now."

Kizzy opens the door.

"It's time to go."

She has my bouquet. She gives it to daddy and pulls the veil over my face. Then she helps me with the gloves and clasps my bracelet over my right wrist.

"You will take this one off to exchange rings," she says, indicating my left hand.

My nerves are back from their brief hiatus. Daddy and Kizzy help me down the stairs.

The photographer snaps away. I notice that we're also being filmed. There's a limo and a Rolls Royce parked in the drive. The drivers are standing outside.

The bonnets of both vehicles are decorated with white flowers. Savannah tells me I will ride in the Rolls Royce with daddy. A few members of staff stand in the hallway, looking at me. I smile and wave. My heart hammers in my chest, and I don't hear anything else being said around me. I do feel it when they give me kisses before they depart.

And then, I'm alone with daddy.

"You ready, Dilly?"

He helps me into the car and makes sure my train is inside. It's a sweet moment seeing the emotions displayed on his handsome face. As we drive along,

Choosing Love

pedestrians stop and stare at the car, waving.

We approach the chapel, and I squeeze daddy's hand. O'Neil is standing at the door to the chapel. He smiles at me and opens the car door. He takes my hand and helps me out as Kizzy comes over to me.

"Breathe, Dilly."

"Is Markus here?" my voice gives away my nerves.

"He wouldn't be anywhere else."

It's O'Neil who answers.

The groomsmen take their places while Kizzy fixes my train and adjusts my veil. She smiles at me.

"Perfect."

I see him the moment I walk inside. Everyone stands. The room goes eerily quiet for a second, and we only have eyes for each other.

The soulful sounds of George Michael singing Jesus to a Child float to me as I move towards my future. Lily smiles, and I touch her hand. Daddy lifts my veil and kisses me, then offers my hand to Markus.

"Hello," he whispers as Kizzy adjusts the veil and the back of my dress.

She takes my bouquet and Markus holds both my hands. We stand facing each other.

"You're unbelievably beautiful."

He kisses my hand. Toby is standing to the side of Markus.

"Ladies and gentlemen, please be seated. Into this holy estate, these two persons come now to be joined. Dearly beloved, we are gathered here in the presence of God to join this man and this woman in holy marriage, which is instituted by God, blessed by our Lord Jesus Christ, and to be held in honour among all men."

The minister's voice echoes in the tiny chapel. That's it, I think to myself, we're married. As if he can read my thoughts, Markus smiles and shakes his head.

Choosing Love

"Who gives this woman to be married to this man?"

"Her mother and I do."

"If any person present knows of any lawful impediment to this marriage, they should declare it now. Marriage joins two people in the circle of love. When two people pledge their love and care for each other within a marriage, they create a spirit which binds them closer than any spoken or written words."

His voice fades, and I feel the presence of Grams and Papa Kit.

"I do," Markus says.

We exchange rings. Markus removes my glove and slips a silver eternity band with tiny diamonds on my finger.

"I, Markus Anthony Matthew Mills, take you, Dylan Francine Weekes, to be my lawfully wedded wife, to share my life openly with you, standing with you in sickness and in health, in joy and sorrow, in hardships and in ease, to cherish and love forever."

The minister repeats the question to me.

"I do."

Toby passes me a slim, platinum wedding band. I put it on his finger and make my promise to this man, telling him I will stand by his side, never forsaking him, to always love and cherish him, forever.

"I now pronounce you husband and wife. You may kiss the bride."

Markus pulls me in gently by my waist and kisses me. Our first kiss as husband and wife. Toby and Kizzy give us hugs, and then everyone surrounds us.

We walk outside in the brilliant sunlight to cheers from our family and friends. We pose for photos at the entrance. Markus lifts me up and spins me in the air, laughing.

"I love you," he shouts, kissing me.

Kizzy admonishes her brother-in-law.

"Dilly has to be picture-perfect for the photos," she says.

Choosing Love

He laughs and gives her a hug. Kizzy fixes my veil, as my wedding party surround us.

"Congratulations!"

* * *

Markus and I are driven back to the house.

"I want to take you away right now."

"What about the reception party?"

"The others can enjoy it for us. I'll enjoy you."

"I see I'll have to be the responsible one in this marriage."

"Okay, have your party, say your goodbyes and then, you come with me."

"My dear husband, it's your party too."

"My wife," he says, trying it out.

I like the sound of it.

"Yes. Forever," I whisper, and we kiss.

* * *

The party is in full swing when we arrive.

Everyone cheers.

"Couldn't wait to consummate?" Toby stage whispers to us.

We've been gone for more than an hour, so it does look that way. Nothing could be further from the truth.

Markus helped me dress in my second outfit of the day. It took him ages to work the buttons on my wedding dress. Once he finally undressed me, there was a bit of canoodling, but we didn't get far.

O'Neil showed up for my bags, thinking we were at the party. I had to run to the bathroom as I was standing there in my corset, looking like a trussed-up turkey. I took the hint and finished dressing. Markus locked the tiara away.

We have our first dance and there is a collective sigh from the crowd as the full extent of my dress is revealed.

"You were wearing something similar when we first met," Markus whispers to me.

Choosing Love

"I'll never forget how you looked the first time I saw you. I hope I never forget the way you look right now."

He rocks me slowly to the sounds of When a Man Loves a Woman.

At yesterday's party, we sat down to have dinner, and it was very formal. Today, we dance and socialise.

I move around, mingling with family and friends. I'm out of time, and even though I'm heading off with the man of my dreams, it is tinged with sadness.

I hug my friend as he spins me around the dance floor.

"I'll miss you, Toby."

"I'll miss you too."

Lily and I have a moment together.

"Thank you for coming and for bringing Gram's gloves. It meant so much to me."

"The chance to see you looking so beautiful was special. I love you, my sweet Dilly."

By the time I hug Markus' family, I'm crying my eyes out. Daddy and Kizzy hold onto me. It's harder with them.

"Will you come back with me, Kizzy?"

"Of course I will."

"I'm so proud of you," daddy whispers, and I'm completely overcome.

My wedding party forms a circle and dances around me. Kizzy brings my bouquet. I turn my back and throw it. Savannah catches it, but I don't think she was trying. She quickly gives it to Holly.

Tim drives us in his Porsche. My sister and I spend the last few moments together. I shower and wash away all the make-up. She picks out my travel outfit: a light green silk blouse, hot pink pants with a wide yellow belt and matching heels.

She brushes out my hair and applies minimal make-up.

"Let's go. Markus is waiting for his bride."

Tim keeps his promise, and we are back at the

Choosing Love

hotel at eight forty-five p.m.

"I'm ready," I say to my new husband.

He has also changed into dark brown pants, a white dress shirt and a khaki jacket, looking effortlessly gorgeous. He picks up a microphone.

The music goes off, and the room falls silent.

"On behalf of my wife and I...." he stops and laughs as the room erupts with cheers.

"Thank you to everyone here tonight for making this a memorable day. A special thank you to my family for organising this celebration. Brandon, Kizzy, and Lily, thank you for my wife. I promise to treasure her. We love you."

The room erupts in more cheers, and Markus looks at me, his beautiful smile on display. We step outside the French doors as the sky lights up with fireworks. The crowd gathers around us. I search for Toby among our friends and family, and notice him looking up at the sky, his arms around my sister.

Markus takes my hand and leads me out into the

night, onto our next adventure.

The end.

Acknowledgements

To my wonderful sister, Mrs O., for reading my drafts.

My Grams, though she is gone, for continuing to be my muse.

My husband for putting up with my imaginary friends.

To the editors that have worked on my manuscript.

> Woodbridge Publishers
>
> The word tank
>
> Fiction Feedback

And last but not least, to the die-hard romance readers for whom a happy ending is a must.

The journey continues...

A note about the author

Marrying the man of your dreams must be a wonderful thing. As a girl, I dreamt of having a fairy tale wedding, but when it was my turn to do the deed, I was so far removed from actually doing it that if not for the pictures, I would doubt whether it happened at all. So it is no surprise that when I started to write a book centred on the intricacies of love, a wedding with all the trimmings was just the thing. My imagination ran wild, and I enjoyed every single moment. That is the power of escapism and

Choosing Love

my inspiration for writing this book.

I thoroughly enjoyed delving into the complicated nature of love. There were so many parallels to draw on from my own personal experiences.

When I was thirteen, I met a boy at camp. His name was Samuel Anthony, and he was beautiful. He lived on a neighbouring Island, and so we communicated by writing each other letters. I recall the thrill of arriving home from school to see his penmanship on a white envelope with stamps. Alas, I turned eighteen, and the relationship fizzled. It was only years later that I realized we had no sexual chemistry.

Markus is a culmination of all the men I've known in my past and present. One editor told me that he was too perfect. I tried so many ways to turn him ugly, but none of it felt true. It was my sister who eventually said to me that he will be whoever you say he is. I loved that idea best, and I hope you agree.

Printed in Great Britain
by Amazon